after hello

C-1

after hello

a novel

LISA MANGUM

Visit us at ShadowMountain.com

Library of Congress Cataloging-in-Publication Data

ISBN 978-1-60907-010-6

Printed in the United States of America
Malloy Lithographing Incorporated, Ann Arbor, MI

10 9 8 7 6 5 4 3 2 1

To Heidi
Fellow writer, fellow dreamer
Friend

Sara

Chapter 1

I shouldn't have noticed him. I wasn't even looking in his direction at first. I was dazzled by the sunlight reflecting off the glass buildings that lined the busy sidewalks of New York. It was only when I turned away that I saw him—though, to be fair, it wasn't him I noticed first. It was his zip-up gray fleece hoodie with the black stripe that ran down the sleeve and around the collar and the faded, fuzzy letters that said *Zebra Stripes* across his chest.

I didn't think anyone but me listened to their music, let alone spent money on swag.

The bookstore door stayed open behind him, though a small bell still rang when he stepped outside into the spring sunshine. He tucked a book wrapped in brown paper into the military green messenger bag hanging at his side, then shoved his hands into the pockets of his jeans. A rolling cart of bargain books hid most of his body, the tops of the titles hitting him hip-high. Tall, then. And lean.

Say what you want, but I'm a photographer so I get paid to

notice details like that. Well, not yet. *Amateur* photographers don't get paid, but the pros do, and someday I'm going pro.

Zebra Stripes twisted slightly, scanning the street, and I caught a glimpse of sandy brown hair cut short and darker brown eyes. Tall, lean, *and* cute.

He stepped back, letting an older woman walking a dog pass by, then fell into step behind her and headed into the crowd.

Almost on instinct, I powered up my point-and-shoot camera and snapped off a picture before he disappeared. I reviewed it on the screen, zooming in as much as I could on the small image, hoping to see more of his face. No luck. I'd missed his face, capturing only a shoulder, a sliver of his back, his leg extended mid-stride. Still, there was something interesting about the picture. Something that spoke of movement and purpose. And isolation. I thought he looked oddly solitary even as the crowd had pushed in around him.

I'd heard stories about the crowds of New York, and so far they were all true. Given that it was lunchtime, there were probably even more people out than usual, but since this was my first day here, it was hard to know for sure. After I'd been jostled and bumped and pushed one time too many, I finally pressed my back against the brick wall of the building behind me, feeling small and trying to stay out of the way.

Thinking about lunch made my stomach rumble. Dad had promised to meet me here at 11:30 sharp for our first big date in the Big Apple, but he was already late—almost a half hour late. I sighed, wondering why I was surprised. He had warned me at breakfast that his meeting might run long, but still, we only had the one day to spend in New York and I didn't want to spend it alone.

Dad was the only family I had. It had been just the two of us for a long time now. In the beginning, Mom had been part of the family dream, but when I was eight, she must have decided she wanted to be part of someone else's dream, someone else's family. And just like that—she was gone.

My cell phone sounded from where it was buried deep in my shoulder bag. The marimba music of an incoming call interrupted my thoughts. Keeping my eyes focused on where the Zebra Stripes boy had disappeared, I fished out my phone. The cars and buses and trucks sped past me like film flickering through an old-fashioned camera. They were just flashes of metal, of color. Blue. Black. Silver. Red. I felt the energy pulse around me like a living thing. I closed my eyes, and the sound transformed from traffic to ocean inside my ear.

"Sara?" My dad's voice echoed through my phone, sounding thin and metallic. Speakerphone. I hated that. Couldn't he just pick up the phone and talk to me? I opened my eyes, and the fleeting moment of inside stillness slipped away like a speeding car. Or like a boy with a book under his arm.

"Hey, Dad," I said. I wondered who was listening in on the other end. Probably his new boss and a room full of company men in suits and ties. The thought made me claustrophobic. I'd much rather be outside than inside on a day like this. The weather was all blue skies and sunshine, and the city was alive around me. I felt the urge to move, to tap into the energy of the day and just *go*. Somewhere—anywhere.

"Is everything okay?" I asked. The whole reason we were in New York was so Dad could finalize the sale of his company. Not only would the sale bring in a nice chunk of change for us, but it meant that Dad would be able to cut back on his hours. He'd been working eighty-hour weeks for a long time, building up his SEO company—FindersKeepers.com—into something a bigger company like SearchEngineDrivers.com would find attractive enough to acquire.

"Yes, everything's fine. It's just that the paperwork is taking a little longer than we planned." Dad hesitated. "Listen, Sara-bear, I'm sorry I'm not there yet, but I don't think I'll be able to get away for lunch this afternoon."

His words dropped on my heart like a lead weight. *So much for our perfect day.* I knew this meeting was important, but I had really hoped that it wouldn't take all day.

I concentrated on the phone and heard the sound of papers rustling against each other, the clink of a glass hitting the tabletop. A door closed—or opened; I couldn't quite tell. A muttering of voices ebbed and flowed, lost in the sounds of a wailing siren that roared wildly in my other ear.

"Sara? Are you there?"

"Yeah." I let the moment stretch out. I heard Dad inhale, prepare to speak. I rushed to fill the void. "It's okay. I don't mind. I'll find something."

This time it was Dad's turn to pause. "Are you sure?" He didn't wait for me to answer. "We're still on for dinner—promise. And I haven't forgotten that you wanted to go to the top of the Empire State Building. We'll do that, too. Double promise. It's just that right now—"

"It's okay, Dad," I interrupted. "Seriously. I know you're busy. Your meeting is more important than lunch." *More important than me.* I didn't have to say it; we both heard it anyway. I looked down the street, clogged with people. "And if I can't find a place to eat in this town on a Saturday, then I deserve to starve."

"But—"

"Dad." The single syllable was enough to kill the rest of his sentence. He knew that tone. The one that said, *Pay attention because I'm only going to say this once.* The one that warned, *Don't push it.* The one that I learned from my mom.

"Okay," he acquiesced. Because he knew I wanted him to.

"I'll call you later," I promised. Because I knew he wanted me to.

"Have fun." It was almost a question, but I chose to hear it as a directive.

"I will," I said. I hung up without saying good-bye. I never said it. Not if I could help it. Good-bye was final. Painful. It was the sound of a door closing. Of footsteps walking away.

It was the last thing my mother had ever said to me.

I shook off the bitter thought. I wasn't going to let her invade my day. Not today. Not this day.

This day was for breathing deep and looking ahead. So I did just that, gulping down a lungful of hot, sweet air until it filled my entire body. I tasted the metallic tang of exhaust, listened to the rumble and thrum of throngs of people moving around me, and drank in the sight of green leaves scattered on the trees hidden between the buildings.

Freedom. That was what I felt standing there on the corner with a park on one side of me and a cluster of shops on the other, the small bookstore with its open door and rolling carts of books beckoning me from across the street. The freedom to go wherever I wanted, do whatever I wanted. I was a single person in a city of millions and the one person who wanted to keep tabs on me had just told me to go to lunch without him.

I absently pushed the power button on my camera, listening to the smooth hum of the lens as it woke and stretched before settling into its standard halfway position. I glanced down at the last picture I'd taken. The one of the boy in the gray hoodie with the gray-green messenger bag. I lifted the camera, lining up my surroundings until they matched the image on the LCD screen. It was like looking into a portal of a moment that had been snatched out of time. The mysterious boy was the only difference. Here, then gone.

I snapped another picture, just to hear the reassuring click of capture, and then looped my camera around my wrist.

Glancing over my shoulder at the steady stream of traffic flowing around me, I headed off into the unknown, trailing the fading footsteps of the boy I'd glimpsed only briefly through my camera eye.

Sam

Chapter 2

Someone was following him. It was a crazy idea; there were always people walking along the narrow sidewalk, so it was impossible to believe there could be just one person intent on following him, but he knew it as surely as he knew the exact contents of his messenger bag. When he glanced over his shoulder, his eyes found her immediately. Yep, that was her. The girl with the camera.

He'd noticed her the instant he'd left the bookstore. Maybe no one else would have paid her any mind, but there was something about the way she leaned up against the building—a black band of sunglasses resting across the top of her head, her hand wrapped tightly around the strap of her shoulder bag—that called out to him. She wasn't just a tourist—those he could spot a mile away and avoid with ease. No, she was something else. Something more. Something—he almost didn't dare think the word—*kindred.*

He hunched his shoulders, ducking to avoid the prickling

sensation running up and down his back. She was still there. He didn't know if that was good or bad.

Approaching the corner, he hesitated. She was close. Turn left and he could duck into Scoops Ice Cream Shoppe and out the back door and be gone. Or he could head straight, linger at the row of concert posters and ads on the makeshift construction wall, and let her catch up.

No. That was a bad idea. He had a job to do.

Paul was waiting for him back at the Plaza, and the sooner he dropped off the book, the sooner his afternoon would be his again. He had no time to spare for the strange girl with the green eyes.

But instead of quickening his step and turning left, he hesitated at the curb, deciding to wait for the official walk sign to flash before he crossed the street. He couldn't remember the last time he'd actually obeyed the crosswalk signs.

The prickling between his shoulder blades intensified, and he shifted the strap of his messenger bag across his chest. Bad idea or not, he lingered at the plywood wall, studying the colorful signs and flyers that had been tacked up there despite the clear instructions prohibiting such postings.

His brain screamed at him to keep going, to move. He hated standing still. Questions bubbled up inside him the longer he stood there: Why was he waiting? For the girl?

Yes. He could admit that now. Just as he could admit that the whole idea was crazy. Crazy, but he didn't care. It wouldn't be the first crazy thing he'd ever done.

His eyes roamed over the posters, the names and addresses and numbers blending together into a steady stream of data.

Buy one lesson, get one free at Moosmuller Music.

The Fall of Night—now playing at Glass and Coasters. Tuesday night is ladies' night.

Missing dog. Black with white paws. Very friendly. Answers to the name of Nedra. Please call—we miss our baby girl. Reward!

She stepped up next to him, pretending to study the posters as carefully as he was. He could feel the nervousness sliding off her body.

He flicked his eyes in her direction. "You stole something from me."

She blinked, almost taking a step back. "What? I did no such thing."

Nervous, yes. But also brave. An interesting combination.

He pivoted on his heel, walking away from her. Fast enough to quiet his inner demand for motion, but not so fast that she couldn't catch up if she wanted to.

"Hey!" she shouted at his back. "I said I didn't steal anything from you." In a flash, she had matched his pace, step for step. She gripped her bag and frowned. "You owe me an apology."

"And you owe me my soul." He stopped, allowing her to outpace him by a step.

She turned, her mouth open in a small, silent protest, confusion in her eyes.

He held her gaze—the green irises were the darkest green he'd ever seen—and gestured toward the small silver camera looped around her wrist. "You took my picture without my permission. That's stealing." He lifted the shoulder not burdened with the strap of his bag. "And in some cultures, taking a man's picture is the same as taking his soul."

"How—?" She clutched the camera close to her chest and shut her mouth. "I'm sorry. I didn't mean to."

He read the lie in the bones of her face as she adjusted her expression. But it was an innocent lie, if such a thing were possible. "Yes, you did. And you're not sorry about it."

She shifted her weight, one hip jutting out just enough to knock her body out of alignment. She looked better that way—more curves, more dimension.

She looked him up and down, then matched his determined gaze with her own. Her eyes were the green of the jungle, of camouflage. "So what if I'm not?" she challenged.

He grinned as though she had passed some sort of test, and held out his hand. "Sam." She looked at him warily, but the nervousness he'd sensed before was gone. "For the caption."

"Sara," she declared, touching his hand quickly, coolly.

"Without the *h*," he murmured. Her palm was smooth and soft against the rough-worn touch of his fingers.

"How did you know that?" she asked, her hand dropping to her hip, her elbow forming a triangle.

"Because you didn't say it." Yes, she definitely looked better with some angles to her.

"I don't know what game you're playing at, Sam, but—"

"I don't play games," he interrupted quietly but firmly.

"Then what do you call this?" She gestured with her free hand to the space between them.

Sam shrugged. "A conversation. You should try it sometime. They can be quite enlightening."

A flash of a smile played across her lips, just a spark of amusement before it was squirreled away.

Ah, so she was a girl who was careful with her smiles. He liked that.

"My dad taught me never to talk to strangers," she said lightly.

"We're all strangers in the beginning."

"Then what are we in the end?"

"We'll have to see when we get there. Walk with me." He'd been stationary too long. It was time to move.

"Where are we going?" she asked.

"Where do you want to go?"

She shrugged.

"I don't believe that. A smart girl like you knows exactly where she wants to go."

"How do you know I'm smart? You don't know anything about me."

"I know you've never been to New York before. I know you appreciate beauty when you see it. And I know you're equal parts stubborn and brave."

His lips twitched upward when her mouth dropped open.

"Before you ask," he continued, "I'm observant. I look. And I see. And, yes, keeping people guessing is one of my specialties."

"I'll say. On all counts." She fell silent for a moment as they reached another intersection.

Luckily, the light was green so he didn't have to wait. He'd never been late on a delivery yet, and today was not the day to start. He stuttered his steps so his pace was in sync with Sara's. Right, left. Right, left. It kept their arms from bumping into each other. It kept the distance manageable.

"You keep looking up like you're afraid the buildings are going to fall on you. That's how I know you're new to the city. And the camera is an obvious clue that you want to remember your visit here, but it's also how I know you appreciate beauty. A camera of that quality means you are serious about your pictures; you have an artist's eye. And the fact that you followed me—and talked to me—and are still walking with me—means that you're stubborn."

"And brave," she reminded him. "Or crazy," she muttered under her breath.

He didn't think he was supposed to hear that.

"So can you teach me?" she asked, tilting her head up at him. She wasn't short by any means, but she still wasn't as tall as he was. "To look? And see?"

"You already know how."

"No, I don't. Not like that."

He raised an eyebrow, a half question, half challenge. "Then why did you take my picture?"

Sara

Chapter 3

Good question. Why *had* I taken his picture? I paused, my hand cradling the camera again. "Because it felt like the right thing to do," I admitted in an unexpectedly soft voice.

"And do you always do what *feels* right—or what is *actually* right?"

"What does that mean?" I bristled. I had been raised to believe that when your feelings led you toward something good, then it was best to follow them. And although taking Sam's picture might have been impulsive, I didn't think it was a bad thing.

Sam fidgeted with the strap of his bag while he walked. "I'm sorry if that sounded confrontational. All I meant was that sometimes it's hard to tell what the right thing to do is. Take this situation, for example. You tagging along with me while I do my job probably isn't the smartest thing either one of us has done, yet—" He hesitated, his eyes focused forward. "Yet it feels *right*."

I matched my pace to his. I knew how he felt. This moment, this meeting, did feel right. Somehow just knowing the name of another person in this big city had made me feel a part of it. And

Sam seemed nice enough. He hadn't tried to kidnap me or steal from me. He hadn't demanded I leave him alone. In fact, he'd invited me along, and I felt like he'd attempted to make me feel comfortable walking next to him by allowing me some space and keeping our pace even.

"So what's your job?" I asked.

His hand drifted down to the body of his messenger bag. "I find things for people."

"You look a little young to be a PI. And a little scrawny to work in repo."

He shook his head. "I'm freelance."

"So who do you work for now?"

"Right now I'm finding something for my brother. His boss is . . . specific about certain things, and when Paul can't find them on his own, he asks me to help."

"He makes you work on Saturday?"

"I work when there's work to do."

"You don't go to school?"

"Graduated early," he said, his words clipped.

"Lucky." I blew out my breath, ruffling the hair above my eyes. "I still have one more year."

We crossed a street, angling past a newsstand. "So the book in your bag is for his boss?" I asked.

"How did you know—?" he started, the faintest sound of panic in his voice.

"I saw you with it." He wasn't the only one who could be observant. I lifted my arm, my camera dangling from the wrist strap. "I stole your soul outside the bookstore, remember? I love books; which one did you buy? Maybe I've read it."

He glanced at me. "I can't say."

"Can't, or won't?"

"Won't." Sam didn't look at me.

"Oh, so it's one of *those* kinds of books," I teased.

Red touched his cheeks. "No, it's not."

"Then why can't—*won't*—you tell me? It's just a book."

"No, it's not," he said again, more firmly this time.

With that, my curiosity was caught. A book that was more than a book? A secret pickup for a mysterious client? And we were en route to deliver it. The sweet burn of excitement filled my belly, and I grinned. Today was going to be a good day after all.

When Sam didn't say anything else, I said breezily, "No, no, attorney-client privilege, I get it."

He sighed. "I take my job very seriously. People need things; I find things. But *need* is something that is private—personal. If you knew what I'd found for this person, then you'd know something about them. You'd know something about what they *needed.* And what my brother's boss needs more than anything at the moment is privacy."

We walked a few more steps together.

"What kinds of things do you find?" I asked.

"I can find anything." He said this rather matter-of-factly. Not a boast or a brag. Just the simple truth.

"Just books?" I asked.

Sam shook his head. "This was a rare request."

The sky above us was a cloudless blue, bright and hot. "What was the strangest request you've had? I mean, if you don't mind my asking. If it's not *confidential.*"

He gave me a slow smile. "That's easy. I once tracked down an honest-to-goodness pirate treasure map."

"Like with 'X marks the spot' and everything?"

He nodded. "It even said 'Here there be dragons' in the margins of the oceans."

"No. Way."

"Way."

"Where did you find it? Who wanted it? A *pirate* map—" My voice trailed off into the high-pitched squeak it hit whenever I was excited about something.

Sam laughed, but not to mock me. "Would you believe me if I said I found it at the pirate treasure map store and bought it for Long John Silver?"

I laughed back. "Not a chance."

"Okay, okay. Here's the story. I was in SoHo on a job for my brother when I stumbled onto a movie set."

"Which movie?"

Sam waved his hand. "Doesn't matter. What matters is that I saw a former client of mine working as an extra in the scene. During a break, he came over and told me that Vanessa was finally ready to trade."

"Who's Vanessa?"

"You ask a lot of questions, don't you?"

I didn't apologize. "I like knowing the answers."

Sam looked at me straight on, his dark brown eyes searching mine, searching *me.* The hairs on my arm shivered to attention. A warm wave shifted inside me under his scrutiny. He tilted his head so slightly I almost missed it—a gesture of acknowledgment and acceptance.

When he looked away, I felt like he had plucked an important bit of information out of my mind and filed it away for future reference.

Oddly enough, I didn't mind.

"So who's Vanessa?" I repeated when the silence between us had stretched almost to the point of being uncomfortable.

"Vanessa is a Creole voodoo priestess. She has an art studio in SoHo, where she lives."

I stopped walking. "She's a *what,* now?"

Sam didn't stop with me. Instead he turned on his heel and walked backward. "She's from New Orleans, originally, but she moved here four or five years ago. Tired of battling hurricanes, she said."

I closed the distance, my mouth hanging open in surprise.

"A voodoo priestess," I repeated. "Like in zombies and black magic and stuff?"

"No, actually, nothing like that at all." Sam looked at me again as though reconsidering where to put me in the filing system in his head. "You really don't get out much, do you?"

"You're the one who noticed this is my first time in the city."

"Where are you from, anyway?"

"Don't change the subject. I want to hear the rest of the story."

"And I want to hear about you," he said. From anyone else, that might have sounded like a bad pickup line, but all I sensed from Sam was genuine interest. I couldn't tell if the flutter I felt was flattery or disbelief.

"No, you don't. Trust me, Vanessa the voodoo priestess is a lot more exciting than I am."

"Trade you for it," Sam said, a shaded gleam in his brown eyes. Even walking backwards, he managed to avoid bumping into people, exhibiting a natural grace and instinct.

"Trade me for what?"

"Your story for Vanessa's story—and the story of the pirate map."

"I don't have a story."

"Sure you do. Everyone does."

"Mine is lame."

Sam shrugged. "You'll never know that if you don't tell it. Maybe Vanessa's story is the lame one and yours is the one filled with zombies and black magic and stuff."

I laughed. "I doubt that. I don't even like zombies."

"But you *do* like pirates. And stories about their treasure maps." He raised an eyebrow as though daring me to contradict him.

"Everyone likes pirates."

"Law-abiding sailors don't."

I mulled that over. "True," I granted. "But law-abiding sailors don't bury treasure, either."

"You might be surprised," Sam said.

"I'm still not sure a story for a story is a fair trade."

"Are you kidding? That's totally a fair trade. It's the very definition of a fair trade."

"Sorry, not interested. Try again."

He stopped in the shadow of an enormous, beautiful gray building. The roof was a light shade of green. Flags snapped above us in the breeze. "How's this: I'll finish telling you the story of Vanessa and the pirates, and, in exchange, you let me buy you lunch."

Sam

Chapter 4

HER FACE TURNED A DUSKY PINK COLOR. She shifted her weight on her feet and hooked a strand of long, blondish-brown hair behind her ear. "Oh, I couldn't let you do that."

"You won't be."

Sam saw her eyebrows start to twitch up and answered before she could say anything.

"You aren't *letting* me do anything. It's a trade, remember?"

"But I thought you wanted a fair trade. What do you get out of it?"

He shrugged. "Lunch. And some company." *And a chance to find out more about you,* he thought.

Still she hesitated. He wasn't used to that. Usually when he offered something, the girl said yes right away.

"It's almost one—past lunch, but not by much. And I'm willing to bet that, even if you had breakfast this morning, you're probably hungry by now."

She pressed her hand to her stomach as though afraid he had heard the growl, which he had. "Okay, I guess," she said. "Deal."

"Good," Sam said and turned immediately toward the building's doors.

A doorman in a long burgundy coat and white gloves sprang into action, smoothly opening the door and nodding them inside.

"Wait—we're having lunch here?" Sara's voice cracked on the last word.

"Welcome to the Plaza Hotel," the doorman said as Sam led the way into the opulent lobby.

"Business first, then lunch," Sam said. "I told my brother I'd meet him here at one."

Sara tugged at the hem of her dark red T-shirt and hurriedly ran her fingers through her hair.

Sam cut diagonally across the lobby, bypassing the check-in counter with a single wave to the afternoon manager and heading directly for the gleaming concierge desk in the corner. Will was on duty, talking to an elderly couple and looking none too happy about it.

"Are you sure we can't just walk to the Statue of Liberty?" the man was asking Will.

"I wouldn't recommend it," Will said in the tone of a man who had said it more than once already. "Considering it's on an island. Like I said, the fastest way would be to take the A train south to—"

"Oh, the subway?" the woman said, placing her hand on her husband's arm. They were wearing matching I Heart NY shirts. "I don't know about that—"

"Then perhaps you'd like me to call a taxi for you?" Will suggested, a strain appearing in his smile.

"A taxi would be terribly expensive, though, wouldn't it?" the woman said, pulling her purse closer to her chest.

Will looked up as Sam approached, his nod acknowledging an equal, but his eyes begging for help.

Sam reached into his bag and pulled out a pamphlet. He stepped up to the side of the counter. "I'm sorry to interrupt," he said, flashing a white smile, "but have you seen the Panorama yet?" He set the pamphlet down and slid it a fraction of an inch closer to the tourists. "It's a little out of the way, but it's a wonderful place to visit if you want to see the whole city all at once. There is a perfect reconstruction of the entire island—but done in miniature. You can see everything from uptown to the Statue of Liberty. You'll never look at New York the same way again."

The man picked up the slick white flyer, flipped it over, and raised his eyebrows in pleasant surprise. "There's a half-off coupon, too." He handed it to his wife. "What do you think, sweetie?"

"I think it's exactly what we were looking for." She gave Will a pointed glare, then reached over and squeezed Sam's arm. "Thank you for the recommendation, dear."

The couple left, heads together, planning out their afternoon.

Will leaned his elbows on the counter and dropped his head in his hands. "Shoot me, Sam. I'm begging you, just shoot me."

"Can't today, Will, sorry." Sam drummed his fingers absently against the marble countertop.

Will groaned and rubbed his eyes with the heels of his hands. "Tourists," he spat. "They couldn't make up their minds what they wanted to do—sightsee, go eat, catch a show—and every suggestion I made, they shot down. You heard them—it was like that for *hours.* This is New York, for crying out loud. There are a thousand things to do—pick one!"

"At least they left happy," Sam said.

"Thanks to you." Will straightened up, peering at Sam through narrow eyes. "The Panorama? Isn't that in Queens?"

Sam shrugged. "I bet the cab fare there is still cheaper than it is to Battery Park. Besides, it's an amazing sight. You should go sometime. I learned about it from a friend of a friend of . . ."

"A friend," Will finished. "Yeah, I know. You never divulge your sources."

"If I did, I'd be out of a job."

Will grimaced. "You could always have mine."

Sam laughed. "And direct tourists to the Statue of Liberty every day? No, thanks."

"Some friend you are. And speaking of friends," Will started, his attention sliding from Sam to Sara, a wicked curiosity gleaming in his blue eyes.

"Will, this is Sara without the *h*. She's a tourist, but don't hold that against her. Sara, this is Will. He's quite the ladies' man—or so he thinks—and you should totally hold that against him."

"It's nice to meet you," Sara said, holding out her hand for Will to shake.

Will did more than that, his fingers lingering on her wrist, his professional smile softening into a grin. His shoulders slouched forward into an assumed intimacy.

The ornate grandfather clock in the lobby chimed the hour and Sam pushed away from the counter, deftly extracting Sara's hand from Will's and angling his shoulder between them.

"And that's my cue." He turned toward a set of elevator doors hidden in the wall. "Don't want to be late."

Will gestured with a sweep of his arm. "Be my guest. Though, a word of advice? Be careful. She's been on the warpath all day. Rumor has it that she made Rebecca cry—twice."

"I'm always careful," Sam said. He stepped forward, Sara right behind him, when Will cleared his throat almost apologetically.

"C'mon, Sam, you know the rules. No one goes upstairs unless they're on the list."

Sam turned back to the counter. "But she *is* on the list."

Will raised one eyebrow and held out a clipboard.

Sam took the board, grabbed a pen from Will's desk, and wrote *IOU One Free Favor.* "See. She's right here—Sara." He handed the clipboard back to Will. "Without the *h*."

Will squinted at the paper. "Hmm, I can't quite make out her last name . . ."

Grabbing the clipboard, Sam crossed out *one* and wrote in *two.* "Happy?"

"Extremely. Have fun. And good luck." Will slid his ID card through a scanner and the elevator doors opened with an austere chime.

Sam stepped inside, pulling Sara in with him. There was only one button on the panel, which Sam pushed.

The doors closed and the elevator ascended silently toward the top floor. "Stay with me. And once we get off the elevator, don't talk to anyone."

Sara's green eyes revealed a mix of nervousness and excitement.

He leaned closer and squeezed her hand. "Don't worry. Everything's going to be fine." He tried to ignore the warmth of her fingers against his, but not very hard.

Sara

Chapter 5

Silence filled the elevator. I couldn't even really hear the hum of the machinery as the cables pulled us upward. Of course, the beating of my heart sounded like thunder in my ears, so that could have caused some of my sudden deafness.

He was holding my hand. I was afraid to move too much in case he realized his mistake and stepped away from me.

No sweaty palms. No sweaty palms, I prayed, concentrating on keeping my hands as cool and dry as the desert. As if I had any control over that. But I had to try—he was *holding my hand.*

A nervous feeling skittered up and down the back of my throat, tasting like questions. Why was he holding my hand? Was it an accident? Had he forgotten? Did he expect something from me? How come no one had ever told me how exhilarating it could be to suddenly be holding hands with a strange boy?

And Sam was strange—but not in a creepy, gotta-get-outta-here way. His strangeness seemed to stem more from the turn of his conversation and his uncanny way of looking at people as though he knew exactly what they were thinking. I hoped he didn't know what I was thinking at the moment, which was a jumbled mess of *hooray* and *uh-oh*.

I opted for *hooray*. Besides, Dad had told me to have fun today.

"Sorry about Will," Sam said quietly.

"What?" I blurted out, hoping he hadn't noticed my distractedness.

Sam's smile was as quiet as his words. Of course he had noticed; I had a feeling he noticed everything.

"Will is nice, but not someone you'd want to get involved with."

"Because he's a ladies' man?" I thought back to Will's bright blue eyes and wondered how many girls had fallen into them.

"Because he can be careless."

"That doesn't sound so bad."

"Said by a girl who has probably never had her heart broken."

I felt my face heat up. "I'm seventeen. I've had plenty of boyfriends," I lied. I didn't know why I did it. I wasn't usually a liar, but I didn't want to admit that Sam had seen right to the heart of me. No serious boyfriend—yet. No real first kiss, either. And besides, I *had* had my heart broken—but that wasn't a story I wanted to tell.

He let the lie slide, though again I got the impression that he knew more than he was letting on.

The doors opened. When we stepped out, I thought for a moment I'd gone to heaven. A sharp white light filled the hallway from floor to ceiling. Thick white carpet unrolled before us, leading to a set of white wooden double doors at the other end of the hallway. I could see the polished gleam of the gold handles from where I stood. A handful of gilt-framed mirrors hung over narrow silver tables that were lining the walls. On the tables stood crystal vases filled with white lilies, the green stems a stark blast of color.

"What is this place?" I whispered.

Before Sam could answer, the large double doors swung open and a short girl in a blue and gray uniform ran through them. Literally *ran* in an all-out track-and-field sprint like the building was burning down behind her.

A howling followed her—a long, mournful wail that set the hairs on the back of my neck to shivering.

"Oh, no," Sam murmured. He dropped my hand in time to catch the fleeing girl right before she crashed into his arms, sobbing and quivering.

"I've had it," she choked out. "I can't take it anymore, Sam. She's a—"

"I know, Rebecca, I know," Sam interrupted, but gently. He reached into his bag and pulled out a water bottle. He handed it to the girl, who immediately twisted off the cap and gulped down a swallow, then two. "What happened this time?"

She barked out a laugh, the water on her lips making them glisten as brightly as the tears in her eyes. "What *didn't* happen? Her lunch was late. Her champagne was the wrong temperature. Bootsie's food dish wasn't full to the brim. Take your pick." She wiped at her eyes with the back of her wrist. "I didn't mean for it to happen, I swear. But I was in such a rush to get back from the kitchen and I didn't see Bootsie—she must have followed me, I don't know—and I tripped and stepped on the dog's leg . . . and I heard something snap." She shook her head, her eyes slightly unfocused. "She said she was going to fire me, Sam. I can't do this anymore . . . I gotta get out of here."

"I know," Sam said again. "Let me talk to Paul. I'll see what I can do."

She laughed again, but the sound was hollow and strained. "Can you set a dog's broken leg?"

The howling rose in pitch and volume, and all three of us looked toward the partially open doors at the end of the hallway.

Sam lifted one shoulder in a shrug. "Never tried. But you never know."

Rebecca seemed to see me for the first time and her mouth thinned. She looked from me to Sam and back again. "I don't know you, but you shouldn't be here. Not today. Not any day. If she sees you, there's no telling what she'll do." She grabbed my arm and turned me toward the elevator doors.

I shot a desperate glance at Sam. Maybe Rebecca was right and I was in the wrong place at the wrong time, but the only person I knew in the whole hotel was Sam. I heard my dad's voice in the back of my head reminding me that I didn't even really know Sam that well, but I ignored the caution. I didn't want to go with Rebecca. I didn't want to wait in the lobby with Will. I wanted to stay with Sam.

Sam, for his part, didn't hesitate. He placed his hand over Rebecca's and, just like that, he had set me free. "I can handle it. Trust me."

Rebecca downed the last of the water and looked at Sam with narrowed eyes. "I bet you say that to everyone—right before everything falls apart."

Sam's face paled and he dropped Rebecca's hand like she'd sprouted claws.

Bootsie's howl had turned into a harsh, labored panting, punctuated by a weird mix of yips and yelps.

"Do what you want," Rebecca muttered. "I'm leaving." She touched my shoulder as she passed me. "Last chance to come with me," she offered.

I shook my head, but it didn't matter. Rebecca had already stepped into the elevator.

"You sure?" Sam asked me once we were alone, the look in his eye making me think he was reevaluating me yet again, finding a new place for me in the filing cabinet of his mind.

I shrugged with more courage than I felt. "You already know I'm equal parts stubborn and brave," I echoed his earlier words back to him, making him smile.

"Sam!" a sharp voice hissed from the suite doors. A man stepped into the hallway, dressed in the same kind of blue and gray uniform that Rebecca had been wearing. A whimpering bundle wrapped in a hot pink blanket was tucked in the crook of his arm. He closed the door firmly behind him before he turned back to us. "What the hell are you doing here?"

"Delivering the book. Like you asked me to, Paul." Sam adjusted his messenger bag but didn't move otherwise. "How's Bootsie?"

Paul and Sam could have been twins—same brown hair, same brown eyes—but because Paul was just that much taller than Sam, I could tell he was the older of the two brothers. That and the way he stormed down the hallway like an angry father preparing to scold a disobedient child.

"How do you think?" Paul snapped, barely sparing a glance for me. "The little rat has a broken leg. Where did Rebecca go? This is her mess; she should be here to clean it up. I swear when I find her—" Paul drew in a deep breath through his nose and exhaled slowly. "I need your help."

Sam looked blandly at the blanket. "Obviously."

"Not with the dog. I have to take her to the vet personally. She'll ask me too many questions I won't be able to answer if I'm not there. And forget going back inside without her pet. She'd have my head."

"Tough day at the office?" Sam asked.

Paul's lips flattened into an unhappy line. "Let's just say I'm already on thin ice."

"Is she okay?" I asked quietly, peering forward and trying to catch a glimpse of the small animal. "Bootsie, I mean. It sounded like she was in a lot of pain." I loved all kinds of furry creatures, and my heart ached at the thought of the poor dog's pain.

Paul rolled his eyes. "Apparently Bootsie likes Valium almost as much as her owner does."

"You drugged the dog?" I blurted out. "Isn't that dangerous?"

"How should I know?" He glanced between me and Sam. A line creased his forehead.

"I'm Sara," I sighed. I was getting a little tired of introducing myself all the time. "And before you say it, yes, I know I'm not supposed to be here."

"I know that look, Paul," Sam said, an edge to his voice. "What are you thinking?"

"You still have the book?"

Sam nodded.

"Good. Give it to her." Paul jerked his head in my direction.

"What?" I asked.

"Why?" Sam echoed at the same time.

Paul shook his head, impatient. "The book is the perfect distraction, which is exactly what she needs right now. And if she thinks someone from the bookstore came to deliver the book *personally*—"

"No," Sam said in a tone that refused discussion. "Not Sara. I'll do it."

Paul huffed out his frustration. "You can't."

"Why not?" Sam folded his arms and lifted his chin.

"Because she's doing a cleanse this month, trying to align her feminine chi."

I was impressed that Paul managed to say that without cracking a smile.

"So?" Sam challenged.

"So no boys allowed," Paul said, biting off each word.

"You were in there," Sam said, his head jutting toward the apartment doors.

I wondered why he was so determined to keep me out of Paul's clutches. It was just a book. How bad could delivering it be?

"Why do you think she's already mad at me?" Bootsie whimpered in Paul's arms. He looked down, grimacing. "I gotta go."

"But—"

"It's not your call, little brother. Give me the book."

Sam

Chapter 6

Paul held out his free hand and waited. Bootsie's whimpers rose in pitch; she panted and squirmed. Sam wondered if the Valium was already wearing off. Paul snapped his fingers, demanding more than patience.

With a sigh, Sam flipped open the top flap of his messenger bag and withdrew the brown-wrapped package from the bookstore. He plunked it into his brother's hand. A muscle jumped in the back of his jaw and the darkness in his eyes turned from brown to black.

Paul immediately passed the book to Sara. "Don't open it. Don't be there when she opens it. Don't ask what it is. Don't invite conversation. Don't sit down. Don't touch anything. If you're not in and out in five seconds, you've done something wrong." He glared at her. "Do. *Not*. Get. Me. Fired."

Sara froze, holding the book unnaturally in front of her as though she had caught it mid-drop but then had forgotten to bring it to her side. Her face had lost the rosy blush she'd had in the elevator. Sam missed it. A little color brought her to life, and seeing her so pale and stiff felt wrong.

Of course, there was too much about this situation that was wrong. The whole day was turning into a disaster. He should have sent Sara away with Rebecca when he had the chance. Or at least listened to Will and left Sara in the lobby. Better yet, he should have cut through the back room of Scoops and disappeared. It would have been safer—for everyone.

Paul shifted his intensity to Sam. "I'll be back in thirty minutes."

"We'll be gone in twenty-nine," Sam said, a weariness in his voice that he hated to hear.

Paul didn't even turn around. "Be gone in two." Then he stepped into the elevator and was gone.

Silence filled the hallway again for a beat or two. Sam shifted his weight, feeling the familiar demand for movement building in his bones. Paul was right; they should be gone sooner rather than later. He reached for the book in Sara's hand. "You don't have to do this, you know. We can just leave the book by the door."

Sara blinked as though waking up from a dream. "I know." She pulled the book close to her chest.

"Let me put it another way: I don't think you should do this."

"I know that too." Sara hefted the book in her hands, eyeing the closed door at the end of the hallway.

He sighed. He knew that look. He'd seen it on his own reflection more than once. "You're going to do it anyway, aren't you?"

Shrugging, she cocked her hip out to one side. "If delivering the book keeps your brother out of trouble, then I don't really see what the problem is. It's like Paul said—in and out. Two minutes flat."

"Paul isn't always right."

"Is he right about this?"

Sam's lips thinned. His silence was his answer.

Sara took a step toward the door.

"Wait," Sam said, catching her elbow. "If you're going to go through with this, you might as well look the part."

Sam's eyes touched Sara at shoulder, wrist, hip, but softly. A glance. A brush.

Sara looked down at her clothes. "T-shirt and jeans. I know. Really original. But give me a break. I'm on vacation. I didn't exactly plan on this."

Sam shook his head. "You look—" The glance moved over her again, but on the opposite side—shoulder, wrist, hip—crisscrossing her body. A swallow moved down his throat.

He gently slid her camera off her wrist and looped the strap around his own. He plucked the sunglasses off her head. A wisp of brownish-blonde hair curled up and away and, without thinking, he smoothed it down by her ear and allowed the edge of his thumb to graze the edge of her cheek.

She glanced up at him in surprise, and he dropped his hand from her face, fumbling at his bag as though nothing was wrong. Instinct screamed at him to step back, to leave, to *move.*

"I think . . . ah, yes." His fingers found what he was looking for at the bottom of the bag, and he withdrew a small golden rectangle with a pin clasp on one side and the name "Sam" printed in black letters on the other.

He held out the name tag for her on his open palm. A gentleman might have offered to pin it to her shirt, but he didn't dare get too close. Not again.

"Do I want to know why you're carrying around a spare name tag?" she asked, tucking the book under her arm and plucking the gold bar from his hand. "I thought you freelanced."

"I do. But you never know when a bit of official-looking identification will come in handy."

"Like today?" She pinched the front of her shirt between her fingers and fastened the name tag just below her collarbone.

"Like today," he agreed, taking a step back and leaning against one of the tables lining the wall.

"Sam," she said, her tone thoughtful and careful.

He looked up, anticipating a question, then realized she was merely reading the name off the tag.

"Short for Samantha?" he suggested.

She tilted her head, considering, then nodded. "Samantha. And I work at . . ." She flipped the book back into her hands and read the name printed on the sticker holding the wrapping closed. "Chasing Pages."

"New York's finest bookstore," Sam added. "With New York's finest employees."

She looked up at him, her eyes meeting his, then shifting away.

He bit back a curse. He'd made her uncomfortable. He hadn't meant to do that. But, on the plus side, that warm hint of color had returned to her cheeks, and there was nothing wrong with that, in his opinion.

Sara took a deep breath and touched her hair with her free hand. "Why am I so nervous all of a sudden?" she asked, her voice filled with a breathy laugh.

His own throat constricted a little at the sound. What was that about? He had only just met her. He shouldn't be reacting like this. But it had been a long time since he'd felt so comfortable with a girl so quickly. And a pretty girl at that. Not since—no, he cut off that line of thought and looked down at his boots.

"Because, Samantha from Chasing Pages, this is your first time making a delivery to Piper Kinkade's personal penthouse suite—and that would make anyone nervous."

Sara's mouth dropped open, and her brown eyes glazed over in shock. "Piper Kinkade?"

Sam relaxed, knowing Sara's attention had been successfully diverted to a safer topic. Though how safe Piper was remained to be seen.

"You lie," Sara accused, her eyes narrowing.

"You don't know me well enough to know when I'm lying."

"*The* Piper Kinkade? As in the *actress* Piper Kinkade? Star of *Graffiti* and *Central Park West* and *Sunflower Girl?*" Her voice slid up in an excited squeak.

"She also had a bit part in *Dance Dance America: A Two-Step Story,* but that was her first movie; she doesn't like to talk about it."

Sara stared down the hallway. "Are you telling me that your brother works for Piper Kinkade, and that I'm supposed to go in there and make sure she doesn't fire him?"

Sam bobbed his head right, then left. "More or less—yes."

Sara swallowed. Her hand touched her hair again, a nervous habit Sam noted and filed away.

"There's still time to change your mind," he said quietly.

His words seemed to break Sara from her paralysis, and she blinked three times. She took a deep breath. "You don't know me well enough yet to know that I never change my mind."

She slung her bag off her shoulder and handed it to Sam. Then she secured the book under her arm and touched the name tag as if for luck. When she walked toward the door, she didn't look back. Her knock was perfectly halfway between a request and a demand. Professional, but courteous.

After a moment, Sara squared her shoulders and opened the door. She stepped through, leaving Sam alone in the hallway.

The afterimage of her shape lingered in his eyes.

Yet. He liked the sound of that.

Sara

Chapter 7

The room I stepped into was an extension of the hallway of light outside. Everything was white. The couch. The carpet. The curtains. I wondered how Piper survived in such a sterile environment without going crazy, but as my eyes adjusted, I noticed that the billowing clouds of whiteness were not all exactly the same color. There were subtle hues and tones to the throw pillows, the paint on the walls, the blanket artfully draped over the back of a chair that somehow gave the room depth and dimension.

Someone had spent countless hours and dollars to make it look like no effort had been spent at all.

Someone else had defied the aesthetic and demanded their own style be seen.

Splashes of hot pink were scattered throughout the room. A dog dish encrusted with sparkling jewels sat near a distant door—I hoped the baubles were glass, but somehow doubted it. A fluffy pink pillow embroidered with Bootsie's name along the edge seared my eyes like a laser. Dozens of pictures of Piper and Bootsie hung on the walls or rested on the otherwise clear tabletops, each photograph framed in hot bubblegum pink. Some frames even had dark pink hearts painted on them.

What decorating madness had I stepped into?

The suite was empty, and I breathed a sigh of relief. Paul hadn't needed to worry about his job. Sam hadn't needed to stay in the hallway. Whatever fireworks they had expected to happen had fizzled. Piper's feminine chi—whatever that was—could be aligned without worry, because wherever Piper was, it wasn't here.

I had to admit it, I was a little disappointed. I had loved Piper in *Sunflower Girl;* she had played Claire, who, at sixteen, finds out she'd been adopted and then spends the rest of the movie searching for her birth mother and the family she hadn't known she had. Claire was so brave and so vulnerable, and I could relate to her feelings of loss and abandonment. I'd seen the movie four times in the theater and had cried every time. And now I was going to miss out on my one chance to meet, in private and in person, the girl who'd brought Claire to life. Just my luck.

And then I heard the sound of sobbing coming from a back room.

The book suddenly gained weight in my hands, the grocery-bag paper rough under my fingers.

Piper was here after all. My mouth went dry.

Piper Kinkade. The darling of the media. The princess of popularity. A trendsetter. What she wore, what she said, everything she did—*mattered.* She was the reigning pop queen, the girl-next-door who had made it big. She was a *movie star.* She couldn't really be as terrible as Paul and Rebecca had made her out to be, could she?

The sob was followed by the crash of glass hitting the wall, the sound as sharp-edged as a scream.

My heart quivered, shot through with an arrow of fear.

Maybe I should just leave the book on the nearest table and quietly slip away like Paul had instructed. She would never even know I had been here.

My hand hovered over the table, my fingers ready to relax and let gravity make the decision for me. But—

But Piper was still crying. She was probably worried about her dog. Who wouldn't be? Paul hadn't struck me as much of a dog-lover. I'd be hesitant to hand over my beloved pet to someone who might not care for it as much as I did.

I took a step forward, my feet somehow more certain than the rest of me was. The lush carpet was the color of eggshells.

Gliding through the white landscape like a ghost, I crept closer to the door that muffled the shrill sounds of anguish.

An echo of Paul's voice yelled at me from inside my head, warning me back and away, demanding that I go—*now.*

But Piper was in pain. How could I turn my back on someone who needed comfort?

I'd just knock. Just once. And if she didn't hear me, or didn't answer, then I'd leave the book by her door and slip away. She'd get her book, Paul would keep his job, I'd get out of here intact. Everyone would win.

My knuckles brushed against the door, sounding like a rasp instead of a cough.

The crying switched off like a radio.

The door fell away from my hand, wrenched open so fast I felt the pull of air past me like an inhaled breath.

Piper Kinkade stood in the doorway, one hand clutching her hot-pink bathrobe at the throat, her other hand wrapped around the door handle in a fist. Her face looked soft, almost like her makeup had melted under the heat of her tears, but her eyes were hard. Angry. I knew she was only nineteen, but the fury in her face made her look older.

"What?" she spat. "How did you get in here? Who are you? Why didn't Paul stop you?" She kept her gaze locked on me and raised her voice in a shrill wail. "Paul-ie! Come here!"

I cringed. It was the same tone most people used when calling their dog or reprimanding a small child.

Piper drew in another breath, but before she could bellow for Paul again, I jumped in.

"I'm Sam . . . antha," I managed, touching the name tag pinned to my shirt. "I'm from Chasing Pages. The bookstore? And I brought you the book you wanted." All my words ran together into one big lump of sound. I hoped they made sense to Piper. I wasn't sure I could repeat them.

Piper relaxed a little. Her hunched shoulders smoothed out, and she stopped strangling her bathrobe collar. She brushed her fingertips beneath her eyes, wiping away the smudges of black mascara. Red spots glowed high in her cheeks, but I couldn't tell if it was leftover rouge or high emotion. Her famous blonde hair had been pulled back into a ponytail, a few wisps escaping like shooting stars. She didn't seem to care that I had caught her at a time when she wasn't all primped and polished and perfect.

Even in her less-than-perfect state, I could see why Piper was a movie star. There was an aura of confidence around her. A sense of expectation, like she knew exactly what she wanted out of life and exactly how she could get it. The sheer force of her presence felt like a hammer blow to my senses. We were only two years apart in age; so why did I feel like such a little kid standing next to her?

I swallowed, wishing I'd listened to Paul and Sam and Will and Rebecca. They'd all tried to warn me, I realized. But I'd walked into the lion's den and there was no going back now. Facing her now, seeing the anger in her eyes, I felt the façade of her movie role persona shatter into dust. She wasn't anything like I had imagined she would be. She wasn't Claire. Disappointment sat like a rock in my stomach.

Her eyes flicked up and down, evaluating me, judging me. She was a sigh away from discarding me altogether when her gaze stopped on the book in my hands.

"Give me that," she snapped, yanking the book from my lax fingers and holding it close. "You didn't read it, did you?"

I shook my head. "I don't even know which book it is," I admitted. Curiosity burned on my tongue. I wanted to ask the title, but I couldn't make myself speak.

Piper relaxed another fraction. "Good. Let's keep it that way."

We stood in silence for a moment, the awkwardness growing between us like mold.

Piper finally sighed and rolled her eyes. She stepped back into her room, tossing the book onto her bed without a second glance. Then, pushing past me, she strode toward the front door.

For one horrible moment, I feared she was going to call security and have me thrown out of her suite. I hurried after her; I didn't want her to yell at me again.

A small table stood next to the front door. I hadn't seen it when I'd walked in, partly because, when the door was opened, the table was hidden behind it, and partly because it was the exact same shade as the wall. A stack of high-gloss, black-and-white photographs appeared to be suspended in midair along with a cup of a dozen identical silver pens. After a closer look, I realized the tabletop was made of clear, polished glass.

Piper grabbed the top picture off the stack and a pen from the cup. She jammed the top of the pen in her mouth, bit down, and pulled the pen free from its cap. Scrawling her name across her head shot, she tossed the pen back onto the tabletop.

"Happy?" She thrust the autographed picture at me, still holding the pen top between her teeth.

I accepted the offering with numb fingers. "I'm sorry . . . I don't—"

"One per person. And no, I don't do personalized autographs." She smiled, but not like she meant it.

"Oh, I see. I mean, okay, that's fine." I hated stumbling over my words in front of people, and to be reduced to a quivering lump of broken vocabulary now—in front of *her*—made me tense and uncomfortable.

"You can go now," Piper said, taking the pen cap from her mouth and waving her hands toward the door, shooing me away from her.

I swallowed. Even though every nerve in my body was screaming at me to accept the invitation and flee from the penthouse, I couldn't not ask, "Are you . . . are you okay? I mean, I heard you crying and—"

Big mistake.

Piper didn't say anything; she didn't have to. Her eyes narrowed and I could almost see the hair standing up on her arms as she bristled with suspicion and anger.

I stopped talking.

She tapped her index finger to her perfectly shaped lips. After a long moment, she said quietly, "Paul sent you here, didn't he?"

"Well, I—"

"Yes. Or no."

"Yes," I murmured. It was almost the truth. And there was no point in bringing up Sam's name. I didn't want *both* brothers to get in trouble.

"And you're new, aren't you? Samantha, was it?"

I nodded.

Her mouth stretched into a smile, but I wasn't comforted by the sight.

"You look like a nice girl. A responsible girl. An *obedient* little girl. So, Samantha, let me tell you what's going to happen next, all right?" Piper leaned back against the door, blocking me from leaving until she gave me permission. "You are going to do me a favor. If you refuse, then when Paul returns from the vet with Bootsie, all that will be waiting for him will be his pink slip. And he'll have *you* to thank for it, Samantha from Chasing Pages. You don't want that to happen, do you?"

I shook my head. My mouth was dry and cold.

She pointed past my shoulder. "What do you see there?"

Turning slowly, I followed the line of her finger. The wall to her left was dominated by an enormous gas fireplace. It was turned off at the moment, but I knew it would take only a small flip of the switch to ignite it into a roar. A marble mantel supported a handful of trinkets—all tastefully chosen—and a framed picture of Piper. It was the same head-shot image I held in my hands.

"Um," I started. My mind raced. What was the right answer? What was she looking for? What would happen if I said the wrong thing? A cold sweat slicked my palms, the backs of my knees.

"Exactly," she said. "You see it too."

I blinked and turned back to Piper. "See what? I don't understand."

She fluffed the collar of her bathrobe like it was a mink stole. For all I knew, it might have been. Reaching for one of the random silver pens, she handed it to me.

"Allow me to explain. And trust me—you're going to want to write this down."

SAM

Chapter 8

TWO PACES TO THE WALL. Two paces back. Two paces to the table. Two paces back.

Sam kept his gaze fixed on the closed white door even while pacing. He hated waiting. Worse, he hated having nothing to do while he waited.

He had returned Sara's camera safely to her bag and had successfully resisted the impulse to see what else she might have in there. He wouldn't want anyone snooping around in his bag; the least he could do was extend Sara the same courtesy.

But now there was nothing left to do but wait.

And he *hated* waiting.

Movement helped. So he paced. And watched. And waited.

He unzipped his hoodie. Zipped it again. The tiny teeth clacked as they met and separated, met and separated. The sound of being devoured was oddly comforting.

His thoughts fractured into multiple, parallel tracks.

Paul: How much time was left until his brother's thirty-minute deadline expired? What would he do when he returned and found them both still there? Would Paul's plan to distract Piper even work?

Sara: He knew deep in his gut that he shouldn't have allowed Paul to drag Sara into this mess—unaligned feminine chi or not. Even though she had agreed to do it, Sam knew Sara didn't really know what she was getting into. How could she? Sam still felt unprepared to deal with Piper face-to-face, and he'd been working with Paul for almost eighteen months now.

Before that—

He stopped that train of thought before it could depart the station.

Turning his thoughts to a safer topic—Bootsie—he wondered absently if a dog could even survive a dose of Valium.

He knew that Valium was fast acting and long lasting. Not from personal experience, of course—Sam never touched anything that would alter his reality, no matter how much he wanted his reality to change—but his mother had once kept a bottle of the pills on the back shelf of the medicine cabinet.

He remembered that dark night and even darker day when the bottle had first moved to the front of the shelf. From there it was a short trip to the bathroom counter, then to the nightstand by her bed, where it had taken up permanent residence.

The level of pills never seemed to go down even though she had taken them like candy.

No.

He stopped his thoughts again. This time, his body followed and he froze in the hallway. Triangulated between the door, the table, and the wall, he was trapped.

Sam inhaled deeply, imagining the white light that filled the air being drawn down into the darkness of his lungs. He swallowed, a part of him hoping that some of that light and air could seep into his bones and his blood. Hoping that it would sate the endless emptiness gnawing inside him.

How long had Sara been in the apartment with Piper? Five minutes? Ten? What was taking her so long, anyway?

Something must have happened. Something bad.

He took a step toward the door, but slowly, like a windup toy not yet up to full speed. A faint jingling accompanied his footsteps. The military-style dog tags around his neck had slipped free of his unzipped hoodie. They chimed against the circular token of St. Christopher that hung on the same chain.

He shoved the tags and token beneath the neck of his shirt, wincing as the cold metal touched the bare skin of his chest.

Yet another thing Sam didn't want to think about.

St. Christopher hadn't provided much protection in the past; why did he still think the future would be any different?

The white door swung open on silent hinges.

Sam caught a glimpse of Piper's blonde hair and her red, full lips above her hot-pink bathrobe before the door closed just as silently.

Sara, disgorged from the apartment, approached Sam on unsteady feet. She clutched a rolled-up paper in her hands. Her eyes were wide, the green darkening to near-black. Clearly, she was still reeling from Piper's gravitational pull.

"How did it go?" he asked. Part of him wanted to touch her arm, to provide some kind of tactile comfort, but the jut of Sara's elbows and the slant of her shoulders offered him only angles and planes. She was prepared to deflect and divert. There was no safe place to connect.

"She . . . she . . ." Sara kept walking toward the elevator, the paper in her hands tightening from a tube to a straw. "That was . . ." She shuddered, then pivoted on her heel to face Sam, who was trailing a few steps behind her.

He spoke before she could. "I'm sorry."

Sara pressed her lips together, rocked her hip to the right in a stance that was both a challenge and a warning. "Have you ever met her?"

"Not in person. I've been in her apartment before, but always with Paul. And never when she was there. Paul doesn't want her to know I exist." Which, at the end of the day, was all right with him. Invisibility had its perks.

"But you knew what she was like—in real life."

Sam hesitated, then said, "Everyone who works for her knows what she's like."

"I didn't. I thought . . . I mean, she was so good as Claire in *Sunflower Girl.* Nice. I thought that was who she was. That she was like me." Sara shook her head. "She's not nice. And she's nothing like me."

"No," Sam agreed. "No, she's not."

A silent beat of time passed, each of them looking down or away. He could feel the air around Sara fluttering as she struggled to maintain control. He didn't want her to cry.

"Thank you for going," Sam said quietly. "And if Paul was here, I know he'd say thanks too. You really helped him out today. You helped us both."

Sara sighed, her shoulders squaring a little. Her angled limbs relaxed into roundness.

"Look on the bright side," Sam said, offering up a smile. "Your work is done here, good citizen, and you'll never have to see her again."

Tension snapped back into Sara's body.

"What?" he asked, frowning. Why did he always manage to say the wrong thing at the wrong time?

"Can we go?" Sara's eyes flicked to Piper's door and then slid to the wall. "I don't want to talk about it here."

"Yeah, sure." Sam knew words weren't going to be enough to unwind Sara from the knot she was in. She needed distance, and time. And a distraction of her own.

And if there was one thing Sam was good at, it was fulfilling people's needs.

"I know a great bistro around the corner. You still hungry?" he asked, already knowing the answer.

Sara grabbed her bag and beat him to the elevator door by two long strides.

Sara

Chapter 9

"You ready to talk?" Sam asked, stirring the slurry of melting ice in the bottom of his cup with his straw.

I shook my head. Meeting Piper had taken more out of me than I wanted to admit. I was still trying to figure out what had happened, what she wanted from me, and what I was going to do about it. I didn't want to think about Piper on an empty stomach, and I was grateful that Sam hadn't pressured me to talk about it on the walk from the hotel to the bistro.

I took another bite of the most delicious hamburger I'd ever eaten. I felt a cool streak of liquid along the edge of my mouth—ketchup, no doubt. I wiped at it with the back of my wrist. Sure enough, a red smudge appeared on my hand. I heard the echo of my dad's voice in my head, telling me that what I had just done wasn't very ladylike, but too bad. Napkins would have taken too long, and there was no way I was letting go of this burger until I had devoured it all.

Sam didn't seem to notice, or care about, my lack of dining etiquette. He just looked at me with those dark brown eyes of his as if he had all the time in the world to wait for me. It was nice. A little unnerving, but nice.

"Can't talk. Eating," I said. I hadn't realized exactly how hungry I'd been until we'd walked through the doors of 24 Frames and I'd been hit with the warm, comforting aroma of grilled hamburgers and French fries.

The bistro was small and unassuming. I would have walked right past it if Sam hadn't led me directly to the door. A dozen or so tables filled the main floor, and a small bar had been wedged into one corner, a handful of dark wine bottles scattered among the jewel-toned liquids on the back shelf.

What made me instantly fall in love with the place, though, was the back wall. Painted black from floor to ceiling, the wall held a single row of twenty-four identically framed, black-and-white pictures.

At first glance, the pictures all seemed to be of the same image: a man caught in mid-stride, walking left to right, one leg extended, one leg bent, his arms frozen in mid-swing. But after the hostess sat Sam and me at our table, I was able to get a closer look.

I leaned back in my chair so I could see the entire row of images. Now I could see the subtle differences from one picture to the next. The rise and fall of his foot, the extension on his arms, the tilt of his head. I ran my eyes fast over the entire row of pictures, delighted by what I saw. What had once been a series of static images now flickered to life.

"He's walking," I said.

Sam smiled, glancing up at the wall. "Persistence of vision," he said. "It's what makes movies work. The pictures go by so fast, you don't notice the spaces in between, and your brain fills in the missing information."

The framed pictures were obviously photographs and not stills from a movie, but even so, I appreciated the sprocket holes painted above and below each image.

Taken together, the artwork was the perfect blend of film and photography, motion and stillness.

Just looking at it made the artist in me happy.

I reached for my camera on the table and snapped a picture of the back wall. Sam leaned out of the way, but not quite fast enough. I caught the side of his face and the top of one shoulder in the image as well. He was blurry, pale as a ghost against the black wall.

My thumb hovered over the ERASE option on my menu, but the more I looked at the picture, the more I liked it. It shouldn't have worked, but the balance of the ordered row of images next to the smeared blur of Sam was pleasing in an offbeat way.

"Did you miss me?" he asked, straightening in his chair.

"Don't worry, I got the shot." I turned off the camera, automatically saving the picture.

Then our food arrived, and for the next twenty minutes I was lost in a haze of deliciousness. Hamburger, fries, soda. The holy trinity of lunch.

Sam had ordered the same thing, only without lettuce on his hamburger.

I raised my eyebrow in a question.

"Lettuce has no taste. It's like a bad stage magician of the food world. No style, less substance."

I laughed. "But it provides texture—a nice crunch. Sometimes that's enough to make a difference."

"Not to me," he said.

"So, no texture in your life? You like everything exactly the same?"

"Nothing is exactly the same."

"Explain," I invited, crunching down through another bite of bun, lettuce, tomato, and hamburger. I finally understood why gluttony was such a popular sin.

Sam shrugged. "Everything's different." He pushed his fork to the center of the table and dragged mine into place next to it. "These look the same. They were made by the same manufacturer. They might have even come from the same box of utensils. But they're not the same. This one has a scratch on the handle. That one has a nick in the tine." He lined up the forks like they were soldiers awaiting orders. "They've been through the wash enough times that they've changed. They've been shaped by the hands that have used them, held them. They are *different*."

"But they're still fundamentally forks. You can still use them—even with a scratch on the handle." I reached for the fork on the left and speared two fries with it. I took a bite and grinned in pleasure.

Sam laughed. "Practical. I like that."

The warmth that filled my mouth had nothing to do with lunch and everything to do with the blush rising up my neck.

His brown eyes met mine, and he tilted his head, filing away another flash of information. I knew I should have been embarrassed at having been caught with my emotions all over my face, but I wasn't. I liked the open honesty I saw in his eyes.

I also liked the comfortableness that surrounded me and filled me. Here, sitting across from a new friend in a small, cozy, crowded bistro on a side street of one of the largest cities in the world, I felt at home. Which was strange, since I often didn't even feel at home when I was at home.

Sam tapped his fingers on the table in an idle rhythm, but I could tell it wasn't the tempo of impatience. He was as comfortable here as I was.

I took the last bite of lunch, closing my eyes to better savor the taste. Wiping my mouth with the napkin, I leaned back in my chair and sighed.

"*Now* I'm ready to talk," I said.

Sam's fingers quickened into a drumroll, and he lifted his eyebrows in expectation.

"No fanfare, please. This is serious."

He flattened his hand on the table, cutting off the sound. "Piper," he said with a nod.

"Piper," I repeated. Just the memory of her made my insides quake.

"She wasn't happy to see you, was she?"

"I don't think she's happy about anything."

"You gave her the book?"

I nodded. "And she gave me this." I reached for the rolled-up, autographed photo that I'd set on one of the extra chairs at the table. I smoothed it out and held it up like it was a piece of evidence.

"A head shot? Classy."

"There's more." I placed the photograph facedown on the wooden tabletop, pinning the corners with my glass, the salt and pepper shakers, and the edge of Sam's plate. Words covered the back of the photo, filling the top third of the space, the letters scrawled and slanted. It looked like a crazy person had written it. Which, I reflected, I might have been at the time.

Sam slipped into the empty chair next to me, leaning forward and angling his head so he could read what I had written.

"'Original but familiar. A fresh look at something ethereal. Signed one-of-a-kind. No fakes. Nothing pedestrian. Unexpected and bold. Needs to be emotionally moving. Inspiring but not sappy. Must match décor.'" Sam scrunched up his forehead. "I don't understand. What is this?"

I set my elbow on the table and leaned my head against my hand. "Piper's latest request. Well, *demand* is more like it."

"Are you supposed to give this list to Paul?" Sam ran his fingertips over the words like they were written in Braille.

I shook my head. I pointed to my chest. "She told me I had to do this for her. Just me."

"Why you?"

"Well, I may have, um, unintentionally made her mad. I think she wants me to do this for her as some kind of payback."

"It doesn't take much to make Piper mad," Sam observed, picking a stray fry off his plate. "But I wouldn't worry about it. She thinks you're Samantha who works at the bookstore. You're not and you don't." He shrugged. "You don't have to find anything for her. Trust me, she'll get over it, and you'll have a great story to tell your friends back home."

I hesitated. "There's more."

He lifted an eyebrow.

"It's about Paul."

He lifted his other eyebrow.

"She, um, she said that if I didn't agree to find this for her today, she was . . . she was going to fire Paul."

Sam blew his breath out slowly in understanding, the air ruffling the brown hair hanging over his eyes. "And so you said yes."

"I had to. If I'd blown her off and called her a psycho—which I was seriously tempted to do—then she would have fired Paul when he got back with Bootsie."

Sam looked at me for a long moment. "You don't even know Paul," he said quietly, a touch of wonder in his voice.

I shrugged. "He said he was already on thin ice with her. And if she fired him, then you'd lose your job too. I didn't want to risk it."

"Then, on behalf of both of us, I'm glad you said yes." He tapped his finger on the words spread between us. "But you don't have to do this, you know. This isn't your problem. This is just some crazy request from some crazy celebrity. Let me handle this, and you can walk away, free and clear."

I bit my lip. My once-delicious lunch sat in my stomach like a rock. "I can't just walk away. I told Piper I would do it, and I'm not a liar."

"It's not your responsibility."

"I know. But I have to at least try. Besides, I'm afraid that if I don't bring her back what she wants, she's going to fire him anyway."

"Piper isn't going to fire my brother; she relies on him too much."

"Are you sure about that?"

Sam's silence stretched past confidence and into uncertainty.

He looked over the list of requirements again. "So what is it she wants, exactly?"

"Artwork. Something that she can hang over her fireplace."

"A one-of-a-kind?"

"Signed." I tapped the paper and exhaled in frustration. "I don't have the kind of money it'll take to buy a signed, one-of-a-kind piece of artwork that is inspirational and moving and original and fresh." I leaned back in my chair. "I barely have enough money to cover lunch."

Sam waved his hand, his attention still on Piper's list. "Don't worry about lunch."

"I can't let you pay—"

"We had a deal," he reminded me. "Lunch is on me."

"The deal was Vanessa's story in exchange for lunch. You never finished the story."

Sam pushed aside the salt and pepper shakers and flipped over Piper's photo. "This is the better trade. I'll tell you Vanessa's story over dinner."

My heart lifted in hope. "And what makes you think we'll be having dinner together?"

Sam rolled up the photo and handed it back to me. "Because a job like this will take all day." He signaled the waitress to bring the bill. "And because you'll need my help."

SAM

Chapter 10

HELP? The word felt slippery in his mouth. Why had he offered to help? He should have just said he would do it alone. He worked alone. He liked working alone. *Alone* didn't invite complications. *Alone* meant no one got hurt. He shut down that thought before it could take root and refocused his attention on Sara.

It didn't matter what he thought or felt. Sara needed his help. Paul needed his help. That was all there was to it.

She was looking at him through squinted eyes as though, if she concentrated hard enough, she could bring him into focus.

"Relax," he said, trying to take his own advice. "I'm sure we can find something for Piper before she does anything drastic."

Jess stopped by the table, her hair pulled back, a pen holding the bun in place. Her name tag was pinned crookedly below the 24 Frames logo embroidered on her white shirt. "How was everything?" she asked, setting down a black folder next to Sam's plate.

"Wonderful, as usual," Sam said. He fished out a few crumpled bills from his bag and tucked them into the folder. Then he reached out and swiped two pink sugar packets from the square black container on the table. "I'm taking two, okay?"

"Two?" Jess's eyebrows rose, and she clucked her tongue in mock disapproval. "I don't think I can let you do that. Especially since you never made good on your bet from last time."

Sam grinned and dropped the packets into his bag. "When have I ever let you down, Jess?" He withdrew a small, white envelope and handed it over.

Sara leaned forward, a line of curiosity wrinkling her forehead. "What is it?"

Jess caught her breath, holding the envelope in both hands as though it were made of gold and lined with diamonds. "You didn't."

"I did," Sam said, leaning back. His grin was effortless.

"How in the world—" Jess shook her head. "No, I know better than to ask."

Sara looked from Sam to Jess. "Open it!" she said as eagerly as a kid at Christmas.

Jess laughed and jerked her head toward Sara. "Where did you find this one?"

"She found me," Sam said quietly. "But she's right. You should open it."

With slightly trembling fingers, Jess lifted the flap of the envelope and withdrew a slim, white rectangle. Her mouth opened, but no words came out, just a soft exhalation of joy.

"What is it?" Sara asked again, her voice reverent.

"A front-row ticket to *The Glass Menagerie.* There's a revival of it on Broadway, but tickets have been sold out for months. It's my favorite play." She looked at Sam with tears in her eyes. "I can't take this. It must have cost you a fortune."

Sam shrugged. "Just the cost of a sugar packet, really." He

stood up and slung his bag over his shoulder. He leaned toward Jess and brushed a kiss to her cheek. "Check the envelope. I think you missed something."

She looked down and withdrew a second ticket. Her gasp was loud in the small bistro. She threw her arms around Sam's neck and pulled him close.

He gently untangled himself and stepped back. "I couldn't send you to the play alone, could I? You should take Donovan." Sam looked over at Sara. Her eyes were wide, a sparkle of light glinting beneath the green.

Jess brushed her wrist across her cheek and made a sound somewhere between a laugh and a cry. She grabbed the black box from the table and dumped the contents into Sam's bag. "I hope you find something good," she said with a smile.

"I always do," Sam said.

Another customer waved for Jess's attention, and she carefully stashed the tickets in her apron pocket, gave Sam one last hug, and then hurried back to her tables.

Sam held the door for Sara and they stepped back into the bustling flow of people. He took a deep breath, noting the layered scents he'd come to love: a deep undertone of exhaust, the light organic scent of people and sour trash, and the high acrid zing of electricity dancing along the top.

"Are you sure you want to do this? You can still walk away, you know. I'm sure Piper won't care if I'm the one to bring her back what she wants. And, as you pointed out, if Paul gets the ax, so do I." He flicked his lips upward in a smile. "And since I happen to like my job, I have way more at stake than you do."

"I told you before—I'm not walking away."

"Why not? This is so clearly not your problem."

She looked down at her feet. "Maybe not, but I still feel

responsible." She swallowed. "I know I don't have to do this for Piper, but if I don't, then, on some level, I feel like she'll be disappointed in me. And I hate that. I know that probably makes me sound crazy, but I just . . . I just don't want it to be my fault. Especially when I could have done something to prevent it." She shook her head, her hair shivering over her shoulders. "I don't expect you to understand."

A point of cold threaded its way through Sam's belly, reaching up through his chest. He swallowed hard, forcing his thoughts to stay still even as his body continued to move forward.

"You don't sound crazy," he said, grateful that his voice didn't break.

"Really? Because I kind of *feel* crazy."

He shrugged, the cold fading deeper into his bones to the point where he could almost ignore it. "That's New York for you. This city inspires its own kind of crazy."

She laughed, light and clear. "I like it, though. So, do you think we can do this? Can we find what we need and save your job? Together?"

He smiled. "Count me in, partner."

A matching smile appeared on her face as fast and as bright as lightning before she tucked it away. But the glow remained in her eyes. "In that case, *partner,* do you have a plan for how we can find whatever it is that will make Piper happy?" she asked.

"I don't know of anything that will make Piper truly happy, but I think I know where we should start looking."

"Where's that?"

"St. John's Cathedral."

"Are you saying we're going to need a miracle?" she said, a hint of teasing in her voice. "Divine intervention?"

"Not exactly." He grinned. "Though it couldn't hurt. C'mon. It's not far."

They paused at the corner as a large red double-decker bus barreled past, the tourists on the top deck snapping pictures right and left. Sam shook his head. The pictures would probably all turn out blurry, but that was tourists for you. Too busy to stop and actually *see* the sights.

Sara reached for her camera and aimed it after the departing bus.

"What?" she said, a little defensively. "I liked the color."

"I didn't say anything." Sam held up his hands.

After they had crossed the street, Sara stashed her camera back in her shoulder bag. "So that thing with Jess—what was that all about?"

"It's what I do," he said, lifting one shoulder and one side of his mouth.

She shook her head. "You help strangers with impossible tasks?"

"I help friends with adventures."

"Semantics."

"Truth."

She hesitated, looking back toward the front façade of 24 Frames. "Am I in an adventure, then?" she asked. She ran her fingers through her hair, pulling the strands into a smooth column and then brushing the entire thing over her shoulder. He wondered if she knew what that did to the line of her neck.

"At the risk of sounding like a motivational poster, *life* is an adventure."

"And the price of an adventure is a sugar packet? What's the story behind that?"

Sam's half smile grew. "A few months ago, I told Jess I could get anything I wanted, and usually for less than the marked price. She didn't believe me, so I explained that it was all about trading."

"Trading? Like how you wanted to trade stories with me?"

"A little. It's more like you give up something small that someone needs for something better that someone else wants. If you keep things circulating, eventually you'll get what you want. Take and trade. Trade and transfer." He turned left at the corner, and Sara stayed in step with him.

"And that's how you get what you want?"

A muscle moved in his jaw. "You've got to keep moving. Stagnation kills."

"Profound," Sara said with a raised eyebrow.

"Truth," he said again. He stepped around a man with a briefcase and fell back into step with Sara. "We made a bet—me and Jess. She bet me that I couldn't bring back her heart's desire if all I could use to trade was a sugar packet."

"And you knew the tickets were her heart's desire."

"I knew *Donovan* was her heart's desire. The tickets were just an excuse to get them together."

Sara tilted her head. "But you could have done anything, then. Movie tickets would have been just as good. It didn't have to be front-row seats to her favorite play."

"You're right—it didn't *have* to be," he agreed lightly.

Her green eyes filled with light—and admiration. "Show me."

"What?"

She tilted her head the other direction. "Show me how you trade. Jess gave you all those sugar packets. Trade one for me."

A smile hovered around Sam's mouth. "Okay. What do you want?"

Sara started to shrug, but Sam held up his hand.

"Don't say you don't know."

"I wasn't—" she started.

Sam ignored the lie he saw on her face. "I can't trade without knowing what's at stake."

"I thought the important thing was to keep things moving." Sara waved her hands in small circles in front of her as though stirring the air into action.

Sam shook his head. "If you don't know what you want, you'll never get it. What's more, if you don't know what you want, you'll never know when you *do* get it." He reached into his bag and withdrew a packet. He offered it to her on the palm of his hand. "So, Sara without an *h*, tell me—what do you want?"

Sara looked from Sam's hand to his eyes and back again. Then she carefully took the sugar packet, turning the small square over and over in her fingers. She was quiet for a few steps. A bike messenger zipped past in the narrow space between sidewalk and street, his bell chiming a shrill warning. A few high clouds skidded across the sun, casting dappled shadows over the trees. Sam and Sara walked past the open door of a German deli, the distinct scent of mustard and bratwurst billowing out in a cloud around them.

"There are lots of things that I want." Her eyes stayed focused on the packet, and her voice sounded softer than he'd expected.

He looked at her sharply; he hadn't meant to strike a nerve—at least not one so clearly close to the heart.

He brushed his hand against her wrist. When she looked up at him, he said gently, "Well, then, pick just one, and let's see where it takes us."

Sara

Chapter 11

I couldn't pick just one.

The moment I'd touched the sugar packet, a thousand thoughts cascaded through my mind.

I want to go shopping in Times Square.

I want to go to the top of the Empire State Building.

I want Dad to finish his meetings and come see the city with me.

I want to travel to Paris.

I want to fall in love so hard it makes me cry.

I want . . .

I shook my head. Sam didn't know what he was asking. How could this small pink square of processed sugar be transformed into my heart's desire?

I want Mom to come home.

But I couldn't tell him that. I couldn't tell anyone that. Because it wasn't true, I told my heart. That wasn't what I wanted. Mom had left. She had made her choice, and she hadn't looked back.

Now that I'd thought about it, though, I couldn't *not*

remember. The late-night fights, followed by mornings of frosty silence. Then, one night, anger filled the kitchen like buzzing flies circling a corpse.

I was only eight, so I didn't understand everything Mom and Dad had said to each other; I didn't understand the significance of the suitcase by the door. Even when she crouched down to where I sat hidden beneath the kitchen table, my stuffed dog clutched to my chest, and said, "I'll talk to you soon, sweetie, okay?" I didn't really understand what was happening.

It wasn't until she was at the door, her suitcase in hand, that I finally understood.

It wasn't until she said good-bye that I started to cry.

I closed my hand in a fist around the sugar packet. No. Not today.

"I want to see the Giants play," I said, blurting out the first thing I could think of. My chin jutted out in a challenge.

Sam blinked. "The Giants?"

"They're famous, right? And they play in New York. We're in New York. So let's go see them play."

"It's not that easy—"

"Why not? I thought you could get anything you wanted."

Sam scratched the underside of his jaw. "I can, it's just—"

"What? It's just—what?" A hard knot of emotion lodged in my throat. I tried to swallow around it. I didn't want to be so aggressively unlikable. I could hear my dad's voice in my head: *Now, Sara, be nice.* I *was* a nice person—most of the time. I hated that the mere thought of my mom could make me feel like this.

And Sam had been nothing but nice to me today even when he didn't have to be. I knew I shouldn't be taking it out on him, but I couldn't seem to stop myself.

He looked at me with those dark brown eyes, surprisingly

serene—and perhaps a little sympathetic—and hooked his thumb beneath the strap of his messenger bag that crossed his chest. "Somehow I don't think going to a football game is what you really want."

"You don't know that. I could be a big football fan," I snapped back.

"That's true. But if so, then you'd know that the Giants aren't playing right now. It's May. Preseason games don't start until August." He hesitated, then added, "And, technically the Giants don't play in New York; their stadium is in New Jersey."

"Oh." I felt as though a trapdoor had opened up beneath my feet. All my hot anger fell through, leaving behind a blush of embarrassment.

Sam was kind enough not to laugh.

"But that doesn't mean we can't still try to see them play," he said.

"How?"

"I don't know. But I know how to start." He stopped walking in the middle of the sidewalk and reached for my hand that was still curled around the sugar packet. "Step one: trade this for something better."

Opening my hand, I saw that the paper had been crinkled and creased from the force of my fist. "Who's going to want a slightly sweaty sugar packet?"

"Are you kidding? Who *wouldn't?*" Sam grinned, and I couldn't help but feel a smile coming on.

"Gotta keep things moving, right? Stagnation kills."

His grin tightened a little on his face. He closed my fingers around the packet again. "You hold on to this. Never know when it'll be time for a trade."

I stashed the sugar packet in my bag next to my camera.

Another red double-decker bus rumbled past us, spewing exhaust. Without warning, I remembered seeing my mom's shoes turn away from me. They had been the same dark-red color as the bus. There had been a small scuff on the left heel. And the sound they had made—a crisp snap, like a twig breaking in two. I shuddered.

No.

I took a deep breath and brushed my hair away from my face. I had promised myself I wasn't going to let my mom ruin my day. I closed the door on those memories and forced myself back to the present.

"You said we were going to a church?" I slipped my sunglasses over my eyes, even though we were partially in the shade. Sam was much too observant for his own good, and I didn't want to take the risk that he would see something he shouldn't in my eyes.

"St. John's." Sam pointed. "It's just up the street."

"Then what are we waiting for? We've got a job to do."

"A job?"

"For Piper," I reminded him. "We have to find something amazing that she can hang above her fireplace—or else."

"Oh, I know. I'm well aware of the 'or else.' It's just that calling it a *job* makes it sound so . . . boring. A job is something you do every day—at least, it's something I do every day—and I'm not sure what we are doing is an everyday sort of thing."

"What would you call it, then?"

He drummed his fingers against his leg in thought. "An assignment?"

I made a face. "Sounds too much like homework."

"A threat?"

"That makes it sound too dangerous."

Sam shrugged lightly. "Then it's gotta be a quest."

"What?" I laughed. "We're not on a quest."

"Aren't we? A dashing hero"—Sam pointed at his chest—"and a beautiful girl"—he pointed at me; I blushed—"are looking for the one object that will appease the wicked queen and save us all."

"Piper," I said with distaste.

"Exactly."

"She is rather wicked," I allowed. "But a *quest?* I don't know—it sounds so . . . silly."

"That's because you're thinking of dragons and magic and elves—"

"Oh, my!" I chimed in and was rewarded with a smile from Sam. His smiles were beautiful. They added just the right amount of curve to his mouth. And they had just the smallest hint of unexplained sadness that kept them interesting.

"But a quest can be for anything—knowledge, love, a ham sandwich—not just a dragon's lair or a magical ring."

"Though I suppose you know where we can find one of those, don't you?" I teased.

"A magical ring? Maybe," he replied. "This is New York. You can find anything here."

"Hmm, while a magical ring might qualify as 'unexpected and bold,' Piper also said 'no fakes,' so it would have to be a *real* magical ring, and that might be tricky."

"True. And unless it was a hot pink magical ring, I doubt it would match her décor."

I laughed again. "So rings are out—"

"Magical rings."

"—*magical* rings are out. Dragons, too, probably." I sighed melodramatically. "I guess we'll just have to find something else to quest for. You mentioned something about a ham sandwich . . . ?"

His smile flashed bright. "So you agree with me. We *are* on a quest."

All my earlier dark thoughts had fled from the force of Sam's cheerfulness. Everything around me seemed brighter; everything inside me felt lighter. I looked up at Sam, noting the line of his jaw and the way his hair curled a little around his ears. I caught a glimpse of a silver chain around his neck, the thin metal disappearing beneath his shirt. When he ran his thumb along the underside of the strap again, I wondered what else he had in his messenger bag.

I had never met anyone like Sam before. I thought he was beyond interesting, and he seemed to offer more questions than he answered. I felt a small bubble of happiness start to swell inside my chest.

"Yes," I said after a moment. "I suppose we are."

SAM

Chapter 12

THE DOORS TO St. John's Cathedral were tall and imposing. The dark bronze appeared almost black against the carved stone panels flanking the doors. Statues of people and stories from the Bible decorated the walls and the doors. Sam recognized only a couple of them—mostly the ones from the New Testament—but he could appreciate the artistry and the work that had gone into them. He especially liked the angels that seemed to soar high above.

Sara leaned so far back, her eyes following the rise of the spires, that, for a moment, Sam worried she might fall over.

"Wow," she breathed. "This is amazing."

"You don't have cathedrals like this where you live?"

She shook her head, her mouth open slightly as she tilted her head even farther back.

"And where is that, exactly?" he asked, fishing for information. "I don't remember . . ."

"That's because I didn't say," Sara replied. She walked up the last few steps, brushing past him on her way to the doors.

"Are you ever going to tell me?" he asked.

She paused on the threshold of the doorway and looked back over her shoulder. "Maybe," she said, a daring edge to her smile.

Sam chose to hear the word as a promise instead of an evasion. There had been a moment—right before she'd hidden behind her sunglasses—when he thought he had caught a glimpse of something unexpected. A deeply hidden pain. Raw anger. And maybe a little fear. Perhaps his first impression of her had been accurate. Perhaps they were kindred spirits after all.

There were layers to her that made her intriguing because beneath those layers of emotions, Sam sensed a core of strength in her. He appreciated that. Most people would have delivered the book to Piper and then walked away from her outlandish demand with a simple, *Not my problem* attitude. Not Sara. Even after he had pointed that out to her, she had accepted the quest, and Sam suspected if anyone could see it through to the end, it would be her.

He followed her into the church, trying to remember if he had ever been as brave as Sara seemed to be. Maybe. Once. Not anymore, though.

Sara hadn't gone far. She stood just inside the doorway, her face lifted toward the high, arched ceilings. "Oh, wow," she said again. She slid her glasses back up onto her head, her face peaceful.

The afternoon light filtered through the stained-glass panels on the walls and touched the floor with color. The rich sounds of organ music filled the church. Deep bass notes rumbled through the air, followed by a flurry of ever-increasing notes that traveled all the way up the scales to a piercingly high soprano pitch. Sam had been gambling that Daniel would be on the bench this afternoon. Sounded like he was right. That was good. But Sam knew they'd have to hurry if they wanted to talk to him before he left for the day.

Sam touched Sara's shoulder and gestured for her to follow him.

They each dropped a few dollars into the donation box—the volunteer thanked Sam by name—and then they walked down the long aisle toward the nave. Tall, arched alcoves lined the aisle on either side. Sara pulled out her camera and looped the strap around her wrist. Her fingers twitched like she wanted to take a few pictures, but Sam tugged on her sleeve and quickened his pace. He wished they could take their time and really explore the church, give Sara the time she wanted to frame up some amazing pictures, but from the sound of the music filling the room, Daniel was almost done with his organ recital.

They reached the choir seats and Sam glanced up into the loft where the organist sat. A group of people stood together in a small cluster, watching Daniel play the final measures of music.

Sara sat in one of the empty chairs facing the loft, her eyes closed, basking in the echoing sound of the organ.

Daniel struck the final, thundering chord. The note held for a moment, then slowly faded away. The smattering of applause sounded weak and small in its wake. Daniel stood up from the bench and shook hands with each member of the tour group who had been watching him, then turned and stretched, lifting his arms high above his shaved head.

Sam raised his hand, waving to catch Daniel's attention. "Not bad—for a beginner," he called up in a loud whisper.

Daniel leaned his elbows on the railing. His dark skin looked even darker against the pale white marble of the balustrade. "Beginner?" he scoffed. "Nah, I *earned* my place here, my man."

"Have a minute?"

"Always. Gimme a sec; I'll be right down."

Sam joined Sara on the front row, leaning back in his chair and stretching out his long legs.

"So, do you like it here?"

She nodded. "It's so beautiful. And . . . quiet."

Sam chuckled. "You didn't appreciate the music?"

"No, it's not that. Honest. It's just . . . this place makes me feel quiet. On the inside."

"I know what you mean. An inside quiet can be a good thing." Sam absently reached for the silver chain around his neck and felt the familiar shape of the dog tags and the token that he wore beneath his shirt. As soon as he realized what he was doing, though, he dropped his hand. He hoped Sara hadn't noticed; he didn't want to invite too many questions. Or conjure up unwanted memories.

"You must come here a lot," she said. "I mean, it seems like the people know you here. The lady at the donation box. The organist."

"Oh, lots of people know me," he said, but he made sure to keep his tone light. He didn't want Sara to think he was bragging. "But I do love this place. When I first got to New York, I would come here at least once a week."

"So you must be pretty religious, then, right?"

Sam swallowed. So much for keeping his memories quiet. He hadn't meant to let the conversation take such a personal turn. Especially not here. He would have to be more careful.

Daniel emerged from one of the archways and jogged softly toward the choir seats.

"Hang on a sec." Sam stood up, grateful for the interruption, and met Daniel partway, knocking knuckles and then slapping his back in greeting.

"Good to see you, Sam, my man. What's on the agenda for today?"

"Sara and I are on a quest for a rather particular client." He gestured at Sara, who sat a few feet away. She offered a small wave, then pulled one leg onto the seat with her, wrapping her arms around her bent knee.

Daniel leaned back on his heels and whistled, low, between his teeth. "You subcontracting your subcontracts now?"

Sam shook his head. "Not exactly. This is an unusually tricky job, and I'm helping out to make sure everyone wins."

"Mm-hmm, I see, I see," Daniel said, his dark eyes dancing. "'Cuz you're all about helping the pretty girls in distress, aren't you?"

"You know it." Sam rolled his eyes. "Listen, I need a favor."

"'Course you do. These days, you never stop by unless you're on a job."

"That's not fair."

"Doesn't have to be fair—just has to be the truth. We're in a church, my man. No lies allowed."

Sam blew out his breath. "I'm not in the mood for one of your guilt trips, Daniel."

"Then stop holding on to your guilt."

Sam had to turn away from the softness in Daniel's voice. His eyes fell on Sara—all angles on the outside, but filled with quiet on the inside—and he had to look away from her as well.

"Aw, hey, man, I'm sorry," Daniel said, touching Sam's shoulder. "I didn't mean—"

"It's okay," Sam said, shrugging off the touch. He heard the snap in his voice and shook his head. "It's okay," he said again, this time softer. "I know what you meant."

"We good?"

"Yeah." Sam shifted his bag. "Always."

"Good." Daniel smiled. "Then tell me what this favor of yours is and how ol' Danny boy can help."

Sam returned the smile, though it still felt a little brittle. "I'll let Sara tell you the details." He slapped Daniel on the back again and turned him toward the choir seats, hoping to regain some of that inside quiet that he'd felt once upon a time.

Sara

Chapter 13

"*This is a tricky one,*" Daniel said, handing Piper's head shot back to me. "And this is all you have to go on?"

"Sam seemed to think you'd have some ideas that might help." I risked a glance at Sam. I hadn't been able to overhear his conversation with Daniel, but whatever they'd talked about had made Sam uncomfortable. A wall had come up around him that hadn't been there before.

"And if you don't make it back with the goods, then Paul's head will roll?" Daniel ran his palm over the top of his shaved head. "That's brutal, man."

"My first thought was to see if you were finished with your sonata yet," Sam said. He sat on the other side of Daniel but kept his eyes fixed on his boots.

"My baby? Naw, I'm not done yet. Why—what did you want with it?" A cautious tone had entered Daniel's voice.

Sam tapped his fingers on his knee in a roundabout rhythm. "When Piper said she wanted something ethereal and original, I thought of your music first."

"You did?" Daniel's face lit up at Sam's compliment. His smile took years off his age. Not that he was old to begin with, but now he looked to be about fourteen or fifteen instead of the mid-twenties I suspected he really was.

"I thought, if your sonata was done, we could make a copy of the score and frame it and give that to Piper."

Daniel's eyebrows came together. "Oh, I don't know about that. My music is personal. And my baby is shy—you know how art is." He bumped his elbow with mine as though we shared a secret.

I liked Daniel instantly.

"You write music?" I asked.

Daniel wiggled his long fingers. "Every day. You can't play for as long as I have without the music in your soul demanding to be released." He reached into his pocket and withdrew his phone. He touched a few buttons, and suddenly the screen was filled with staff lines and notes crowding together. "I'm still working on this one, but I think it'll be my best one yet."

I took Daniel's phone and scrolled through page after page of music. Partway through the last page, the notes stopped, but clearly Daniel had more he planned to write.

"I wish I could do that," I sighed.

"Write music?" Daniel retrieved his phone and slipped it back into his pocket.

I nodded.

"You play at all?"

I shrugged. "I used to play the piano—a little. Took lessons when I was a kid and everything."

"Why did you stop?" Daniel angled his body toward me, but I could see over his shoulder that Sam had sat up a little straighter as well.

"I stopped because—" My words caught in my throat. *Because my mom had been my teacher and when she left, she took the music with her.* "Because I just did, I guess," I finished, feeling lame. Heat encircled my neck. I ran my fingers over the camera in my lap, wishing I could delete a bad memory as easily I could delete a bad image.

"And because you found something else you were good at?" Daniel suggested kindly.

"What?" I looked up. "Oh, this? Yeah. I started taking pictures a while ago. It's fun, and I *am* good at it."

"I bet. Here. Take a picture of us." Daniel leaned in close to me. The scent of his cologne on his skin—something woodsy—mingled with the faint tang of fabric softener from his clothes was nice. "Cheese!" he said in preparation.

Laughing quietly, I lifted my camera and angled it as best I could, hoping to catch both of us in the frame. The flash blinded me for a moment, and I rubbed my eyes, trying to ease the afterglow I still saw.

"How'd we do?" Daniel asked. He left the camera attached to my wrist but turned it over to see the back screen. "Aw, that's pretty good."

I leaned over the screen to see for myself. The picture was pretty good, considering that I had essentially shot it blind. We were both in the frame, but our foreheads seemed huge from the forced perspective angle. Daniel's smile was wide and bright, and his dark skin looked like chocolate next to my tan. The top of Sam's head rose up behind us like a slightly blurry ghost.

I laughed. "Yeah, but I can do better. Here." I adjusted some of the settings on my camera, then reached for Daniel's hand and held it tight. I zoomed in and took another picture. When the image flashed on the back screen, I studied it, then turned the camera toward Daniel. "See? This is much better."

It was a shot of our hands clasping, but since his hand was much larger than mine and his fingers were longer than mine, my hand was almost completely lost in his. And since I had taken the picture in black and white, the contrast in our skin color was even more pronounced. But there was a gentleness in Daniel's fingers as they were wrapped around mine that came through even in the picture.

He whistled low. "You're right. That is better. Hey, Sam, take a look at this." He leaned back so Sam could take a peek, but Sam didn't look at the camera; he looked at me as though he had to once again change where he placed me in the filing cabinet in his head.

I cleared my throat and withdrew my hand from Daniel's. I hadn't done anything wrong; why did I feel like I had? I tried to shake off the feeling, but Sam wouldn't stop looking at me.

"You know what, Daniel, I just remembered," Sam said, his voice curt. "Piper wants an original, so framing a copy of your sonata won't cut it. You can keep your music all to yourself after all. I guess coming here was a bad idea."

"Don't say that," I said, saving the picture of our hands. "He didn't mean that," I said to Daniel. I leaned around to glare at Sam. "Tell him you didn't mean that."

Daniel waved his hands in front of him as though washing away Sam's insult and my words. "No, no, it's okay. I understand." He looked at me and touched the back of my hand. "I'm sorry I couldn't help you more. But, here—" He turned my hand palm up and fished a pen out of his back pocket. He wrote down a name and an address on my hand. "Go see Aces. He's always working on something new and original."

Sam muttered something under his breath, then stood up and walked across the aisle to the other side of the choir seats.

"What's his problem?" I asked Daniel. Even writing on my palm, Daniel had very meticulous handwriting.

"For as long as I've known him, Sam has been trying to outrun his demons. But he can't see the truth. His problems—they never sleep, never take a break. They'll wear him down before he can wear them out."

I studied Sam, trying to see him through Daniel's eyes. He was still the same tall, lean boy I'd met earlier outside the bookstore, but now that I knew him a little better, I could see the fatigue in his shoulders. The ragged cuffs of his jeans. The scuffs on the heels of his boots. It was like Sam said: gotta keep moving. I wondered how long Sam had been moving. I wondered if he would ever feel like he could stop. And if he really believed that if he stopped, he would die.

"How long have you known him?" I asked Daniel quietly.

"About eighteen months. He showed up at the church one day, looking for all the world like the devil was on his shoulder, whispering in his ear." Daniel slouched, stretching his arm around the back of my chair. "He's better now—a little—but some days I wonder if he's really getting better. Or if he's just getting better at hiding it."

I nodded slowly. I knew how that felt. I had been a single exposed nerve after Mom had left; the smallest thing set me off. Dad learned to walk on eggshells around me or else suffer days on end of my wild crying. He wasn't prepared to deal with that—not after the divorce—so he did his best to pretend like nothing was wrong. Eventually I followed suit, and eventually I stopped crying, and eventually we both learned to hide what we couldn't bear to talk about.

"Thanks for your help," I said again. "And I didn't get to tell you this before, but I really enjoyed your music."

Daniel ran his hand over his smooth, shaved head, eyes downcast with a hint of false modesty. "Thanks. When you find something you love, you just gotta share it, ya know."

I watched Sam take a few steps toward the massive altar at the front of the cathedral. "I know," I said. But I wondered if I was really telling the truth, or if I was just getting better at hiding the lies.

Sam

Chapter 14

HE KNEW THEY WERE TALKING about him. He couldn't hear their words, but he could hear the hissing whispers of his name as it passed between them.

Coming here had been a mistake. He knew in his bones that it had been a mistake. But learning that Piper might fire his brother had added an unexpected danger to the day. If Paul lost his job, then Sam was out of luck too. No job meant no apartment meant no more living in New York. And Sam wasn't ready to move back home—not now. Maybe not ever.

He wondered which was the worse sign: that he felt like he needed help, or that Daniel had been the first place he had turned to for help. Daniel had been a good friend in those first bad days after Sam had arrived in New York, and Sam had found plenty of solace and peace sitting in the quiet of the cathedral, but things were different now. He didn't need so much help anymore. He had figured things out and moved on.

The metal dog tags burned with a cold fire beneath his shirt. He deliberately kept his hands at his side.

He drew in a deep breath and held it, tasting the faintest trace of incense and smoke from the candles. He closed his eyes for a moment, trying to center himself, before he exhaled.

"Sam?" Sara touched his arm. He flinched and she jumped. He hadn't meant to react like that and he felt bad that he had startled her.

"All done?" he asked, though he immediately berated himself for the stupid question. It had been his idea to come here. Stupid all the way around.

"Daniel suggested we talk to someone named Aces. He said you would know him." Her voice rose up at the end, but hesitantly, as though she didn't want to burden him with too many questions.

"I do know him. We probably should have gone there first."

"I don't know . . ." Sara looked around at the giant golden cross, the towering candelabras, the small arched hallways leading away from the altar in orderly spokes. "I'm glad we came here. I'm glad I got to see this."

He looked at her sharply, wondering if there was a double meaning to her words, but her gaze had traveled back down the length of the hallway and lifted toward the massive stained-glass circle above the bronze doorways.

Daniel stood as they returned to the choir seats. "Always good to see you again," he said, holding out his hand.

Sam clasped it on instinct, gripping firmly, before Daniel surprised him by pulling him in for a rough embrace. "Hold on, my man. Things will get better. And this Sara-girl? She's something special. I know you know what I'm talking about."

"Thanks," he said, hating the scratch in his voice.

"See you Sunday?" Daniel asked, releasing Sam and clapping him on the shoulder.

"Maybe," Sam said.

"I'm going to pretend you said yes." Daniel smiled, then extended his hand to Sara. "A pleasure to meet you, too. Wish I could have helped more."

Sara quirked her lips in an almost smile. "Well, there is something I wanted to ask you . . ." She dug in her shoulder bag and offered up a slightly crumpled pink sugar packet. "What will you trade me for this?"

Daniel looked from the sugar packet to Sam to Sara. His laugh echoed in the high rafters of the cathedral. "Sam told you the secrets of his trading game, too? Man, girl, he must really like you."

This time it was Sam who turned red. He felt the heat of it in the back of his neck and along the tops of his ears. "Daniel—" he warned.

But Sara just laughed too. "He hasn't told me any secrets yet. Not really. I just thought I'd get a head start on the game."

"Good plan, good plan. Let me see what I have." He dug in his pockets, but didn't turn up much. His phone. A pen. His wallet. Thumbing through the contents of his wallet, Daniel suddenly stopped. "Aha! How's this?"

He handed Sara a slip of paper with the words "Good for One Free Manicure at any Knives and Nails salon."

"A gift certificate for a manicure?" she asked, turning the paper over in her hands as if there might be something printed on the other side. "Why do you even have this?"

"How do you think I keep my hands looking so good? Besides, I need to take care of these babies; it's how I make my living." Daniel held up his fingers and wiggled them in her direction. "Call it an occupational requirement."

"But this doesn't expire until the end of the year. Are you sure you don't want to keep it? It seems like it's worth more to you than the sugar packet."

"I thought all girls liked getting their nails done. And for free? That's too good to pass up."

"But I—"

"This is the part of the trade where you say thank you and move on," Daniel mock-whispered.

"Okay. Thanks," Sara said. "I mean, really—thanks!"

Daniel took the sugar packet from her hand and tucked it into his pocket. "You have a free manicure, and I have something sweet to remember you by. We both win."

"If you two are about done, we've gotta go," Sam cut in. His hand was wrapped around the strap of his messenger bag so tightly that his knuckles had turned white. A familiar tingle had started in the bottoms of his feet. It was time to move. And fast.

Sara giggled and rose up on her toes to brush a kiss against Daniel's cheek. "Thanks again."

Grunting, Sam turned and headed for the main doors. He'd been wrong: it was past time to move. His lungs burned with the need for fresh air. Despite the wide open spaces of the cathedral, he felt like the stone bones of the building were closing in on him. He knew that if he didn't get out under the wide blue sky, he'd be trapped forever.

On the edge of his hearing, he could hear Sara quick-stepping along behind him.

On the edge of his memory, a darkness stirred.

"Don't be a stranger," Daniel called out after them.

Sara caught up with Sam, a little out of breath. She brushed her hair back behind her ear. "That was rude. What's your rush?"

He couldn't speak. He couldn't breathe. The doors were coming closer with every step, but they still felt so far away. Too far.

He was alone and afraid and the darkness in his memory was coming closer—too close—and he wasn't going to make it—

The doors crashed open beneath the force of his hands.

He was through. He was safe.

"Sam, are you okay?" Sara touched his arm and a zing of electricity passed through him, obliterating the darkness and grounding him back to the present.

He drew in a long, shuddering breath and dragged the back of his wrist across his eyes. He managed to pull an "I'm fine" out of his throat.

"No, you're not," Sara said flatly. "I—"

A ripple of marimba music sounded, a repeating measure that announced an incoming call.

"What now?" Sara muttered, letting go of Sam's arm and digging into her bag. She grabbed her phone and held it up to her ear. "Dad? What's up?" She pressed her free hand to her ear and turned away slightly, her shoulders raised like hackles.

Sam concentrated on breathing—in and out—and pushing away the panic attack that had threatened to overcome him in the cathedral. It had been a long time since an attack had come on that strong, that fast.

"Yes, Dad, everything's fine." Sara glanced at Sam as she said that, and he tried to reassure her with a smile. "Yes, I've been having a good time." A pause. "I did have lunch, yes. . . . Now? I'm at St. John's. . . . Yes, that's the one." She caught Sam's eye and mouthed *Sorry.*

He nodded and rolled his shoulders forward, then back. He almost felt back to being his normal self. At least, as normal as he ever felt.

"Really? Still?" Sara sighed. "No, no, it's okay. I understand. No, Dad—Dad—" Her voice took on a sharper tone; Sam looked up in concern. "Listen. It's fine. I'm *fine.* I'll just . . . see the sights. Have dinner somewhere. Whatever." Her body tightened, her elbows jutting out like flared wings. "I don't know what to tell you, Dad. Just . . . do what you have to do, okay?"

She threw her phone back in her bag. Her wings fluttered and folded back on themselves. Her shoulders rounded under a weight Sam couldn't see, but still shared all the same.

He took a step toward her, wondering how close he could come—how close *should* he come?—without scaring her away. But without knowing exactly how it happened, the distance between them closed—halved, then halved again, then dissolved, disappeared.

When he put his arms around her, it felt like the most natural thing in the world. He held his breath, hoping she wouldn't pull away. Or push him away.

The zing he had felt before returned, but this time it traveled from him to her. This time she was the one who needed to be grounded.

"Are *you* okay?" he asked.

Sara

Chapter 15

No. I wasn't. And I said so. And once the words started, I couldn't seem to stop.

"I know this meeting is important, okay? I get it. Good things will come from it. He brought me with him on the trip so we could celebrate when all the papers were signed. But then we didn't have lunch together—and we're not going to dinner together—or to the Empire State Building even though he *promised* . . ." I groaned in frustration and squeezed my eyes shut.

Having Sam's arms around me was both good and bad.

Good because it felt nice to be surrounded and protected. I couldn't ignore the fact that he had more muscles beneath his T-shirt and hoodie than I'd suspected—that was nice. And he smelled nice, too. Not like Daniel, with his shaved head and sweet cologne. No, Sam smelled like the city—of sweat and people and movement.

Bad because I knew if I relaxed my guard for even a moment in his arms, I would start to cry, and I knew no guy wanted to deal with a sniveling, whining crybaby.

"Can't you just do all of those things tomorrow?"

I shook my head, my face rubbing against the fabric of his hoodie. "We're just here for today. We flew in last night; we leave again first thing tomorrow morning."

"Oh," Sam said, a strange tone in his voice.

I opened my eyes and stared at the gray walls of the cathedral. I wished I could go back inside and leave behind this mess with Piper and my dad and everything else. I wished I could stay. In New York. In Sam's arms.

"What kind of business does your dad do?"

"He's selling his Internet company to a bigger Internet company so the bigger company can make finding stuff on the Internet easier and faster."

"That sounds like a good thing."

"It is, I guess."

"So, what's the problem?"

"The problem is . . ." I sighed. "Things . . . haven't been good between us for a while. A long while, really. And Dad thought if I came on this trip with him that it would not only give us a chance to celebrate something really great but that we could use it as a way to start over. He wanted to 'spend time together' and 'really talk'—you know how parents are—but instead, he's not done with this meeting yet and I'm wandering around the city without him." I felt a familiar burn of anger smoldering in my chest. "It's just . . . for the last couple of years, all he's been focused on is this business. I feel like I have to fight for his attention, or wait until he wants to spend time with me. I hate feeling like I'm invisible in my own house. I hate feeling like I'm an afterthought to him." I said it quietly, but the words still tasted like acid.

There was a long pause. I felt the curve of Sam's cheek brush the top of my head. "You're not an afterthought," he said in my ear.

"Then why does he make me feel like one?" I asked. Tears threatened and so I stepped out of Sam's arms and pulled my bag across my chest, as though the patterned cloth could deflect his words.

"Why do you let him?"

Sam's pointed words arrowed their way straight to my heart. "What?" I gasped. "I don't—"

"No one can *make* you feel anything. Emotions are whatever *you* choose to feel. It might be an instantaneous decision—to choose to be happy or sad or offended or hurt—but it's still a decision."

I opened my mouth, then closed it again. "I don't believe that."

He shrugged. "That's your choice. Just like how you have chosen to react to your dad's phone call with anger."

"Are you saying I should be *happy* that my dad abandoned me today? That he *left* me—" I bit down on my lip, refusing to say anything more. Nothing good waited for me at the end of that sentence.

Sam took a step toward me, and I countered, moving back the same distance.

"He didn't abandon you. It sounds like he's trying his best to spend time with you."

I waved my hand at the emptiness around me. "Well, he's doing a great job of it, don't you think?"

"I'm not sure it's his fault—"

"Why are you defending him?" Tears were threatening again, but for a different reason this time. "Why can't you just say, 'Gee, Sara, sorry your dad is being a jerk,' and leave it at that?"

I ran down the steps and headed down the sidewalk blindly. I didn't know where I was going, but I didn't care. Sam had been right about one thing—you had to keep moving. No matter what.

"Sara!" Sam called out. "Sara, hey! Wait!"

I didn't wait, but I also hadn't gone very far. Sam caught up to me in two or three steps.

"Look, all I was trying to say is that emotions are tricky things. If you don't control them, they will control you. And if you're living your life out of control, you'll never be able to make clear and rational decisions."

I slowed my steps and watched a bird swoop down and settle into a high tree branch.

"And if you give your dad power over your feelings, then you've given up power over yourself."

The bird hopped from branch to branch, its head tilting with sharp, almost erratic movements.

"But if you choose to see where your dad is coming from—try to understand his perspective, even a little bit—then maybe you can take back some of the power and control over your life. Make your own decisions. Make your own choices."

Another bird joined the first one, settling close enough that their wings fluttered and touched. I raised my camera and took a picture. The familiar action was soothing, comforting.

Sam took a deep breath and sighed. "Sara, I'm sorry about your dad."

I stopped. "Do you really mean that? Or are you just saying what I told you to say?"

"I really mean it." Sam shoved his hands in his pockets. "I really am sorry about your dad. He's stuck in a meeting instead of spending the whole day on an adventure with his daughter."

I took another picture of the birds in the tree. One of them was bright blue, the other was brown, but they still managed to look like a matched pair.

"You asked me to teach you how to look, how to see things clearly." Sam shrugged and looked down at his boots. "That's one way I do it. By trying to see the world through other people's eyes."

"My dad did sound frustrated that the meeting was taking so much longer than he'd thought," I said slowly. I recalled his voice on the phone: *I'm really sorry, Sara-bear. I'll make it up to you. I promise.*

Sam looked at me, his brown eyes almost the same color as the bird in the tree. "That's all I was trying to say."

He was right, and I knew it. He knew it too, but he was nice enough not to rub it in.

"How'd you get to be so smart?" I asked it a little tongue in cheek, so I was surprised when Sam answered me seriously.

"Because my life used to be out of control. I used to do whatever my emotions told me to do without thinking it through. I don't do that anymore."

As if on cue, we both started walking in step. I tried to avoid the cracks in the sidewalk. A silence fell between us, but one that suggested closeness, not awkwardness. My anger seemed to diffuse with each step.

"What do you do instead?" I asked quietly, not looking at him. Sometimes it was easier to talk about important things from the side instead of straight on. I'd learned that trick from my dad.

"I look. I see. I try to help people find what they need. I listen to music. I read. I try to make choices for my own life. And I try to make those choices count."

He offered me his words as slowly and carefully as he took his steps.

My heart softened, and I was sorry I had snapped at him

earlier. He had just been trying to help. And if he was right, if I could choose my emotional reactions, then I wanted to choose peace. I wanted to make amends. I knew I should apologize to my dad, but that would require me taking out my phone and I didn't want to let go just yet of this closeness I felt with Sam.

I reached out and tugged the sleeve of his hoodie. "I like the Zebra Stripes too, you know."

"Serious?" he said, lifting an eyebrow along with the timbre of his voice.

I smiled a little, and for the moment, debates about emotions and complaints about parents and confessions about the past were shelved. I felt like we had been skirting the edge of a deeper, more serious conversation—one that we weren't perhaps fully prepared to have—and had maneuvered our way to safer territory.

"Keith Kimball rocks it out," I said. "And don't get me started on Tom Jackson—no one can play the drums like he can."

"Where did you hear the Z Stripes?" Sam asked.

"Internet. Maybe you've heard of it? They popped up on Pandora one day, and I've been a fan ever since. Oh, and by the way—'The Z Stripes'? Abbreviating their name doesn't make you any cooler, you know. It actually makes you kind of lame."

Sam shrugged. "I don't mind being lame once in a while. Besides, Tom didn't seem to mind the nickname when I talked to him backstage at their last show."

"Shut. Up." I shoved him in the shoulder. "You were backstage at their show? I didn't think they were touring."

"They're not. It was a private engagement."

"And you got tickets? How—?" I held up my hand. "Wait, let me guess. You traded for them, right?"

"I know a guy who knows a guy . . ." Sam ran his fingers through his hair as if scoring tickets and backstage passes to a private concert was no big deal. I was starting to suspect that, for him, it wasn't.

"Is that where you bought your hoodie? I totally want one."

"Actually, this was a gift from the band."

My mouth dropped open. I knew I looked like a star-crazed groupie gobbling up any small crumb of information, but this was too much.

"A gift?"

"Keith forgot his wife's birthday. So, after the show, I helped him find a gift for her. This was his way of saying thanks."

"What did you get her?"

"Diamond earrings. I heard they were a girl's best friend."

"Wow. Just . . . I mean, wow. That's an amazing story. I bet your life before you came to New York was super boring compared to the kind of adventures you've had since."

Sam kept his hands in his pockets and adjusted his bag by shifting his shoulder. He tucked his chin close to his chest and muttered low, "Not exactly."

I was sure he didn't mean for me to hear him.

And I was sure he didn't know that I had.

Sam

Chapter 16

THE CROSS STREET OF Columbus Avenue was straight ahead, and beyond that was Central Park.

"What address did Daniel write down for you?"

Sara looked down at her hand, angling her wrist, and read, "'Aces. Cathedral Parkway 110th Street station.'"

"Sounds like he's moved since the last time I saw him. Let's hope he's still by the station, though even if he's gone into the park, he'll probably have left a note."

"Who is this guy, anyway?"

"Aces? He's a street performer and an experimental artist. Last time I talked to him, he was working with oil and canvas, so he might have just what we are looking for. I don't know how 'emotionally moving' his work will be, but it will definitely be original and one-of-a-kind."

"And you and Daniel know him . . . how, exactly?"

"Last Christmas I stopped by the cathedral one night, and Aces had come by for a hot meal and some spiritual enlightenment. Daniel was there and we ended up talking for like an hour about the reality of God."

"What did you decide?"

"Daniel said yes; Aces said no. I said I'd have to wait and see."

"And?"

"I'm still waiting to see." Sam stepped off the curb. He didn't notice right away that Sara wasn't following.

"You don't believe in God?"

"I didn't say that."

"So you *do* believe in God."

"I didn't say that, either. I said I'm waiting to see."

A car honked and Sam jogged out of the way. The dog tags around his neck chimed softly as they struck the St. Christopher medallion beneath his shirt. He ignored the sound they made.

Sara waited until traffic cleared and then darted across the street.

"What are you hoping to see? Do you think that God is going to make a personal appearance just for you? I thought the whole point of belief was that you *didn't* see things first."

Sam stopped and turned to Sara. "Do *you* believe in God?"

"Yeah, I guess so."

"But you don't know?"

"Well, I know I'd *like* to believe."

"Then why don't you?"

"I—" Sara closed her mouth. A small dimple appeared in her left cheek, a divot of frustration. After a moment, she pulled her sunglasses down over her eyes and continued walking. "Where did you say Aces was? At the station?"

Sam squeezed his eyes shut. When would he learn to stop provoking people? They had been having a very nice conversation—she liked the Zebra Stripes; who knew?—and then he had to go and ruin it. Again. First that thing about her dad, now this thing about God. He should stick to safer topics. The weather. The city. The price of tea in China. Anything but what was actually on his mind.

And that was what was killing him. Sara was smart and funny. She seemed genuinely interested in spending time with him. He could admit to himself that this was the best day he'd had in ages. Plus, she was easy to talk to—which was exactly what made her so dangerous.

He hadn't connected with a person so quickly since he'd met Alice. If he wasn't careful, he would tell Sara about his life *before* New York. About Alice and the night that—

No, he told himself firmly.

But then, without warning, he added, *Not yet.*

That word—*yet*—echoed in his mind and filled him with dread. It meant that some part of him had already decided to speak the words he had held silent for all these months. What's more, it meant he had decided he would speak those words to Sara.

Maybe that was why he kept directing the conversation to difficult topics even when Sara worked to pull them back to neutral ground. If she could handle a hard, point-blank conversation about God, then maybe she could handle an equally hard, point-blank conversation about him.

Could she? Could he? He wasn't sure he wanted to risk it.

Not yet.

"Sara," he called out, running to catch up with her. His heart thudded in his chest out of rhythm with his steps. He reached out to touch her arm but stopped short of making actual contact. "Not that way. The station is this way."

She pivoted on her heel and followed him silently down the walk.

The station bustled with activity. A large sign announced the different trains that stopped at the hub—B and C—and the staircase descending into the underground was wide with green rails.

Sam grabbed the banister and hopped up on the bottom rail. With the extra few inches of height, he scanned the crowds. "I don't see him," he said after a moment. "He has really bright red hair, so he should be easy to spot."

Sara joined him on the rail, twisting and scanning alongside Sam. The ends of her brownish-blonde hair brushed past his face. It was soft, and he could smell her shampoo—something fruity and floral—along with the tang of exhaust. Even a sunshine girl like Sara couldn't last long in New York without being touched by the city.

"What's that?" she asked, standing on her toes and pointing to a small playing card that had been taped to the bottom of the subway sign.

"Ah! Aces' calling card." Sam hopped off the rail and moved closer to investigate. "Told you he'd leave a note. Looks like he's gone to the park. Heading south."

Sara raised one eyebrow. "It's the ace of clubs."

"Spades are north. Hearts are east. Diamonds are west." Sam shrugged, settling his bag more comfortably on his shoulder. "Clubs are south."

"That's kind of vague. Doesn't he want people to find him?"

"Codes and clues are part of what he does. Don't worry—Aces will leave out another card if we need to change direction." Sam headed into the park and turned south on the first pathway he came to.

Even on the leading edge of Central Park, the trees were huge and green. The wide canopies of leaves cast soft shadows over the hard concrete. New York was a vertical city, no two ways about it, but Central Park had its own unique verticality. Trees instead of buildings. Monuments and statues instead of lampposts and street signs. Wide, rolling lawns spread like green paint, pooling around bridges, ponds, and pathways. The green evoked a strange mix of calm and excitement in Sam, a color that felt all the more shocking and refreshing to his eyes after days of staring at mottled gray sidewalks, rust-colored bricks, and tinted glass buildings.

They walked deeper into the park, past picnickers and Frisbee players and a pack of bicyclists. The afternoon sun was falling lower in the sky, adding some pink and gold to the blue. The sounds of the city—the cars, the sirens, the background hum of endless activity and energy—faded along with the light and were replaced with the sounds of nature: the wind in the trees, a birdsong chorus, a barking dog.

Sara inhaled deeply and wiped her fingers across her cheeks.

"Are you crying?" he asked quietly, pierced with the pointed edge of his lingering guilt.

She shook her head, but he wasn't quite sure he believed her. Those sunglasses of hers were an effective barrier.

"I was just thinking how this place makes me feel like I did at St. John's."

"Quiet?"

"Yeah, but a different kind of quiet. I mean, there it was all about an inside quiet. Like I should whisper, even in my thoughts. But here, I feel like running across the grass and shouting—but I still feel quiet on the inside. It's strange." She shook her head. "I'm not explaining it well."

She reached up and touched a branch of a nearby tree. A

few small leaves came away in her hand, three tiny green buds clustered together. She stashed them in her bag.

"I think I understand," Sam said. "It's kind of like how you feel during the first big snowstorm of the season. Part of you just wants to stay inside and watch the snow fall—and the rest of you wants to go outside and build a snow fort."

"I've never seen snow."

"Never?"

Sara cocked her head at him and placed her hand on her hip. "It doesn't snow in Arizona, you know."

Sam grinned. "Aha! I knew you'd tell me where you were from eventually."

She clapped her hand over her mouth, the tops of her cheeks turning pink. "Oh, man, I wasn't going to say that."

"Why don't you want me to know anything about you? Is it embarrassing? Scandalous? Are you really a Russian government spy sent to uncover my secrets?"

Sara lifted her sunglasses and slanted a look at him. "Do I look Russian to you?"

"I wouldn't have guessed you were from Arizona. You could have gotten that tan anywhere."

She looked away, rubbing her arm as though attempting to smooth away the caramel color.

"So what secrets are you keeping?" she asked, a tease in her tone. "You know, so I can report back to the KGB at the end of my mission."

Sam swallowed the words that weighed down his tongue. *Not yet.* Instead he shook his head and tsked in mock disapproval. "Look at you. Asking me for the information outright. Some spy you are."

"Gimme a break. I'm new to the espionage game."

"Then what game *are* you good at?"

"Well," Sara began, holding up her hand and ticking off her answers one by one. "I'm good at Scrabble and Twister and Pictionary and Clue and Uno, but the game I'm best at is—" She slapped his arm with her open hand. "Tag—you're it!"

And then she ran.

Sara

Chapter 17

I laughed. I couldn't help it. The look on Sam's face had been priceless. His eyes had opened so wide, and his eyebrows had drawn together so fast, he'd looked like a cartoon character. His mouth had even dropped open enough that I could see the tops of his teeth.

He'd been acting weird the last couple of hours—running hot and cold. Sometimes he was fun and friendly, and our conversation was the same. But then he'd brought up all that talk about emotions and God and stuff. The topic seemed to be important to him, and I felt like maybe he was really trying to tell me something else, but I wasn't sure I understood.

What I had understood, though, was the playing card tied to the tree. The ace of hearts. That meant we were supposed to head east. So I did. And the part of me that thrilled at the thought of running through this glorious park didn't hesitate for a moment to accept the invitation to change direction.

I laughed again, this time for the sheer joy of taking flight across the green, green grass. I took all my negative emotions of the day—my memories of my mom, my frustration with my dad, Sam's weirdness, Piper's threat—and pushed them out of my mind. I turned my face to the light and closed my eyes for a brief moment, relishing the sense of freedom that filled me.

Then my foot slipped and I squeaked. I flung my arms out, trying to regain my balance.

A hand reached out to steady me. I squeaked again, laughing. "Sam—no—let go—" But it wasn't Sam who had grabbed my arm.

He had the thickest, brightest, most fire-engine red hair I had ever seen. Below that was a face lined with wear and weather. His hazel-brown eyes were framed with smile lines and a thick pair of black-rimmed glasses. He wore a white shirt with the words "Aces Wild" printed across the front and a pair of tattered jeans with a hole in the left knee. He was barefoot in the grass. He had to be at least sixty years old, but he still looked lean and fit.

"Are you Aces?" I gasped, stumbling over my feet as I tried to stay upright.

"The one and only. I see you followed the cards and found your way. Thus, you have earned the right to ask what you may."

"What?"

Aces chuckled. "Not the best question, I suppose, but I am obligated to answer it as best as I can."

"I don't understand," I managed, my chest heaving as I tried to catch my breath.

"Clearly." He clapped his hands around my shoulders and set me on my feet.

"Hey, Aces," Sam said, coming up to join us. His breath came short and he ran a hand through his hair.

I noticed that Sam's silver chain had come free during the chase, and what appeared to be a pair of dog tags rested on his chest along with another silver circle I didn't recognize.

"Samuel." Aces inclined his head like a reigning king.

"Samuel?" I echoed, looking over at Sam.

He waved away my question and kept his attention on Aces. "Daniel sent us. He said you had some new art?"

"I see. And I do. And I create—yes, indeed I do."

I stepped back from Aces so Sam was closer to him than I was. The old man seemed nice enough, but he was a little strange.

The three of us stood in silence for a moment. I edged even closer to Sam.

"May we see it?" he finally asked. "Your art?"

"What will you give me in return?" He leveled a gnarled finger at Sam. "And no sugar packets."

Sam held up his hands in surrender. "Wouldn't dream of it." He lifted the flap on his bag and rummaged through the hidden contents. He held up a small plastic bottle. "What about an unopened jar of red paint?"

Aces looked horrified. "You would threaten me with an unopened jar of possibilities? That is not a trade, that is a burden. Take it away!"

"O-kay." Sam and I exchanged a glance.

I thought paint for an artist would have been the perfect choice. And what was Sam doing with a jar of paint in his bag, anyway?

Sam dove back into his bag and withdrew a white envelope, similar to the one he had given Jess at 24 Frames. "Movie tickets?"

"Bah!" Aces shook his head. "I have no interest in dreaming other men's dreams."

Again, Sam and I exchanged a glance. "What about a . . . a pair of socks?" he asked with hesitation in his voice.

I raised an eyebrow at Sam. "You have socks in your *bag*?"

"You have *socks* in your bag?" Aces repeated in delight. He held out his hand. "Produce."

Sam handed over a pair of brand-new Christmas-themed socks, complete with two small jingle bells sewn along the top edge.

Aces studied the bells carefully, then examined the reindeers stitched along the sides before counting the individual toes on each sock. "I find these socks to be acceptable. Come with me."

I stifled a giggle. I couldn't help it. The whole situation suddenly struck me as slightly unreal. I was standing in Central Park in New York City bartering Christmas socks with a potentially crazy man in order to see if his original artwork would appease the ridiculous demands of mega-superstar Piper Kinkade or else the brother of the boy I kinda-sorta liked would lose his job.

"Sara," Sam warned under his breath.

"Sorry," I managed. Another giggle surfaced and I barely managed to turn it into a cough. I didn't want to offend Aces, who was clearly everything that had been promised—a true original—but now that the laughter had hold of me, I could feel my resolve slipping away.

Aces led us deeper into the park and literally off the beaten path, pushing past bushes and branches.

"I thought you said he was an oil painter," I said, sucking in a breath as a particularly sharp thorn scratched my arm.

"He was," Sam replied, worried.

A few minutes later, we reached a small patch of grass where a red-white-and-blue-striped blanket had been spread out into a perfect square. Sitting on the blanket was a picnic basket containing a porcelain Dalmatian dog and a stuffed black cat; a carved wooden bird had been clipped to the side of the basket. Lined up in a row leading to the basket was a parade of plastic green army men. The last man held a miniature American flag instead of a gun.

The entire thing had been cordoned off with bright yellow caution tape spread on the grass.

Aces stood tall and proud, gesturing to the blanket. "Behold," he declared. "My latest work of art."

It was so amazing and absurd at the same time that I couldn't contain my amusement. Giggles poured out of me like bubbles, each sound lighter and louder than the last, until I was engaged in a full-fledged belly laugh. Tears ran down my cheeks from the corners of my eyes.

"Sara," Sam hissed. "Stop it!"

Aces turned to regard me with his hazel eyes, a strange expression on his face.

"Sara!"

But Sam's tone only made me laugh even more.

My laughter spent itself in one last burst before finally dribbling into short chuckles and then into bemused silence. I used the hem of my shirt to dab away the last of my tears. "Oh, wow. Oh, man. I'm sorry. I don't know what got into me." I had to force myself not to look at the picnic blanket; I didn't want to risk collapsing into laughter again.

"I'm sorry too, Aces. I—" Sam began.

"No, it's all right," Aces said, his attention still on me. "Art should always produce some kind of visceral reaction, and laughter is as good as revulsion." He frowned for a moment, then smiled widely. "Better, actually."

"Okay, I think I'm better now," I said, clearing my throat and squaring my shoulders. I pulled my hair back with both hands, smoothing it over my head, and then shook out my fingers. "Okay."

Sam glanced at me as if to make sure I was telling the truth, then cleared his own throat. "Um, Aces? Do you, by any chance, have any other artwork you could show us? Something like you used to do? You know, something on canvas?"

As Aces' lips creased in displeasure and his eyes narrowed, Sam hurried on. "I mean, not that this piece isn't amazing, because it is, it's just that we're looking for something you can hang on a wall, and, well, you'd have to admit, this would be a little difficult to frame." Beads of sweat dotted his forehead by the time he was done speaking.

Aces' displeasure morphed into sadness. "Art should be alive. Three-dimensional. I no longer work in a medium that requires my vision to be flat and lifeless, good only to be trapped under glass like a dead insect." He tucked the Christmas socks into the waistband of his pants. "Thank you for the socks, but this is all I have to give you."

My good humor folded in on itself. We had struck out yet again. I was starting to worry that we might not be able to fulfill Piper's demands. And if not, then this day would end in disaster. I couldn't let that happen.

"Are you sure?" I asked Aces. "I mean, you don't have *anything* else you could show us? We really need something original and special. It's important."

Aces folded his arms across his chest and peered down his nose at me. At first, I thought I had made him mad, like Sam had, but then I saw the sparkle in his eyes and the hint of a smile on his lips.

"Ah, but for you, cheerful sprite, I still owe you an answer to your question."

"What?" I asked, pulled off track by the apparent change in topic.

"Exactly."

I looked to Sam, confused.

"Just go with it," he whispered in my ear.

Aces crossed to his art installment, stepped carefully over the yellow tape, and reached into the basket. Returning to us, I saw that he was cradling something in his hands. He nodded to me, and I cupped my hands below his.

"The answer, O lady of laughter, O damsel of delight, O girl of the giggles, is passion." He opened his hands, and a stream of glittering red beads poured into my palms. "Passion is what makes the world go round. Passion is what drives us to be better than we are. Passion is what makes our emotions—whether love or hate or laughter—ignite and blaze into life." The last bead fell onto the pile with a soft click.

Without warning, Aces grabbed my shoulders and pulled me to him. He kissed me on both cheeks in quick succession. "Passion is the answer to your question. Remember it!" Then he kissed my forehead as though searing the word into my brain.

When he released me, I stumbled backward, but Sam was there to steady me with a hand on my arm.

"I will," I said to Aces, and I meant it.

Aces turned to Sam. "When next you see Daniel, tell him hello for me, will you?"

As we turned away, I dumped the beads into my bag. They slithered and shook past the other contents with a sound like falling rain.

Sam and I were silent as we made our way through the park, heading back toward the main walkway. I had so many questions I wanted to ask him—about his dog tags, about Aces and his artwork, and about what we should do next—but he seemed absorbed in his thoughts. I didn't dare interrupt him.

We reached the path and I stepped up onto the road. I turned, my mouth open to break the silence and say his name.

And that's when the bike ran me over.

Sam

Chapter 18

He came out of nowhere.

It happened so fast—she didn't even have time to scream.

Later, when Sam had time to review the events and the courage to examine them up close, that was what he kept coming back to. Her silence.

One minute, Sara was on her feet, her sandy-blonde hair shifting as her head turned toward him, her mouth open. Her eyes were as green as the trees around her. He could almost hear his unspoken name on her lips.

The next minute, she was down, fallen into a crumpled heap at his feet. Her bag slipped from her shoulder, a few red beads scattering and bumping down the path like frozen, isolated drops of blood.

That's when he saw the real blood welling up from her scraped-up knee, staining her blue jeans black.

Sam froze. He didn't breathe. He didn't blink. He didn't move.

The bicyclist screeched to a stop a few paces away. Dropping his bike, he ran back to Sara's side, ripping off his helmet and his gloves. He crashed to his knees next to her.

"Hey, are you okay? I'm sorry. I didn't even see you—"

Sam closed his eyes, the words echoing loud in his mind, in his memory. He could feel his fingers trembling. Sweat lined the back of his neck.

"Hey! Hey, you! Don't just stand there—come help me!" The guy's voice rattled Sam back to reality.

He blinked and saw that a small crowd had gathered at the scene of the accident. He told his body to move, to go to Sara and help her, but all his joints felt disconnected. Nothing in his body seemed to work properly.

The biker crouched next to Sara, supporting her back as she struggled to sit up.

"It's okay," she said over and over. "It's okay. I'm okay. I'm not hurt."

Sam couldn't stop looking at the blood. Another scratch was oozing blood down by her ankle, soaking through the hem of her jeans, turning her white socks first pink, then red.

"Yes, you are," Biker Man said, his hand hovering over her leg. "Looks like you're scraped up pretty bad. Are you hurt anywhere else?"

Sara started to shake her head, then stopped, wincing in pain.

"Here—can you follow my finger?" Biker Man moved his index finger in a slow pass in front of her eyes. "Good. Okay. That's good."

"My hands hurt," Sara whimpered.

Biker Man touched her wrists and turned her palms face up. The heels of her hands were scraped and scuffed. He made a frustrated noise in the back of his throat. "Not as bad as your knee, but still—" He fumbled in the pack at his waist and pulled out his cell phone.

"Oh, you don't have to call anyone," Sara said, trying to smile through a grimace. "I'll be fine. Honest."

Sam finally moved. "She's right. You don't have to call anyone. I have a first-aid kit."

Biker Man lowered his phone, frowning in doubt. "Really?"

"Yeah, I bet he really does," Sara said, hissing a breath between her teeth. "He has everything in that bag of his."

Sam thought he knew the exact placement of everything in his bag, but he couldn't seem to find the first-aid kit. *No. Not again.* The thought came unbidden, though he knew exactly where it had come from. And why.

Biker Man shook his head. "She needs help. I'm calling—"

"If you do, I'll say it was your fault," Sam blurted out, still frantically searching for the bandages. They were in there somewhere, he knew it. They had to be.

"It *was* my fault," Biker Man said.

"No, it was *my* fault," Sara said. "I was on the road—"

"I'll say you did it on purpose," Sam barked. A dark heat had seized his heart. The edges of his vision wavered with black spots. "I'll say you saw her and you ran her down anyway."

"What? Why would you say that? Chill, man, it was just an accident."

"No! It wasn't! It was your fault—you even said so," Sam shouted. His head pounded with two different images. It was hard to tell which one was the real one and which one was the memory.

His fingers found the kit, and he yanked it out of his bag with unexpected force. "Here. I'll do it. I can take care of her."

The crowd had slipped away, the few pedestrians in the area clearly unwilling to get involved in an ugly confrontation with strangers.

"Sam," Sara said, "calm down."

"You"—he jabbed a finger at Biker Man—"get away from her."

Biker Man hesitated. He looked down at Sara. "You okay?"

She nodded.

"You sure?"

She nodded again.

"Who is this guy, anyway?"

Sara's green eyes met Sam's brown ones. Sam held his breath and wondered what she would say. "He's my friend."

"Okay," Biker Man said. "If you're sure—"

"We're friends," she said again, her voice strong and firm. "Aren't we, Sam?"

He felt tears burn in his eyes, but he forced them not to fall. It was all he could do to nod.

"Fine. Then she's all yours, man," Biker Man said, leaning back and rocking to his feet.

"I'm all right," Sara said again. "You don't have to stay. It was just an accident. A couple of Band-Aids and some Tylenol and I'll be back on my feet in no time. Promise. I didn't dent your bike, did I?"

Sam knelt by her side and cracked open the kit. His hands shook; he hoped Sara wouldn't notice.

Biker Man's mouth quirked in a wary smile. "No, you didn't." He took a step away. "Are you sure you—?"

"Go!" Sam snapped. "Just go. You don't need to be here. You aren't wanted here. I can take care of her. I can fix this. I can. I will." He muttered the last few words under his breath.

Again, Biker Man looked to Sara for permission.

She mouthed the word *Go* but softened it with a smile.

He picked up his helmet and his gloves, clearly unhappy at being sent away, and wheeled his bike down the path. After a few steps, he jogged back and set down a water bottle next to Sara's hand. "At least take this. You'll want to wash out those scrapes."

"Thanks," Sara said. "I will."

Biker Man left for good, and then it was just Sam and Sara, alone on the pathway. The wind blew through the high trees.

Sam sorted through the kit with hurried fingers. Sorting and discarding and choosing what to use. Bandages. Gotta have those. Gauze—might help stop the bleeding. What else? What else could he do to save her? Scissors—yes—he'd need those to cut her out of—

He curled his fingers into a fist, concentrating on steadying his breathing and his heart rate. Now was not the time to panic. *Not yet.* Now was not the place to break down. *Not yet.*

"You're going to be okay, Alice," he said. "I promise." His voice caught, but he didn't stop. "Just hold on, okay? Just stay with me."

"Sam."

He ripped open one bandage and reached for another.

"It's going to be okay. Help is on the way."

"Sam."

"No, don't talk."

"Sam."

Her voice cut through the noise that filled his head with static. The sound of a siren in the distance. The sound of metal screeching in protest. The sound of wind sighing down a dark highway.

She touched his hand, her fingers warm.

He hadn't realized how bad the quake had been until her touch stilled the aftershocks.

He looked down at where they had made contact. The polished dog tags swung free in the space between them. St. Christopher looked up at him from the circular medallion with unforgiving silver eyes.

"Sam?" Sara's voice was gentle and soft. "Who's Alice?"

Sara

Chapter 19

I wasn't sure if he'd heard me so I asked it again. "Who's Alice?"

Something was very wrong with Sam. I'd never seen him like this. Granted, we didn't have a long history together, but I hadn't expected him to crack at the sight of my blood. Sure, I had some decent scrapes, but I had come home with worse when I was learning to roller blade.

Sam blinked and leaned back on his heels. His eyes looked blurry. His face paled. "Where did you hear that name?"

"From you. Just now. You called me Alice."

"I did?" For a moment, his eyes started to clear, and then he looked down and returned to the work of bandaging the cuts on my knee and ankle. I worried he wasn't going to say anything else. Then he said, "I might have to cut a bigger hole in your jeans—is that okay?" His voice sounded hoarse.

"That's fine. What happened to Alice?" I tried to keep my tone low and even, gentle. I didn't want to spook him even more.

He still wouldn't look at me. He picked up the scissors and

snipped the air a few times as though practicing. He placed the blades next to the hole in my jeans, trying a few different positions but never actually closing the handles.

"Here. I can do it." I took the scissors from him. Even with my scraped-up hands, I was able to snip three or four times, enlarging the hole enough so I could rip the ruined pant leg away from my actual leg. I clipped through the side seams as well and tore again. I handed the scissors back to Sam. "Now will you tell me about Alice?"

Sam took his time, fussing with the first-aid kit, arranging and rearranging the bandages, tucking the scissors point-down through an elastic loop. He drew Biker Man's water bottle closer. Aligned it parallel to his knee. Turned it a quarter of the way around.

He took a deep breath.

"She had just turned sixteen." The words slipped from Sam's mouth, as quiet as a confession. As he spoke, he carefully pulled on my shoelaces, unraveling the knot.

Cradling my wounded hands to my chest, I held my breath. I watched Sam's fingers gently smooth the laces long and straight. He stayed focused on his task, as if making sure they were perfect was the most important thing in the world.

"I never saw her without a smile." He loosened the top cross. "You should know that about her—she was *always* smiling." The second cross.

His hands, which had been shaking before, became steady whenever they touched me.

"Her family had this huge house on the edge of this wide, wide field. There was a barn out back. It was the perfect place to have a party. Everyone came."

He slipped one hand around the back of my ankle, supporting

it in his palm while he carefully gripped the heel of my shoe with his other hand.

"My three best friends were there: Todd Saunders. Chris Allred. Jeremy Davis." With each name he listed, he wiggled my shoe a little looser, a little looser, a little looser, until he could slowly slip it off my foot. "But that night it was all about Alice."

He set my shoe to the side but continued to hold my leg. His hand was warm where it touched my skin, but his fingers were cool and strong.

"It seemed like she was everywhere I looked that night. Her parents had decorated the barn for her birthday with streamers and banners and lights. They'd hired a DJ. There was dancing. Music. Cake."

He hooked the tip of his finger under the edge of my sock, being careful to avoid the blood spots that had soaked into the white cotton.

"I had a massive crush on her. But then again, so did Todd Saunders, Chris Allred, and Jeremy Davis."

Again, with each name he listed, he peeled my sock a little lower on my foot.

"It wasn't until the party was almost over that Todd brought up his idea. He said the four of us should drive Alice into town for a late-night ice cream run. One last unexpected birthday present from the four of us to her."

He brushed some of the loose gravel away from the path before setting my foot down carefully as if it might shatter on contact.

"I think we were all a little crazy that night."

Sam slipped his hand up the back of my leg, all the way to the bend of my knee. He unstoppered Biker Man's bottle with his teeth and, holding me steady, he poured lukewarm water over my wound. The clear liquid turned pink as it ran down my leg, over my foot, and through my toes. Setting the bottle down, Sam reached for a cloth in his bag and wiped away the water and the blood with long, smooth strokes.

"I know what you're thinking, but we weren't drunk. We weren't high. We weren't anything—just sixteen and stupid."

The skin around the scrape on my knee had turned a dark pink, striated with faint white lines; the wound oozed a few more sluggish drops of blood. The thin scratch on my ankle itched with fire.

"My car couldn't hold all five of us—it was just an old VW bug—but we all crammed inside anyway. Alice sat in the front with me. Jeremy sat behind her, then Todd in the middle, then Chris behind me."

His voice adopted a flat tone, cool and professional, as though he was recounting details he had told many times before. He peeled the backing from a salmon-pink Band-Aid and positioned it over my ankle.

"Having Alice near me made Todd jealous. The trip was his idea to begin with, so why did I get to sit next to the pretty girl?"

He opened a packet of gauze pads, withdrew one, and covered the wound on my knee with it, pressing lightly along the edges to make sure it was secure.

"Todd kept leaning between us, trying to talk to Alice, make her pay attention to him, make her like him. When she started laughing at his jokes . . . that made *me* jealous."

He covered the square of gauze with a larger bandage, smoothing the sticky wings with the edge of his thumb. I could feel the small, rough calluses as they brushed against my knee.

"But then Alice touched my arm, she said my name, and

I didn't care what Todd did or said or thought. I just . . . kept driving."

He moved closer to me, his knees on either side of my leg. When he leaned over to reach for my hands, the silver dog tags landed gently against my newly placed bandage.

"I remember driving through the intersection where the back road crossed the main road, and I remember turning to her and saying her name, and then . . ."

He held my hands with one of his and poured a small measure of water into my cupped palms with his other.

"He came out of nowhere."

His hand beneath mine began to tremble, a faint fluttering like a bird not quite ready to take flight.

"One minute, she was turning toward me, her hair backlit against the oncoming headlights. I knew her mouth was open, but . . ."

Reaching for the cloth, he used a clean corner to wipe the palm of first one hand, then the other.

"It happened so fast—she didn't even have time to scream."

Sam

Chapter 20

Sam's heart was on fire.

His skin had turned to paper. His bones had turned to glass.

He felt strangely disconnected from himself. Like there was no body around him anymore—just a heart, charred and blackened, beating in space.

It had been a long time since he had said anything at all about the accident, let alone said Alice's name out loud.

He drew in a long, deep breath, inhaling the scent of Sara's hair, trying to remember that this girl who sat before him smelled like sunshine and spring.

Focusing on the task before him—cleaning Sara's wounds—he kept his hands moving. *Gotta keep moving; can't stop; stagnation kills.*

"The front of the pickup truck looked like it had been crumpled by a giant fist. There were pieces of metal and broken glass everywhere. I heard a sound like screaming in my head. It wasn't from Alice—she never made a sound—and it wasn't from anyone else. Todd and Chris were pinned in the back, moaning, but not screaming. Jeremy was strangely quiet; he had been sitting behind Alice, and . . . I don't know—maybe I was the one making the noise."

Sara's fingers shivered delicately in his. He had told this part of the story so many times. So why did it still feel like it had happened to someone else?

"Do you still hear it?" she asked, low and careful.

Sam looked at her. Her eyes were *green*. Alice had had blue eyes. As long as he stayed focused on the green, he wouldn't confuse Sara for Alice again. "Sometimes," he admitted after a long minute.

Her shiver turned into a tremble.

She licked her lips, biting down on the bottom one. "I'm so sorry," she whispered, her eyes never leaving his.

"I felt like my whole body had been scratched up and torn. I couldn't move my hand. Blood filled my eyes."

He unconsciously touched the spot where a neat row of stitches had once closed up the gap between his forehead and his hairline.

"But I could still see enough to dial 911. After calling for help, I blacked out. When I came to, the police and the paramedics had arrived. They had to cut my car apart to get to everyone. Chris had broken his arm in two places. Todd had a broken arm too, plus lacerations all over his face and neck and hands—like me. Most of the paramedics were working on Jeremy. When they wouldn't tell me what was wrong with him, I knew it was bad."

He folded and refolded the blood-spotted cloth into ever-smaller squares.

"I remember looking at my friends, battered and bleeding, and at the single white sheet covering a gurney off to the side, and . . . and then the police officer pulled me aside and asked me a few questions about the accident. About Alice. He told me that the four of us were lucky to be alive. He said that the other driver had admitted to hitting my car and was already in custody." His voice cracked. "The police said it wasn't the guy's first drunk driving charge."

"What happened to him?" she whispered.

Sam looked away. "We should probably get you off the ground and someplace more comfortable. Do you think you could make it to that bench?" he asked, nodding to a spot across the way.

Sara's eyebrows came together, her frown clearly communicating her displeasure at his deflection. That small dimple appeared again. "I think so. You'll have to help me, though."

Standing up, he reached for Sara's forearms, careful to avoid her scraped-up hands, and pulled her to her feet. Helping her to the bench, he quickly returned to the side of the path, gathered up the scattered bits of the first-aid kit, and shoved everything into his bag.

He wished he could gather up his scattered thoughts and hide them away as easily. He had always believed in moving forward, but sometimes he wished he could go back. Back to before he had called Sara by the wrong name and all those words had spilled out of him like sand from a punctured bag.

As much as he wished that, though, there was another part of him that didn't mind being rid of the weight of those words.

He wondered if the fact that Sara's green, green eyes had never blinked, never wavered, while he had told her the story that had burdened—and burned—his heart for the past eighteen months meant that he could tell her the rest of what had happened.

Was he strong enough? Was she?

Lots of people knew pieces of the puzzle—both at home and

here in New York—but only Sam knew the entire story, top to bottom, inside and out.

Not even Paul knew all the details. All he knew was that Sam had graduated early and Mom and Dad had sent Sam to live with him "for a change of pace." Sam didn't offer; Paul didn't pry.

Paul had allowed Sam to help him with his job, and Sam had started finding things for people. He had started keeping his eyes open, always on the lookout for those small but special things that would fill the hole in someone's life, always looking for that elusive item that would fill the hole in his.

He sat down next to Sara, who wiped at her eyes with swift fingers. The high color in her cheeks was a dusky, dark rose, hinting at a deeper, sadder emotion.

"What happened to Jeremy?" she asked.

"He slipped into a coma. He woke up a few months later, but the doctors said his head injury was bad enough that he'd be in rehab for a long time."

"And the others? Todd and Chris?" She touched the torn and frayed edge of her jeans where it ended above her knee, straightening the threads into neat lines.

"Chris was in rehab for a while too, for his broken arm, but his injury was bad enough that he couldn't play on the tennis team anymore. Todd did better—his injuries weren't as bad as the others—but he had a hard time with the scars."

She stretched out her wounded leg, wincing, and propped up her ankle with the toe of her other shoe. "You seem to have made it through okay. That's good, right?"

"I guess." Sam reached for his bag, pulling it closer to him on the bench. "After Alice's funeral, her parents wanted to celebrate the good things about her life. They opened up their house to the whole neighborhood. Everyone came." He closed his eyes, remembering the lights, the crowd, the sounds. "Her parents thanked me for calling 911. They said they understood that it was too late for Alice, but that they didn't blame me, and that they were glad I had been able to do something to help everyone else."

"It was good that you could help your friends. It sounds like it was a really hard time for you." She leaned against his shoulder.

Sam's burning heart cracked open with heat and guilt and shame. The blood drained from his face.

What would happen if he told Sara the secret that lay beneath the smoldering coal of his heart? What would she do with the information? He feared he already knew. He had only met her today, but he wasn't sure he was ready to lose her just yet.

He wanted to shift Sara off his shoulder, turn her so he could see her eyes. If he did tell her, then he wanted to be able to see the exact moment if things changed. That way, in that split-second flash of time, he could decide what to do next. To brace himself—or to bolt.

Sam's muscles along his shoulders, his arms, braced for action, and his legs trembled with the tension of holding still for so long. Time to choose. Time to move? Or time to stay?

The remaining words coated his tongue like ash, choking him.

"There's more," he managed.

Sara shifted, sitting up a little straighter and turning to face him.

A slight breeze passed over them. Sam heard the sounds of the park as static through a tunnel: the whisking zip of a kid passing by on skates, the chattering laughter of children, the hurried click-clack of a dog on the run.

"You don't have to tell me if you don't want to," Sara said, her voice barely louder than the breeze.

"I know I don't." He leaned back against the bench. "But I want to."

He realized suddenly that those four small words were the truth. He had been circling around the truth for some time now. Avoiding it, but knowing that it was time to take hold of it and see if it still hurt. And how much.

And who better to tell than Sara? A girl he'd never seen until today; a girl he might never see again. In this one moment, he was free.

The words wouldn't come, though. No matter how many times he framed them in his mind and held them in his mouth, he couldn't make himself say what he had never said to another soul.

She must have sensed his struggle to find the words he needed, because she bit her lip again and said, "I'll trade you for it. A story for a story—wasn't that the deal?"

Sam shook his head. "You don't have a story like this. It wouldn't be fair."

After the moment of silence had dragged on into minutes, Sara shifted on the bench. "It's okay. You don't have to tell me. Or you can tell me later." She touched the dog tags resting on his chest. "Tell me about these."

He lifted the tags in his hand and fanned the three silver ovals across his palm. "I had them made once I came to New York."

Sara touched each tag with the pad of her finger, reading the names out loud one by one. "Todd Saunders. Chris Allred. Jeremy Davis." She swallowed. "You wear them as a way to honor your friends?"

Sam shook his head. "I wear them as penance."

She looked at him silently, confusion written across her face.

He wrapped his hand around the tags, grateful for the sharp bite of the metal. He looked directly into Sara's green eyes and saw what he needed to see. He let the pent-up words tumble out of his mouth.

"That night. The night of the accident. When Todd was flirting with Alice. I knew I couldn't let Todd win. I knew I had to raise the stakes. So before we reached the main road . . ." He cleared his throat, trying to draw in enough air to breathe. "I . . . I turned off the headlights. It was just for a minute—a second. It was a dark night, and I thought it would make me seem cool and dangerous. I wanted Alice to be impressed by what I thought was bravery. But she wasn't. She grabbed my arm and screamed my name. She begged me to stop."

Noise filled Sam's ears, a whirring whine that might have been a distant siren, or the moment before a worried whimper broke into a shout.

"Everyone yelled at me to turn the lights back on. Everyone said I was crazy. But I kept driving. I kept saying, 'Don't worry. I can handle it. Trust me.'" He let go of the dog tags and his hands fell, empty, into his lap. "That was the last thing I said before the truck hit us."

He stopped speaking, breathing heavily through his nose, his lips suddenly as cold and heavy as lead. He had taken his locked-away memories and traded them for something else. Something that, to his surprise, felt like a kind of freedom. He hadn't known that letting part of yourself go like that could be so liberating.

He hadn't known this kind of inside quiet existed.

"It was my fault," he said simply, finally—gratefully. "All of it was my fault."

Sara

Chapter 21

"*But I thought you said* the other driver was drunk?" I asked. I was having a hard time processing everything Sam had told me, but I could sense that telling me the whole story had made him feel better.

"He was."

"I don't understand. How could it have been all your fault, then?"

The lines around Sam's eyes tightened a little, and I wished I'd kept my mouth shut. He had just busted through some heavy emotional walls. I didn't want to give him a reason to put them up again.

"Because if I had kept the lights on, he might have seen us. He might have had time to swerve, or maybe even stop. Things might have been different."

Before I could say anything else—what did you say to something like that?—Sam's phone rang, a utilitarian chime of three repeating notes. I had a lot of questions about what Sam had told me, but it didn't seem like I was going to have a chance to ask any of them.

He yanked the phone from his pocket, swiping his finger across the screen with look of trepidation. "Hi, Paul," he answered carefully. "How—?" Sam's voice cut off and he shot me a look. "Yes. . . . What? When? . . . No, Paul, listen—"

Sam angled his body away from me, pressing the phone closer to his ear. All of his earlier open vulnerability was gone, freezing like ice the longer he listened to his brother. The walls were going back up; I hoped they wouldn't be built as high or as thick as before.

"Paul, listen to me, I'm sorry. No. . . . Yes. . . . Would you let me explain?"

It sounded like bad news. And if Paul was calling, there was only one thing it could be. Piper. My head reeled. My leg throbbed at knee and ankle. Sam had done a good job bandaging my wounds, and I didn't think the cuts would get infected, but I still felt banged up both physically from being hit by the bike and emotionally from listening to Sam's story. And now this? I wasn't sure I could handle another disaster.

Sam turned off his phone and clutched it in his fist. He squeezed his eyes shut and ran his free hand through his hair.

"What is it?" I asked, my heart sinking lower in dread with each passing moment. I was afraid I knew what he was going to say before he even opened his mouth.

"She did it. She fired Paul."

My heart hit bottom, where it shattered. "But she said—"

"I know what she said."

I drew my bag closer to my side, my hand automatically touching the spot where Piper's head shot was stashed. "I agreed to help her," I said, clinging to the one thing that seemed to matter most.

"She said she wouldn't fire Paul if I agreed to help her. I did that. So why would she—"

"Paul said that Piper told him she had given you until six o'clock to bring back the artwork. You weren't there when time was up, so she handed him his walking papers." He turned his phone toward me. The clock showed 6:37 in stark, white numbers.

Tears of anger, frustration, and fear burned in my eyes. "That wasn't the deal. She never said that. If she had said I had a six o'clock deadline, I would have written it down."

Sam chucked his phone back into his bag. "It doesn't matter anymore."

"Yes, it does." I swung my legs off the bench, wincing as the movement pulled at the bandages. "It's not fair! She's a liar and a . . . a cheat!"

"She's Piper Kinkade. She can do whatever she wants." Sam scrubbed the back of his wrist across his forehead. He exhaled and rolled his shoulders. Then he grabbed the dog tags and shoved them back under his shirt. "Paul's already home. We need to get there as soon as we can so I can explain. Do you think you can walk?"

"I think so. Do you have my shoe?"

Sam checked his bag and withdrew my shoe and red-stained sock. He handed them back to me with a quiet "Sorry about the blood."

"Not your fault," I said, leaning over to slip the sock back on and then tying the shoelaces with a vicious knot. I was still fuming about Piper's betrayal. What she had done wasn't fair. It wasn't right. And I wasn't going to let her get away with it. But how did you stop something that had already happened? *Gotta keep moving.*

I levered myself up off the bench, making sure to keep as

much weight off my bad leg as I could. I looked down at my knees, one still covered by my jeans, the other bare but bandaged.

"Pretty fashionable, huh?" I asked, pointing my toe and modeling my torn jeans. "The half-pants, half-shorts look will be all the rage next season, I'm sure."

Sam didn't laugh at my dismal attempt at humor. He held my arm just above the elbow, keeping me steady and making sure I didn't fall.

I took a tentative step forward. It hurt to walk, but I could do it. I had to. I hated feeling like everything was my fault, and I had to find some way to make it right.

"I'm really sorry, Sam," I said. "Piper talked so fast. I thought I had written everything down."

He sighed heavily. "It's okay. We'll figure something out."

"Was Paul mad?"

Sam shrugged. "Paul doesn't like it when things are broken and he can't fix them. This . . ." He sighed again. "This is a pretty big break in his life."

I grimaced again, but not from my injury this time. "Did you tell him we can fix it?"

Sam slipped his arm around my waist and let me lean on him. "I didn't have a chance."

I shuffled along next to Sam, trying to hide my pain. We managed to make our way out of the park and back to Central Park North. I concentrated on matching my breathing to my steps. At least now I was only wincing at every fourth step.

When we paused at the corner, I asked, "How far away did you say your apartment was?"

"Not too far. The subway station is west of here. We can take the subway to 125th Street and walk from there."

"Oh. Okay." I tried not to let my despair color my voice. There was more walking? How big was this blasted city?

Sam turned to look at me, concern drawing a line across his forehead. "Are you sure you're going to make it?"

"Yeah, I'll be fine." I felt a light tickle of liquid start to slide along my shin. Oh, no. "Um, Sam? Do you have a tissue I could borrow?"

His glance dropped to my knee and his eyes widened. "Sara!"

"I'll be fine," I said again, bluffing. "Look—the light's green; let's go. Paul's waiting for us. We don't want to be late."

Sam frowned, the movement pulling his jaw tight. "Hold on."

He made sure I was steady on my feet, then stepped to the curb and scanned the street in both directions. Raising his arm, he signaled, and a bright yellow cab pulled out of traffic.

Sam helped me hobble forward and opened the back door for me.

"I can't afford a taxi," I whispered as he slid into the seat next to me. "We can take the subway, it's okay."

"It's not okay. And don't worry about the taxi." Sam leaned forward and rattled off an address to the cab driver. As the car merged back into the stream of traffic, Sam opened his messenger bag and handed me a pack of tissues.

I blotted up the thin line of blood seeping from beneath my bandage, then kept as much pressure as I could bear on the spot.

"Would you rather I just take you back to your hotel?" Sam asked, looking out the window at the buildings passing by. "That might be for the best anyway. I'm not sure you should be walking around anymore with that scrape. I'd hate for it to get worse."

For a moment, I considered saying yes. Going back to the hotel sounded so nice. I could take a hot bath, eat a hot meal, and fall asleep in a soft, comfortable bed. But then I thought about Paul and Piper. And Sam. And I shook my head.

"No. I said I'd see this through, and I will." I closed my eyes and rubbed at my forehead. "Though if I had just left the book on the table like I'd been told to do instead of trying to be nice to Piper, none of this would have happened."

The setting sun filled the back of the cab with light.

Sam hesitated, then said, "What if it's too late to fix it? I don't know that anything we do will appease Piper enough to make her give Paul his job back. It's not like we already have what she wants and we just have to deliver it to her." He fell back against the seat. "And the longer we wait, the harder it will be to convince her to change her mind, no matter what we bring her."

"We can't give up now," I said. "We just need to find that magic ring and take it to the wicked queen and save . . . well, Paul isn't exactly a damsel, but he is in distress, right?"

Sam's mouth lifted in a small smile that faded almost as soon as it appeared. He sighed and rubbed at his eyes. "I feel like I'm running out of ideas," he admitted in a low voice.

"But you're not *completely* out of ideas, are you?"

Sam slanted a glance at me, that smile peeking through again. "No, not completely."

"And didn't you say that you could find anything you wanted in New York?"

"I did say that."

"Then I'm staying," I said, my anger at Piper solidifying into determination. "This"—I nodded to my knee and assumed an air of noble confidence—"is just a flesh wound. It can't stop me from completing my quest." I bumped his shoulder with mine. "What do you say, partner? Are you going to give up? Or are you still in?"

Sam

Chapter 22

THE CAB FARE TOOK THE LAST of Sam's money. He handed it over, feeling guilty that he had to short the driver a decent tip. He slipped in the envelope of movie ticket gift certificates from his bag to make up for it.

"This is where you live?" Sara asked.

Sam looked up at the gray stone building. Metal fire-escape ladders and landings crisscrossed the outside walls. The middle of the building was set back from the sidewalk, creating a front walkway that was flanked by two towers. A couple of trees stood guard along the sidewalk. Most of the windows were open, and Sam could hear music drifting down from an apartment on the third floor. The apartment he shared with Paul.

"Yes," Sam said. "I live here. Is there something wrong with it?"

Sara shook her head, her eyes sparkling. "No, nothing. It's just so . . . I don't know. It just looks the way New York buildings do on TV."

Sam laughed lightly. "It should. This *is* New York."

She laughed back and slapped him lightly on the arm. "That's not what I meant."

"What did you mean, then?"

"Just . . . that it's nice. That's all. It looks like someplace you could call home."

Sam noticed that she kept shifting her weight off her bad leg, and that she was clutching her bag with both hands.

"Are you nervous about something?" he asked.

"I'm just imagining what my dad would say if he knew I was about to go alone into the apartment of a boy I just met today." She covered her mouth with her hand. "Oh, that sounds really bad."

"But you won't be alone," Sam pointed out. "Paul will be there. And from the sounds of it, he brought friends."

"Great. So I'm going to a *party* at the apartment of a boy I just met today. This is sounding better and better."

Sam glanced up at the open window. "Something tells me it won't be much of a party."

"How can you tell?"

"Paul is listening to Fall of Night. He only plays their music when he's depressed." Sam held out his hand to Sara. "C'mon. At least my building has an elevator."

Sam was grateful they only had to go up three floors. The sooner Sara could sit down again, the better. He helped her down the hallway and then unlocked the apartment door.

As soon as he opened the door, he heard Paul shouting from the living room. "Sam? Is that you?"

"Yes, it's me." He hung his bag on a nearby wall hook. He opened the bathroom door and ushered Sara inside. "Give me ten minutes. Then come into the living room. It'll be okay. I promise."

"Wait—" she started, her face pale, but Sam closed the door.

Taking a deep breath and squaring his shoulders, Sam crossed the small foyer and walked into the living room.

"Sorry I'm late—" He stopped in his tracks.

Paul was stretched out on the couch, his eyes closed, an ice pack on his head. Will sat on the chair next to the couch, the jacket of his Plaza Hotel uniform unbuttoned and open, displaying the plain white T-shirt beneath. He had kicked his feet up onto the coffee table. Rebecca was standing in the small kitchen, pouring out several glasses of water and setting them near a stack of plates that stood on the counter. Her eyes were swollen and a little red, like she'd been crying.

"So glad you could join us," Will said with a tight grin. "We're always ready to welcome another member to our illustrious party of the recently unemployed."

"What?" Sam looked around the room. "Were you all—"

"Fired?" Pointing his index finger at Sam like a gun, Will lowered his thumb. "Bingo."

"But Piper can't fire all of you," Sam protested. He sat down in the open chair across from Will.

"Can and did." Will shrugged his shoulders. "One of the perks of being a monster is that you can devour whoever you want, whenever you want, and no one will stop you."

Sam pressed his fingers to his eyes and rubbed, hard. "This can't be happening. This is impossible."

"It was bound to happen, I guess. We all knew Rebecca was on the chopping block after the Bootsie fiasco—" Will lifted his head and called out, "Love you, Becky," to which she replied, "Drop dead." Will laughed, then returned his attention to Sam. "But Paul was totally blindsided by whatever it was your little friend stirred up." Will shook his head. "I told you not to take her upstairs."

"And I told you to leave as soon as the book was delivered," Paul said from the couch. "I'm not surprised the girl screwed it up, though. She didn't look all that bright when I met her."

"Hey, be nice," Rebecca said. "I'm sure she was trying her best."

"If this was her best, then I'd hate to see her worst," Paul retorted, lifting his ice pack and glaring at Rebecca.

Sam clenched his jaw. "Shut up, Paul."

"Where did you even find her, Sam? I thought you avoided tourists. And bringing her on a job? That was stupid. I hope you ditched her the first chance you got."

"Leave it alone, Paul. You don't understand anything." Sam turned to Will. "Why did Piper fire you? How? You don't even work for her."

Will plucked at the collar of his uniform. "But I work for the hotel where she is staying. And when a guest is as rich and unhappy as Piper was, then someone has to take the fall. And since yours truly was on duty tonight . . ." He drew his hand across his throat and made a face.

"Oh, man, I can't believe it," Sam groaned.

"I wouldn't worry about Will too much. He always lands on his feet," Rebecca said. "I bet he already has a job interview lined up."

"I hear there's an opening at the Plaza. Maybe I'll apply for my old job again," Will said, buffing his nails on his shirt.

Rebecca made a face. "Count your lucky stars, boy. You can work at any hotel. It's not so easy for the rest of us. It's not like celebrity personal assistant jobs open up all the time. And if Piper decides to blacklist me and Paul?" She shuddered and downed a glass of water in one swallow. "We'll be lucky to find work in Manhattan by Christmas."

"There's always Jersey," Will suggested.

Rebecca stuck her tongue out at him.

"Guys—Paul, Will, Rebecca—I'm so sorry this happened," Sam said. "I'll make it up to you, I swear. I just need—"

"Stop," Paul said. "Just . . . stop. I don't want to hear about it." He moved the ice pack from his forehead and sat up on the couch. "I just want to have dinner with my friends, listen to some music, and not think about how I don't have a job to go to in the morning."

"That's not necessarily a bad thing," Rebecca chimed in. "Working for Piper wasn't the best job in the world."

"No, it was *exactly* the best job in the world. It paid my rent." He stalked into the kitchen and threw the ice pack into the sink. "Do you know how long I've worked for Piper Kinkade? Four years. All I've done for *four years* is take care of her, and I'm damn good at it. The best. I didn't deserve to be dismissed like some stupid errand boy because of someone else's mistake."

Sam refused to take the bait. "We'll figure something out," he said again, feeling like his words were stuck in a loop.

"Really? We will?" Paul said, turning on his heel. "Think you can trade enough junk from that bag of yours to cover the gas bill, too? If not, you might as well pack up now and head back to Mom and Dad."

Sam flushed hot and looked away, only to see Sara standing in the entrance to the living room.

She looked so much younger than seventeen. She gathered up her hair, smoothing it with her hands and then flipping it over her shoulder. Strange that her nervous habits had already become familiar to him.

Paul looked up. "What is she doing here?" he growled.

"I brought her with me," Sam said. "I couldn't just abandon her."

Paul closed his eyes and was silent for a long moment. Then he fixed Sam with a hard gaze and pointed a long finger at his brother. "I don't want to talk to her. I don't want to look at her. You keep her away from me."

Sara shifted her weight as though preparing to dart toward the door, her eyes wide and shimmering with unshed tears.

Rebecca set down her glass and gasped. "What happened to your knee?"

Sara glanced down quickly, but before she could answer, the front door rattled as someone on the other side banged hard three times.

Rebecca hurried around the counter, giving Sara a concerned look. "That'll be Jen," she said to no one in particular.

Sara stepped back to allow Rebecca to pass and then remained pressed up against the wall as though desperate to disappear.

Paul walked over to the stereo, switching it off midsong. "It's about time. I'm starving."

Rebecca returned to the kitchen, followed by a girl with short brown hair and glasses. They both carried white plastic bags with a few characters of Chinese calligraphy marked on the outside.

Will wrinkled his nose. "Chinese? How original."

"Paul said I could order what I wanted," Rebecca said. "And I wanted egg rolls." She turned to Jen. "Thanks for picking up dinner."

Jen set her bag on the counter. "No problem; it was on my way. Oh, and Becca, I got that green curry you like."

Will's eyes lit up in appreciation and he grinned at Jen. "I love green curry. Is there enough to share?" He joined Paul in the kitchen. As the girls began unpacking the containers of food, Sam moved to Sara's side. She had wrapped her arms across her chest as though trying to hold herself together. Her eyes kept darting to the bathroom; Sam could see where she had left her sunglasses with her bag. He knew how unpleasant unwanted exposure could be when all you wanted to do was hide.

He touched her arm, just above her elbow. "You hungry?"

"I should go—" She made a move toward the door, but he increased the pressure of his hand and kept her in place.

"You should stay."

"But Paul—"

"Will get over it."

"But . . . I don't know what to do or say . . ."

Sam held her eyes, trying to set her at ease without letting her know how much he wanted her to stay. *Needed* her to stay. After what had happened at the park, he wasn't sure he was ready to let her go. "Say you'll stay."

Sara

Chapter 23

I held his gaze for a long moment. "Okay. I'll stay," I said. The words were out before I could pull them back. I'd heard what Paul and Will and Rebecca had said about me, and I really didn't want to hang around and hear anything else, but Sam's eyes were surprisingly persuasive. Gentle. Soft.

He had opened up to me at the park with a story that was so personal and painful. The least I could do was grant him this favor in exchange.

"Sam? Sara?" Rebecca called over. "You guys hungry? There's plenty."

I took a quick breath, tasting the flavor of ginger and soy in the air. "I'll stay," I said again. "But you go first, okay?"

Sam nodded and led the way into the small kitchen, careful to keep himself between me and Paul. I mirrored Sam's movements almost exactly. He took a plate; so did I. He dished up a spoonful of rice, a scoop of chicken, and a serving of some dark noodles; so did I. He grabbed two egg rolls; I took one.

Jen held out a set of chopsticks to me, and I hesitated. "Um, is there a fork I could use?" I asked her quietly, trying to ignore the fact that everyone else had taken a pair—even Sam—like it was no big deal. I felt stupid and clumsy, but it wasn't like I used the chopsticks at Panda Express back home, either.

"I know—I hate them too," she said, pulling out two black plastic forks from the bag. She handed one to me with a kind smile as she headed toward the couch to sit next to Rebecca.

"Thanks," I said, grateful to think that at least one person in the room didn't hate me. Sam had balanced his plate of food on top of his glass and reached out to pick up a second glass for me. I amended my thought: at least *two* people in the room didn't hate me.

Rebecca lifted her hand in our direction. "Sara, come sit by me and Jen."

I glanced at Sam, who nodded for me to take the lead, and we made our way across the small room. *Three.*

I took the last spot on the couch while Sam sat on the floor next to me. I could feel Paul's hot anger and Will's slightly less-abrasive annoyance, and, for a while, we all ate in semi-uncomfortable silence. My stomach churned with more than just the unfamiliar spices.

I was twirling a strand of noodles around my fork when my phone rang. The marimba music sounded loud in the quiet apartment—even though my phone was still in my bag, which was still in the bathroom. I blushed in unnecessary embarrassment and quickly set my plate down on the coffee table.

"Sorry," I apologized to the room in general and limped as quickly as I could to the bathroom to answer my phone. I was going to have to do something about my ruined jeans, and fast. I felt awkward enough without sporting such unflattering fashion.

Paul muttered something under his breath behind me, and I heard Sam's quick response, demanding that his brother be quiet.

Fumbling open my bag, I yanked out my phone. "Hello?" I answered as I swung the door partially shut behind me.

"Sara!" Dad's voice was loud on the other end.

"Dad? What's wrong?" I pressed my hand to my stomach, hoping he didn't have bad news. Though, if he did, maybe it was good that I was already in the bathroom in case the few bites of dinner I'd managed to swallow didn't stay down.

"Nothing's wrong, baby. I signed the papers. The deal is done."

"Really?" A wave of relief passed through me. "That's great."

"I know. I'm so glad it worked out. Now, where are you? We need to celebrate."

"Oh, um . . ." It had been a long time since I'd heard that level of happiness in my dad's voice. I didn't want to ruin this moment for him, but, at the same time, I couldn't just leave Sam and Paul to face their fate with Piper alone. I still had to fix it; it was still my responsibility.

"I know that 'um.' What's going on? Are you in trouble?" Dad asked cautiously.

"No, nothing's wrong, Dad. I'm fine." I didn't look at the bandage plastered across my knee. "It's just . . . well, I'm kind of in the middle of something and it might be a while before I can wrap it up and—"

"Sara." Dad's voice deepened, his good humor fading fast.

"I promised a friend that I would help him with something, and I really need to see it through to the end. You understand, right?"

"No, I don't understand. What are you talking about? What friend? What are you doing?"

My anger flared, hot and sudden. "I'm having dinner without you—like you told me to." I winced at the harshness in my tone. I remembered what Sam had said about choosing my emotional reactions and I decided to choose to be nice. Or at least *nicer.* Dad had called with good news, after all. Taking out my own frustrations on my dad wasn't the answer; it wasn't like it was his fault Paul was mad at me. "Sorry—I'm having dinner," I said again, calmer. "With some friends."

"Friends? What friends? You don't have any friends."

I told myself that he didn't mean it the way it sounded, but I wasn't sure I believed it. "I do now. I met some people today while I was out. They're nice"—*some of them,* I thought to myself—"and they invited me over for dinner." It wasn't exactly how it had happened, but I didn't want to go into all the details with my dad.

"And you said yes? I thought you knew better than to talk to strangers."

"This is New York, Dad. *Everyone* is a stranger."

His sigh clogged the line. "I knew I should have kept you with me today. If you had just stayed in the hotel, you wouldn't be in this kind of trouble."

My choice to be nice felt slipperier with every word he said. "What kind of trouble do you think I'm in?" I turned my back to the bathroom door. I could hear the low murmur of voices from the living room. I wondered what they were saying, then decided I didn't want to know. It was probably about how mad everyone was at me. Well, they could get in line. My hand shook around the phone pressed tight against my ear.

I could practically hear Dad gritting his teeth. "Please don't be difficult, Sara. I don't want to fight with you. I thought you'd be happy that I sold my company. It's kind of a big deal to me."

"I am happy for you, Dad. But I made someone a promise, and I can't just walk away from that."

Dad was quiet for a long moment. "It's been a long day, and I'm exhausted. Just tell me where you are so I can come get you."

"You don't think I can make it back to Times Square on my own? I'm not a child, you know."

"I know that, and I'm sure you can go wherever you want—you always do—but I don't want you wandering around the city *alone* anymore. It's late. It's getting dark. And I want you to come home."

I didn't say anything. My mind caught on his last word. I picked at the edge of the bandage on my knee with restless fingers. I knew Dad meant the hotel we were staying at in Times Square, but that wasn't home. I thought about all the places I'd been today, all the people I'd met and the things I'd done and seen. It had been an incredible day—not counting the most recent disastrous turn of events—and maybe even one of my best days ever.

Why did New York feel more like home to me than *home* did? I'd heard of love at first sight, but I didn't know it could happen with a whole city.

Arizona was nice enough. I loved the heat and the desert and the days when the sky turned so blue it almost hurt to look at it. I loved the fiery sunshine and the smoky clouds that warned of late-afternoon storms.

But I hated that when Mom had left, she'd taken the warmth with her.

"Sara?" Dad's voice was quieter now. "You still there?"

I nodded, then, realizing he couldn't see me, I said, "Yes. I'm still here." And, I realized, I wanted to stay here. I'd told Sam in the cab that I wanted to finish our quest, and I did. I would—even if no one cared about it but me. I wanted to finish what I'd started instead of abandoning it, leaving it undone. I just didn't know how. I didn't know what to do next.

"These friends of yours? They're nice? You feel safe with them?"

"Yes." I looked at the bathroom door as though I could see through the wood all the way to where Sam sat in the living room. I sighed and summoned the tone of voice I had perfected in eight years of being raised by a single dad. "Everything is okay, Dad. Honest. I'm not in danger. I'm perfectly fine."

"When are you coming back?"

I heard the echo of my own voice asking that same question once, long ago. It was the question I had asked my mother the night I'd sat underneath the kitchen table and watched her shoes turn and walk away from me. From us. But she'd never answered me. She'd only said good-bye.

Dad and I had never talked about that night—not in any meaningful way—I realized. We'd never talked about how she was there one day—and gone the next. I wondered if he still had as many questions as I did.

When I didn't answer right away, Dad sighed again, but I could tell that his earlier irritation—and his earlier joy—were gone. This sigh sounded of defeat. Of acceptance.

This was how most of our fights went: a flash of anger and accusations, then resigned silence, followed by unrelenting guilt.

"After dinner, okay? I'll come back after dinner. I promise." I peeled back a corner of the bandage, revealing a small triangle of angry red skin. "I won't be long."

"You'll be careful?"

"Always. And Dad?" I sensed his attention pick up through the phone. *Be nice. Try to see it from his perspective.* "I'm sorry if I made you worry about me."

"I'm your dad, Sara-bear. Don't you want me to worry about you?"

And there was the guilt, right on schedule. Some things never changed.

A soft knock opened the bathroom door an inch. "Sara?" Rebecca peeked around the corner.

"I gotta go, Dad," I said. "I'll see you later, okay?" I turned off my phone and tossed it on my bag, grateful for the distance in both space and technology.

I opened the door wider and gestured for Rebecca to come in. She had changed out of the blue and gray uniform she'd worn when I'd first met her at Piper's place and into a dark purple sundress and strappy sandals that looked easy and comfortable.

She glanced at my phone. "Is everything okay?"

"Yeah, just . . . family stuff. Sorry." I looked down and away. I didn't want to cry in front of Rebecca.

"Sam thought you might need these." She placed a pair of folded, dark blue jeans on the counter. "He wanted me to make sure you knew they were clean."

I smiled, touched by his thoughtfulness.

"How's your knee?"

I straightened my leg out in front of me. The bandage was a little ragged around the edges where I had picked at it, and some blood had seeped through the gauze and dried, creating a dark red bull's-eye marking the epicenter of my wound.

"Does it hurt?"

I shook my head. "Sam did a good job."

"He always does." Rebecca opened the medicine cabinet above the sink and rummaged through the boxes and bottles. "It's about the only thing he has in common with Paul."

"Aren't they brothers?"

"Sure, but they're nothing alike." Rebecca pointed for me to sit on the edge of the bathtub, which I did. She tossed me a box of bandages and then turned on the sink faucet and ran a washcloth under the water. "Paul is seven years older than Sam, did you know that?"

"No, I didn't." I wasn't even sure I knew how old Sam was. He had to be at least sixteen if he'd been driving the car that night . . . I forced my thoughts away. I wasn't sure I could process everything he'd told me about Alice and his friends, and now wasn't the time to try. I remembered that Daniel had said that he'd known Sam at least eighteen months. Could it be we were the same age? Then why did Sam seem older than I was?

Rebecca handed me the damp cloth and leaned against the sink. "Paul is nice, don't get me wrong, but he's so . . . focused, you know? Single-minded. Give him a goal and then get out of his way."

I picked at the torn corner of the bandage until I could peel the whole thing off. I winced as the gauze pulled away from the wound. "Sam can be pretty focused." I thought about how he sometimes looked at me like he was trying to figure out where I belonged in the world. I was starting to wonder that myself.

"Sure, but Sam has a different kind of focus. He'd rather make other people happy instead of himself."

"You don't think Sam is happy?"

She lifted her shoulders in a gesture that was both an answer and a dismissal at the same time. "Sam is who he is." She glanced down at my leg. "That's a pretty bad scrape. You might need to use two bandages."

I followed her advice and dabbed at my knee with the washcloth. "Why are you being so nice to me?" I asked as I fixed the new bandages to my leg. "I mean, you lost your job because of me. You and Paul and Will."

Rebecca shrugged, leaning closer to the mirror to check her lipstick. "Do you have any idea what it's like to be around someone like that all day, every day? It drains the life right out of you."

"So why does Paul want to work for her?"

"Are you kidding? Paul and Piper are made for each other. They both like things to be perfect. He likes things to be organized and then he likes to keep them that way. He had a gift for making all of Piper's problems go away—and then keeping them away. She doesn't know what she lost today."

"Do you . . . do you think Paul would go back to her? If I got him his job back, I mean?"

"Oh, sweetie, that's nice of you to think you could change Piper's mind, but you're way out of your league. I've worked for her for almost two years, and as far as I know, she's never rehired anyone to her staff."

My heart sank. So even if I completed Piper's quest for the perfect piece of art, she might not care. It might not matter. It might already be too late.

"I have to try," I said quietly, firmly.

Rebecca smiled kindly and patted me on the shoulder. "Don't worry about it, kid. You didn't know; it's not your fault." She reached for the doorknob. "Change your clothes and come on back, okay?"

She breezed out the door, closing it behind her.

I kicked off my shoes and picked up the pair of jeans she'd left on the counter. Slipping them on, I looked down at the cuffs puddling around my feet. I hadn't thought I was that much shorter than Sam.

I sighed. Maybe I wasn't who I thought I was at all.

Sam

Chapter 24

Sam looked up as Rebecca returned to the living room, picking up her plate from the kitchen on her way. He glanced back to the bathroom door. Still closed.

"She's fine," Rebecca said over her shoulder, a smile on her face. She sat on the couch next to Jen and kicked off her sandals. "You can stop worrying."

"I—" Sam's chopsticks clattered together as he fumbled and dropped a bite of food.

Rebecca and Jen exchanged a look and a small laugh.

"What's so funny?" Will asked.

"Boys," Rebecca said, and Jen rolled her eyes in agreement.

A few minutes later, Sara emerged from the bathroom, the cuffs of her jeans rolled up to her ankles. She tugged at the hem of her shirt as she took her place on the couch again.

"Thanks," she said to Sam in a low voice. She flicked a glance at Paul, who was in the kitchen scooping up another serving of chicken and rice. "What did I miss?"

Sam shook his head. "I told him what had happened with Piper—and how—and why—and we came to an understanding."

"What kind of understanding?"

"He won't bring it up if you don't."

Sara zipped her finger and thumb across her lips. "Consider it not brought up, then."

Sam reached for her plate of food. "Are you still hungry? I can warm this up for you if you want."

She waved it off. "No, thanks."

"So, Jen," Will said, scraping together the last bite of curry on his plate. "What's your story?"

"Will!" Rebecca said, glaring at him.

"What?" He blinked in innocent surprise. "A girl as pretty as Jen has got to have an interesting story." He grinned. "What can I say? I'm interested."

Rebecca nudged Jen with her elbow. "Feel free to ignore him."

Jen adjusted her glasses. "I'm afraid my story isn't that interesting. Becca and I went to school together back in Ohio. She convinced me to move here and even helped me find a place to stay. Paul and Sam helped me move in last month."

"No wonder we haven't met yet," Will said. "Though I'm a little surprised Paul didn't tell me he had a beautiful new neighbor. I thought we were better friends," he called over his shoulder to Paul, who rolled his eyes.

Jen blushed and cleared her throat. "Becca's told me a little about Piper. She sounds like a terrible person."

At the sound of Piper's name, Paul dropped the serving spoon with a clatter. Everyone turned to look at him, but he reserved his glare for Sara.

"It wasn't me," she whispered to Sam. "I didn't bring it up. You heard me not bring it up."

Sam cleared his throat, drawing everyone's attention away from Paul. And Sara. "Jen, did you know Will is a huge soccer fan?"

She sat up a little straighter. "Really?"

"Never miss a match," Will boasted.

Rebecca groaned. "Count me out of this conversation." She took her plate into the kitchen and started helping Paul put away the leftovers.

Will seized the opening and took her place on the couch. "A girl who likes green curry *and* soccer? Where have you been my whole life?"

Jen laughed and looked down. But she didn't move away when Will stretched his arm across the back of the couch and leaned closer.

Sam tapped Sara's leg and gestured for her to follow him. Edging away from Will and Jen, and giving Paul and Rebecca an equally wide berth, they ended up by the still-open window.

The sun had mostly set and the sky was cooling into lavender and blue. The air was warm and comfortable.

Sara leaned toward the window, a soft breeze stirring her hair.

"Would you like to go outside?" he asked, nodding to the fire-escape landing that was on the other side of the window.

"Can we?"

In answer, he opened the window a little wider and stepped out.

She grinned and climbed out after him. She gripped the rail and turned her face to the sky. The sound of cars and people and music blended together and rose up to meet them, surrounding them with an almost tangible energy.

He leaned back against the slanted fire-escape ladder and watched her watch the city.

. love it here," she said with a sigh.

"I can tell."

"You are so lucky to be able to live here."

"Most days, it doesn't feel like luck."

She tilted her head at him, jutting out her hip. "What about today?"

He liked how she looked, standing there in her dark red T-shirt and borrowed jeans. She looked like she was on the prow of a ship, ready to sail away, ready to face anything. She wore the same look on her face as she had when he'd first seen her outside the bookstore—had it only been that morning? it felt like a lifetime ago—but now he knew what it meant.

Sara was ready for an adventure.

"Today?" he said, watching her face. "Today feels like luck."

Her smile lit up her eyes, and he felt a matching spark of light come to life inside of him.

"You know," she said, turning around and leaning her elbows against the railing, "you still owe me a story."

"I do?"

"The long-promised-but-never-delivered story of Vanessa and the pirate map. You said you'd tell it to me over dinner, remember?"

Sam leaned his head back. "Ah, yes, I remember. But"—he shrugged—"dinner is over. Guess you missed your chance."

"That's not fair!" she protested with a laugh.

He laughed with her, and the spark of light grew a little warmer. "Hang on, I'll tell it. We made a deal, and I always keep my word."

She settled back, attentive and eager. "So, you said Vanessa had a pirate map . . ." she prompted.

"Actually, Vanessa *didn't* have the pirate map. But she *did* have something to trade." Sam sat on a step of the ladder, hooking his heels over the edge of the step below him. "I'd had my eye on this item for a long time, but Vanessa had never been willing to let it go. Until now."

"What was it?"

"A ticket stub from when the Beatles played at City Park Stadium in New Orleans in 1964."

Her eyes opened wide. "Wow."

"I know. After my friend told me Vanessa was ready to trade, I headed to her studio as fast as I could. I had a necklace I knew she wanted, so we made a deal. I left, ticket in hand. From there, I headed straight to the law offices of Durham and Little, where Mr. Little himself traded me his pirate map in exchange for the Beatles ticket."

"You got a *pirate* map from a *lawyer*?" Sara threw back her head and laughed, her happiness moving along the smooth column of her throat.

"Ironic, I know."

"Where did he get the map?"

"I didn't ask. Besides, you know you can't trust lawyers. Some people say they're almost as bad as pirates."

Sara laughed again, a bright, happy sound; Sam had to look away.

"So Vanessa traded away a priceless piece of Beatlemania for a necklace? That doesn't seem like a fair trade."

"It may not seem fair to you, but it doesn't have to. It only has to be fair to the person doing the trading. It's about what you're willing to give up in order to get what you want. For Vanessa, the necklace was more important to her than some old piece of paper with the Beatles' name printed on it." Sam shrugged and tucked his hands into his pockets. "And sometimes it's about sacrifice.

Giving up more so that the other person can get what they need. Vanessa knew I needed that ticket in order to get the map. And I needed the map to finish the job. She traded with me, in part, to help me."

Sara swallowed hard and the laugh lines along her mouth and throat disappeared. She turned away from Sam and looked back up at the night sky.

He watched a ripple of tension move through her body, down her neck, through her shoulders, past her hips and legs. Clearly something he'd said had struck a nerve. He wondered if he should ask her what was wrong; he wondered what she would say if he did.

Sara

Chapter 25

Sacrifice. Sam's words echoed in my head. *Giving up more so that the other person can get what they need.*

I had been trying hard not to think of that night when my mom left, but after my conversation with my dad, I couldn't seem to stop thinking about it. Now another memory surfaced—my mom's voice saying, "I feel like I'm the only one giving anything in this relationship. Why couldn't you at least meet me halfway?"

What had my mom needed that my dad hadn't been able to give? Was that why she had left? Was that why he'd let her go? If they'd been able to meet halfway, would they still be together?

I shuddered again, gathering up those dark thoughts and shoving them away.

"Sara?" Sam's voice was close to my ear, and I turned quickly to see him standing next to me at the railing. I hadn't heard him move. But then, he was good at that.

"That's an awesome story," I said. "Thanks."

Concern furrowed his forehead as his eyes searched mine, as though he could trace the path of pain that wound throughout me. His lips parted, a question ready to come to life on his breath. I knew what he was going to ask, and I didn't want to go there. Not right now.

"Vanessa sounds like a cool lady." I shifted away from Sam. A shiver took me, but I chalked it up to the night air and nothing else. I didn't want it to be anything else.

He tapped his fingers on the rail between us. "She is. You'd like her. I think you guys would have a lot in common."

"Because my life is full of zombies and dark magic, right?" I offered up a lopsided smile, but he didn't take the bait.

"Because you've both left behind something you love."

I gasped, feeling like I was teetering on a ledge, ready to fall.

Sam pretended not to notice, though I knew he had. He noticed everything. "Vanessa may live in New York—she may even like living in SoHo—but her heart is still in New Orleans. Always will be." He looked down at his hands, touching his thumbnails together. "She left her home, and she's been looking for a way back ever since."

The gasp I had swallowed turned to ice in my stomach. "Why doesn't she just move back, then? Why does she stay here?"

Sam looked at me, his brown eyes almost black in the shadows. "Because you can never go back. You can only go forward." He shrugged. "Maybe her path will loop her back to where she started, but for now, she's here. And, for what it's worth, I think she's happy here."

"Even without her heart?"

"Happiness can be close by, even if your heart is far away."

I felt like our conversation was suddenly as precarious as the landing beneath my feet. It looked solid enough, but there were dangerous gaps between the rails, places where uncertain feet or unspoken words could slide through.

"I don't know if I can believe that," I said quietly.

"Then don't," Sam said with an equally quiet shrug. "You don't have to believe in happiness for it to exist."

I clasped my hands together and let them dangle over the edge of the railing. When my mom had left, she had taken a part of my heart with her, and the hole she had left behind had only grown wider and deeper over the years. I kept trying to fill it with happiness, but it never seemed to be enough.

"I believe that happiness is always there," Sam continued, looking up and away at the faint stars struggling to peek through the night. "That's why we have to keep looking for it. Because we can't always see it."

"And is that why we have to find it? Because it doesn't always find us?"

He turned to me, the light reflecting like stars in his eyes. "Sometimes it does, though. Even when we aren't looking for it."

Another shiver ran through me, but this time it was a warm wave that traveled from the top of my head all the way down to the tips of my fingers and my toes. I tried to take a breath, but I couldn't seem to convince my lungs to work, and what little air I managed to inhale smelled like Sam.

I suddenly remembered holding his hand in the elevator to Piper's place, the brush of his thumb against my cheek, the pressure of his fingers on my leg. My skin tingled everywhere he had touched me today, a sharp prickling like my body was waking up from numbness.

"Maybe Vanessa could make us a voodoo doll of Piper that we could poke with pins until she gave Paul his job back." I said it as a joke, hoping to bring the conversation back to safer ground and, I'll admit, to make Sam smile. It worked: his lips pulled upward and a quick chuckle escaped. I felt like I could breathe again. Like I had been released.

He slouched against the railing, his attention shifting away from me, diffusing in intensity but not entirely disappearing. "You want to resort to black magic to complete your quest? That doesn't seem very noble."

"Nobility is overrated. Piper made this personal. I'm out to win."

"Winning is overrated," Sam countered.

"Said by the boy who wins all the time." I rolled my eyes good-naturedly. I was glad to be back on familiar ground, joking and teasing with Sam. His earlier intensity and seriousness made me feel unsettled; I didn't know what to do with my emotions. "Okay, so maybe the voodoo doll isn't the way to go," I said, feeling my way through a new idea. "But what if we've been looking at Piper's request all wrong?"

"What do you mean?"

"We've been looking for something we could frame and hang on a wall. Art or sheet music, right? And we've been looking for something local—or at least, we've been talking to people you know, like Daniel and Aces—but what if what will make Piper happy isn't artwork at all? What if it's something else? And she never said it had to be from New York."

"Are you saying you want to go to *Jersey?*" he asked, his humor laced with disbelief.

I waved my hands in front of me, the idea continuing to crystallize in my mind. "No, no, I'm wondering if you think Vanessa would have one of those elaborate masks people wear during Mardi Gras."

"You've been to Mardi Gras?" Sam asked with raised eyebrows.

"No, but I watch TV."

He nodded, granting me the point, and then cocked his head in thought for a moment. "It's not a bad idea."

"Are you kidding? It's a great idea!" I grinned, elated. I pushed away from the railing and gestured as the words spilled out of me. "Piper said she wanted something bold and unexpected, right? Well, there's no way she'll be expecting this. If it had some of those fancy sparkling crystals on it, and, oh, maybe we could find one with hot-pink feathers, and—" I stopped at the look on Sam's face. "What? What is that look for?"

He held my eyes with his and didn't let go. The lines in his face softened as his earlier smile returned, but this time with an unexpected shyness. "I was just thinking that I've never met anyone like you before."

"Oh." I felt heat rise in my cheeks, and I was grateful for the cool night shadows.

"You're wrong about one thing, though," he went on.

"I am?"

"I don't always win."

I twisted my lips down. "I seem to recall you saying that you can get whatever you want, so forgive me if I don't believe that."

Sam shook his head, suddenly serious. "I said I can *find* anything I need. That's a long way from getting whatever you want."

I leaned against the metal ladder and looked at Sam out of the corner of my eye. With the glow of lights from the apartments around us and the streetlights below us, Sam's brown hair seemed closer to gold, but his eyes remained that warm, chocolate brown. The play of light and shadow on his face made him look foreign and familiar at the same time.

My heart picked up a step, and I swallowed, my mouth

suddenly dry. The prickles returned to my fingers, my cheek, my leg. "So . . . what is it that you want?"

For a moment, his face was open and unguarded. I saw a thousand answers pass through his eyes before he managed to control his expression. He took a step away from me.

A bang on the window shattered my thoughts and made me jump.

"Hey," Will called out, knocking on the window again. "If you two lovebirds are done out there, Paul says to come back in."

I looked at Sam, but he was back to being all business. The vulnerability I'd seen and the closeness we'd shared was locked away. His fingers twitched on the railing, unsettled and unable to stay still. "We should go in," he said, his tone and his words clipped. "I'll call Vanessa about your mask idea. See if she has anything that we can use."

He brushed past me, leaning down to step back into the apartment.

I stood for one more moment on the landing, looking up at the sky above me and feeling the tingling spot on my body where our shoulders had touched.

Sam

Chapter 26

Sam stepped into his bedroom, the phone already at his ear when he heard Sara climb back in through the window. As he listened to the ringing go unanswered on the other end, he pressed his back against the wall, grateful for the momentary isolation. It was a small apartment, and there were altogether too many people in it.

Will and Jen were still on the couch, talking, and Paul had flipped on the TV, watching the news with a glazed expression. Rebecca was wiping down the kitchen counter. He reminded himself to thank her later for that as he closed the door to his room.

The phone buzzed one more time in his ear, followed by a click as Vanessa's voice mail picked up.

"If you know who you're callin', then you know what to do," her throaty voice purred on the recording.

"Vanessa? Yeah, it's Sam," he said after the beep. He quickly explained about the Mardi Gras mask but didn't go into detail about why he needed it. "Call me back if you get this message tonight, okay? Doesn't matter what time. It's important."

He hung up and shoved his phone back into his pocket. He scrubbed his hands through his hair.

What was his problem? He thought back to that moment earlier in the day when he'd had the chance to walk away and didn't. It was too late to go back and change that moment, so the only thing to do was to take his own advice and move forward.

But he wasn't sure moving forward with Sara was a good idea. He'd seen her face out on the landing, and when she'd asked him what he wanted, he'd heard her unspoken words.

What did he want? It was the easiest—and the most complicated—question in the world. If he was being honest with himself, then, at that moment, standing there on the landing with Sara so close, there had been only one answer. And he knew she had seen it written all over his face.

He should have taken that step forward—toward her—instead of away.

But again, it was too late to go back and change it.

Story of my life, he thought, a bitter taste in his mouth.

Through the wall, he heard Sara say something, followed by Rebecca's muted reply, and just the sound of her voice made him close his eyes, frustrated with himself. What was it about her that made him feel like he could say whatever was on his mind to her? And why did he suddenly have so much to say?

Eighteen months he'd lived here with Paul. Eighteen months he'd worked in the city and wandered the streets, looking and searching and finding. He'd been from Battery Park to Washington Heights and all points in between. He'd met all kinds of people. But no one in all that time and in all those places had clicked with him the way Sara had.

Was it because he knew that she was literally here today, gone tomorrow? Did knowing she was just passing through make it easier to trust her? Was he giving her bits of his story, his past, so that when she left, she would take them with her?

He drew in a slow, deep breath. He pulled his hands away from his head, his face, and concentrated on stopping the trembling in his fingers. *Don't look back. Gotta keep moving.*

"Rebecca?" Sara's voice was clear, close to the door to his room. "I just wanted to say thanks. For being so nice to me."

He cocked his head, listening, hating the lift he felt in his chest knowing she was just on the other side of the wall.

"What's this?" Rebecca's voice wasn't as close, but it was still as clear.

"It's a coupon for a free manicure at Knives and Nails. I know it's not much, but . . ."

"You don't need to give me anything. Honest. I can't take this."

"Then don't take it," Sara said. "Trade me for it."

Rebecca laughed. "Sam has you trading now?"

Sam rolled from his back to his shoulder and pressed his ear closer to the wall.

"Maybe." Sara's voice was a touch defiant.

"I don't think I have anything to trade. Well, wait—let me see . . ."

Sam heard the faint sound of Rebecca rummaging in her purse, of keys clicking together.

"Ah, here. What about this?" Rebecca asked.

There was a brief pause, then Sara said, "You're sure you want to trade that?"

"For a free manicure at the best salon in the city? You bet."

"But it's so pretty—"

"It's not really my style."

"Okay. If you're sure. Thanks."

"You already said that," Rebecca's voice held a smile.

"I still mean it," Sara said.

"Hey, Paul," Rebecca called out. "Where did Sam go? He didn't leave, did he?"

Sam stepped back from the wall and ran his hand through his hair one more time. He opened the door and reentered the living room. "Nope, still here."

Sara hurriedly shoved something into the pocket of her jeans.

He offered her a curious look, but she didn't quite meet his eyes.

"Good," Rebecca said. "I didn't want to leave without saying good-bye." She leaned in and kissed Sam on the cheek. "Take care of your brother for me, okay?"

Sam glanced at Paul, who had leaned back in his chair, his eyes closed and his hands folded on his chest. "I will."

"And take care of Sara, too. Make sure she gets home okay," Rebecca continued, pulling Sara in for a quick hug. She leaned close and spoke in a mock-whisper. "And forget about Piper, sweetie. She's not worth your time."

Sara's eyes darted to Sam, and even though she said, "I know," he saw in them the determination that she would finish the job.

"Jen," Rebecca called out, looping her purse over her shoulder. "It's late. Let's go."

Jen didn't look up from where she and Will were kissing on the couch, but she waved a hand indicating that she would be happy to be left behind.

Rebecca rolled her eyes. "Oh, for the love of—" She crossed to the couch and yanked the back of Will's shirt. "She'll call you tomorrow."

He coughed and rubbed at his throat. "Enough with the manhandling, Becky."

Rebecca swatted him on the back of his head. Jen laughed, and the two friends swept out of the apartment with a final wave at Sam.

Will scooped up the remote from the coffee table and stretched out on the couch with a grin that would have made the Cheshire Cat jealous. "Well, aside from the whole losing-my-job thing, this turned out to be a pretty nice day."

Sara giggled behind her hand.

Sam nudged her elbow with his. "Hey, so I had to leave a message at Vanessa's. Do you want to wait for her to call back, or—"

She shook her head. "I promised my dad I'd check in with him—in person—once I was done with dinner. I . . . I don't suppose you want to come with me?" Her green eyes were bright with hope.

"To meet your dad? That seems a little sudden."

She narrowed her eyes in mock anger. "No, *not* to meet my dad."

"What? You don't think I'm good enough to meet your folks? Are you ashamed of me?"

"Should I be?" she countered.

"Not today." He looked over at Will, who had kicked off his shoes and was flipping through channels on the TV. "Hey, Will? Sara and I need to run an errand. Keep an eye on Paul for me, okay?"

Will waved the remote without breaking his gaze from the flickering lights. "Have fun. Don't get arrested."

Sara giggled again as Sam led her back to the front door. He was careful to match his steps to hers, careful to keep some distance between them. He had let himself get too close too quickly.

He reminded himself that she wasn't going to be there in the morning. He still didn't know if that was a good thing or a bad thing.

Sara detoured into the bathroom to grab her bag and her sunglasses, and then, at the door, she paused, one hand on the doorknob, one hand on his arm.

"Sam?" she said, and he felt that lift in his chest again at the sound of his name. "Thanks."

He nodded, not trusting himself to speak, not daring to look at her hand on his arm but acutely aware of it all the same.

She smiled and slipped out the door into the hallway.

He grabbed his bag from the hook by the door and slung it across his chest, like it was a shield that could protect him, before following her out.

Sara
Chapter 27

"*Are you sure we're on the right* subway?" I asked. I found the different colors and numbers and letters for the trains confusing and was glad Sam was still my guide; I wondered how long it had taken him to master the intertwining transportation system.

"We are, if you still want to go to Times Square." Sam and I sat facing each other along the row of seats that lined the wall of the train, our feet propped up on the middle seat between us, our toes and our knees almost touching.

A handful of people were scattered in seats throughout the train, but most everyone else was listening to music or reading or sleeping. The bright fluorescent lights that ran down the center of the ceiling cast a brightness over us that felt harsh and artificial.

"I don't mind going to Times Square," I said, absently folding and unfolding the frames of my sunglasses.

"You mind seeing your dad." Sam spun his subway metro card between his fingers.

"I mind having to *check in* with my dad," I clarified. "I told him on the phone I was okay. It's like he only believes me when he wants to."

"Maybe he needs to see it to believe it," Sam said with a shrug and a smile. "He's your dad; he'll always worry about you."

I grimaced. "He said that on the phone too."

"How'd his deal go? Did he say?"

"Yeah, it's all good. Signed, sealed, and delivered."

"You don't sound that happy about it."

I flipped my sunglasses over in my hands, staring down at my reflection in the curved lenses. "No, I am, it's just that his business took up so much of his time. It dominated everything. Some days it was all we talked about. When we bothered to talk at all, I mean."

Sam's fingers tapped against the side of the seat. "Sounds like, now that it's gone, you'll have more time to spend together."

"That's just it. Now that it's gone, what are we going to talk about?" I looked out the darkened window. "What if we don't have anything left to say? What if all we have is worry and silence and guilt?" I nudged his toe with mine. "It must be nice not to have your parents worry about you all the time."

"Are you kidding? All my parents do is worry about me."

"But they let you move to New York and stay with Paul."

"It was more like they were relieved when I said I wanted to move here and stay with Paul."

"They didn't want you at home anymore?" My heart stung at the thought.

"*I* didn't want to be at home anymore." Sam looked out the window at the passing black walls of the tunnel. "The worse things got at home, the more attractive the option of sending me away became. It's why I worked so hard to graduate early.

Everything changed after the accident—and not for the better. I had to get out of that life. I had to get away."

I curled my fingers around my sunglasses, hiding my reflection from sight. "How bad did it get?"

Sam's hand reached for his throat where the dog tags hung hidden beneath his shirt. "Bad."

I was quiet for a moment. An automated voice announced the next stop.

"I hadn't told anyone the truth about that night, you know," Sam said, still staring out the window. A tiled wall appeared, the street name written in blue blocks and surrounded by green squares. "I wasn't sure if Todd and Chris remembered what I had done, and there wasn't exactly a good way to ask. Jeremy was still in the hospital, so . . . anyway, if I brought it up and they *didn't* remember, then what could I possibly say? And if they *did* remember, then I didn't want to risk bringing it up and making it worse. Besides, after a month or so, I figured if no one had said anything by then, they weren't going to."

"You didn't tell your parents?"

He met my gaze, hard, and didn't look away. "Would you?"

I tried to imagine what it would be like to carry around a secret so big and so bad and not be able to tell anyone.

People shuffled in and out of the train. The doors hissed closed, and we continued through the underground.

"I think Todd and Chris remembered something—maybe not everything, but they started avoiding me. They still hung out together, and once Jeremy was out of the hospital, they would go see him, but never with me. I remember I saw them at the mall once, but before I could say anything, I saw them see me, and they ducked into the nearest store so they wouldn't have to talk to me."

"Are you sure? Maybe they were—"

"Somehow I doubt they were shopping the sales at the Baby Gap."

"Oh." The walls slid by almost silently, the black flickering past like film. I looked down at my hands, picking at my fingernails. "That's why you wanted to get away. Because it's easier to be the one to leave instead of being the one left behind."

Sam didn't say anything. Then he bumped my foot with his until I looked up at him. His eyes had lost the hard edge they had held and had softened in surprise. "Yeah," he said. "It is."

I cleared my throat, hoping it would also clear my mind. Memories crowded in close: Mom and Dad singing together at my birthday party. Mom twirling, showing off a bright blue dress, her toenails painted to match. The sound of Dad mowing the lawn on a hot summer's evening. The rumbling of the motor suddenly transformed into the grating sounds of arguing, yelling. I always thought the brittle silence that followed a fight was somehow worse than all the noise.

My thoughts and emotions knocked against each other like rocks and flint. I didn't know which one would be the spark that would ignite them all, but I could feel the pain coming.

"You know, you never told me about the medallion on your chain," I said, shoving my glasses into my bag. My fingers closed around my camera and I pulled it out almost on instinct.

The understanding in Sam's eyes just about undid me. Clearly, he knew a desperate evasion when he saw one. He didn't call me on it, for which I was profoundly grateful, and instead he pulled the chain free from his shirt, separating out the circular medallion from the oval dog tags.

"It's St. Christopher," he said reverently. "It was my grandpa's. He wore it while he was in the Navy during World War II. He died almost five years ago and left it to me in his will."

"St. Christopher is supposed to be good luck for travelers, right?"

Sam turned the metal circle over in his fingers before letting it drop to his chest, where it clanged against the dog tags. "Supposed to be."

I winced. Here I had been trying to avoid emotionally touchy subjects, and I'd blundered headlong back into the worst one possible.

"I think it's cool that you have something from your grandpa," I tried, hoping to steer the conversation to safer ground. "What was he like?"

"He was amazing. He loved to hunt and fish and hike in the mountains. He could speak four languages—well, he could *curse* in four languages, at least." Sam tucked the medallion and the tags under his shirt again. "He was the one who taught me how to trade."

"He did a good job," I said.

Sam leaned his head against the window, his reflection only a sliver of a face in the shadows of the subway. His eyes were distant, his expression lost in thought.

The shadow-Sam had darker hair, black holes where the eyes were supposed to be. The strap of his bag was a band of shadow bisecting his chest before tapering off into nothingness.

I carefully and quietly lifted my camera, angling the lens through the narrow space between my knees and his, and pushed the button, grateful that the rumble and clack of the train was loud enough to cover the click.

Checking the back screen, I caught my breath. The image that flashed past me was quiet and honest and strangely intimate. I felt like I really had stolen part of Sam's soul. And there was a part of me that didn't want to give it back.

We rode in an unexpectedly comfortable silence for another stop.

After a new group of people had boarded the train, I knocked his knee with mine. "Hey, can I ask you a question?"

I waited until Sam roused himself from his thoughts and settled back against his seat.

"Is there anything you wouldn't trade away?"

"No," Sam said instantly. "Everything is on the table. Everything is up for grabs."

"Really?" I asked in suspicion and in surprise. "There's nothing you would keep for yourself? What about St. Christopher? You'd trade him?"

"It only has value because I say it does. If something came along that I thought had more value, I'd trade it."

I stared at him in disbelief. "You'd trade away part of your past, just like that?"

He shrugged. "You've got to keep things moving. If leaving behind the past means you can have a better future, then, sure, why not?"

Why not? I repeated to myself. The answer dropped on me without invitation: *Because when all you have is the past, it's hard to let it go.*

My mom had left when I was eight. I had lived more than half my life without her, but she was still there, present in my mind and my memories. Even today, when I had promised myself I wouldn't think about her, I couldn't seem to let her go. Yes, it had been bad—those days and weeks and months before she had left, and the days and weeks and months after she'd left—but before that, there had been some good as well. That was what I wanted to hold on to: the good memories of my past. Even if they sometimes felt more like a dream than reality.

"You know," I started slowly, wondering if Sam would believe what I was about to say. I wondered if I believed it. "Sometimes it's okay to hold on to the good things—like your grandpa's medallion—and not trade everything. Sometimes it's okay to slow down and be still."

"Is that why you take pictures?" he asked.

I looked down at the camera where I cradled the captured image of Sam in my hands.

"Because when you take a picture, you can keep it forever?"

I hadn't ever thought about it like that before, but Sam was right. There was something comforting about knowing that once I had taken a picture, it wasn't going to change unless *I* changed it. I could keep it or delete it, but whatever I did with it, it was *my* decision. My choice. I was in control.

"So, I have a question for you," he said.

"Yeah?" My thoughts were filled with an assortment of fractured images, pieces of puzzles that didn't want to fit together.

"Which one are you?"

"Which one of what?" I asked, confused.

"Were you the one who left, or the one who was left behind?"

I swallowed hard, ignoring the rush of tears that threatened to surface.

The subway slowed and the automated voice announced that the next stop was Times Square. I stood up, my knees wobbling, and reached for the pole in the center of the floor. Adjusting my bag over my shoulder, I stared at the doors, willing them to open faster. I needed fresh air. I needed to be outside, up and away from the dark tunnels and the fake light and the questions that hurt to answer.

When the train slid to a stop, Sam stood up, placing his hand next to mine on the pole. "Sara?"

"I was left behind," I said, fast and quiet. The words tasted strange, hard-edged and metallic. I doubted I had ever spoken them aloud before. The tears I had struggled to keep at bay spilled over and raced down my cheeks.

The doors split apart, and I bolted from the train.

Sam

Chapter 28

SAM'S BAG BOUNCED ON HIS HIP as he ran after her. She was quick, darting and dodging through the crowds like a pinball set loose from its track.

He knew how she felt. His own thoughts jumped from point to point, sometimes bouncing past, other times sliding away. The tags beneath his shirt chimed along with the metal rings and undone buckles on his bag. If he hadn't been so focused on Sara, he might have paused to appreciate the music.

She pounded up the stairs, her camera swinging from the wrist strap.

"Sara!" he called out, but she didn't stop.

Shoving past a couple walking hand in hand, he took the stairs two at a time. He reached out his hand but only brushed the trailing ends of her hair as she rounded the corner.

"Watch where you're going!" a voice shouted, but Sam was already gone.

That was his problem, he realized. He never watched where he was *going;* he only paid attention to where he was *right now.* If he had been able to see even a few steps ahead, he would have noticed how quiet Sara had been on the train, how quickly she had grown introspective. Something heavy was weighing on her mind, but he had barged in and demanded to know her soul because that was what he was thinking about *right now.*

He was thinking about what he wanted. Not what *she* wanted. Not what she needed.

So much for being observant.

He emerged from the subway station and was immediately assaulted by the sights and sounds of Times Square.

There was a reason why he avoided the area as much as possible. Huge video screens lit up the night sky with a false dawn. Neon lights flickered in staccato accompaniment to the never-ending hum of conversation that filled the square. Cars inched their way through the narrow streets crammed with pedestrians.

For once, Sam was grateful for the countless tourists weighed down with shopping bags and maps and cameras: they had unwittingly created a wall that had stopped Sara's flight. She stood on the corner, looking down both cross streets as though debating which way to go.

He grabbed her elbow and spun her around to face him. "Sara, what the—"

Tears streaked her face, and she brushed her free hand across her cheek.

"I can't," she choked out.

"Can't what?"

She shook her head.

Sam kept his hand on her arm, partly because he didn't want her to bolt again, and partly because he liked the feel of her skin beneath his fingers. He took a deep breath and reminded himself to not only stay in the moment but look forward just a little.

"Sara," he said again, his voice soft despite the roar of the crowd around them, "why did you run?"

"Gotta keep moving, right?" she said with a lopsided smile.

"Not like that. Not when it's dangerous."

The crowds parted and flowed around them.

"I knew where I was going," she said. The tears had dried on her face.

He raised an eyebrow and shifted his bag on his shoulder.

"I could have figured it out," she muttered.

"Which way is north?"

Sara hesitated, then pointed in one direction. A moment later, she switched and pointed in another direction.

His smile was gentle. He reached out and took her wrist, swinging her arm to point in a third direction. "*That's* north."

She pulled her hand from his grasp. She shifted her weight, kicking her hip out, and blew her hair off her face. "So?"

"So . . . I don't want you to get lost."

"Now you sound like my dad."

"Maybe your dad has a point."

She scrunched up her face. "The only point he likes to make is that I'm not old enough to take care of myself."

He touched her wrist. "Is that such a bad thing?"

A shadow darkened her green eyes.

"I just meant," Sam hurried to explain, "is it so bad to have someone want to help take care of you? It can be nice to know that someone is in your corner, looking out for you. You don't *have* to take care of yourself all by yourself." His words stumbled to a stop. He wasn't expressing himself very well, he could feel it. He tried to take back the words, turn them into something else. "Back there"—he jerked his head toward the bustling and brightly lit subway station—"you said you had been left behind. I don't know that story—I don't expect you to tell me that story—but I know how that feels. I know that when I first saw you today, I recognized something about you. I thought then that we might have something in common. And I know now that we do. We're a lot alike, you and I." He took a breath. "You haven't been abandoned. Someone still cares about you—your dad. Even if it doesn't always seem like it." His hand slipped from her wrist to her fingers. "You're not alone."

The shadows in her face softened along with the corners of her mouth. Her fingers twitched, but she didn't withdraw.

She held his gaze for a long time. "You're not alone either," she said, her voice almost lost in the swirl of noise and lights. "Paul cares about you. And your parents. And . . . I—"

Someone bumped into Sam from behind, jostling him forward. His hands flashed to Sara's shoulders to keep himself steady. He felt an electric zing pass through her and into him. His cheeks burned, but he didn't mind the heat.

"Sorry," he managed, stumbling back. He lowered his hands to his sides, but they felt oddly heavy there. Useless. He rubbed his thumbs against his thighs and then shoved his hands into his pockets.

Sara's mouth moved, but a truck rumbled past, the horn blaring, so he missed her words. He thought she said "I'm not" but he couldn't be sure. He didn't dare ask in case he was wrong.

He didn't think he could survive making that kind of mistake again.

Sara

Chapter 29

I'm not, I said again in my head. I'm not sorry you put your hands on my shoulders. I'm not sorry you looked at me like you knew everything about me. I'm not sorry I took your picture this morning. I'm not sorry about today.

I wanted to let the words spill out of me, but I couldn't. I didn't want to break whatever spell had been woven between me and Sam. I was afraid that if I said anything, did anything—if I took a single step away from him—this connection we had would turn as thin as silk, as fragile as a whisper, and break.

"Sara!" I heard my name, but Sam's mouth hadn't moved. Strange.

His gaze jerked away from mine with an almost audible snap. He stared past my shoulder, his face sliding behind the same mask he'd worn when I'd first seen him outside the bookstore.

A hand grabbed my arm and spun me on my heel.

"Dad?" I squeaked.

He was mad. I hadn't seen him this mad in years. Maybe not since the days before Mom left. His thinning brown hair was dark with sweat, stray strands standing up in all directions. His cheeks were flushed as though he had run a long distance. His green eyes—the same color as mine; everyone said so—were bright with emotion.

"I thought you said you were coming back right after dinner." The veins in his neck bulged beneath the open collar of his button-down shirt. The muscles on his arms flexed. He'd rolled up his sleeves almost to his elbows. The sparkling lights caught the gold glint of his wristwatch.

"I was. I mean, I did," I stammered. "We had to wait for the subway, and we were kind of far away—"

Dad's eyes glared past me. "Who's that?" he snapped.

I twisted around as much as I could without breaking free of my dad's grip. He wasn't going to let me go, and I knew better than to push my luck at the moment.

"That's Sam," I said. "He's my friend. The one I was having dinner with."

Sam nodded in a neutral greeting. "It's nice to meet you."

His body was tall and straight, but I saw the exact moment when he shifted his weight forward on his toes. He was ready to run.

Some of Dad's anger faded when he saw how normal Sam looked. He drew in a shaking breath and ran his free hand over his head, messing up his hair even more.

"I told you I was okay," I said to Dad. "You didn't need to freak out about anything."

He barked out a short laugh. "I've been walking around Times Square for almost an hour looking for you. I've been checking my phone every two minutes. Why didn't you call me?"

"I didn't think I needed to," I snapped back. "I told you I was coming back. Why didn't you believe me?"

"You're seventeen years old, Sara. You're too young to be out in the city alone."

"You didn't seem to care that you left me alone this afternoon." I yanked my arm free from his hand and took a step back. "Besides, I wasn't alone; I was with Sam."

"It's true, sir," Sam said, his voice cool and professional. "I showed her some of the sights—St. John's Cathedral, Central Park—and then she asked me to bring her back to Times Square."

Dad relaxed a little more, reserving his irritation for me instead of Sam. "Thanks," he grunted. "I'm sorry if she bothered you."

"She wasn't a bother," Sam returned. He swallowed, then looked down at me. A flash of emotion appeared in his eyes. Regret? Relief? "I'll see you around, Sara." He shifted his weight again, his body pivoting away from me.

"No! Wait!" I shouted, lunging for Sam's arm and not caring what anyone thought. My own thoughts had boiled down to this one truth: If Sam disappeared into the crowds right now, I would never see him again. I couldn't let that happen.

"Sara!" My dad grabbed for me again, but I was already out of reach.

I latched onto Sam and he froze. His gaze darted between my hand on his arm and my eyes that stayed focused on his face. "Twenty minutes," I pleaded with him. "Give me twenty minutes. Then I'll be back."

"You will not, young lady," my dad said. "It's late, and I don't want you going out any more tonight with some boy you just met." He thinned his lips and looked at Sam. "No offense."

"None taken," Sam said, lifting a shoulder coolly and straightening his bag across his chest.

I increased the pressure on Sam's arm until he looked away

from my dad and back to me. When I knew I had his attention again, I spoke quietly, fiercely. "I promised to fix things with Paul and Piper. *We* promised. I can't walk away from that. Twenty minutes. I'll meet you"—my eyes scanned the square—"outside the toy store." I pointed at the huge multicolored sign that dominated the building's storefront.

Sam followed my gaze. His face showed the most uncertainty I'd seen from him all day. "I don't know. I—"

"I'll trade you for it," I blurted. "You give me twenty minutes, and I'll give you the story. My story."

"That's enough," Dad growled, closing the space between us and grabbing my arm again. He dragged me backwards, my feet tripping over themselves as I alternately tried to keep up with Dad and stay closer to Sam. "Good night, Sam," Dad said, his voice the sound of a closing door. "And good-bye."

I held Sam's gaze for as long as I could, silently pleading for him to wait. And then the masses swept between us like a wave, and he was gone.

I found my footing and pulled my arm away. "Let go, Dad. I can walk by myself."

He clamped his hand on my shoulder, steering me through the narrow pathways that opened and closed as the flow of people shifted and spun. We threaded our way toward a tall gray building plastered with signs and lights. Our hotel. Our home away from home.

The last thing I wanted to do was walk through the opulent lobby, ride the elevator to the nineteenth floor, and stay locked in my room until morning. I had things I needed to do tonight. Things that couldn't wait.

But Dad was mad. Too mad to let me out of his sight again?

Probably. I stumbled along next to him as he stomped his way forward. Change that *probably* to *definitely.*

We reached the glass doors of the lobby. "Dad," I tried. "Dad—wait—"

He staggered to a stop just to the side of the revolving doors and faced me.

"What, Sara? What?"

That's when I noticed that the rims around his eyes were red with tears and not anger. The high color in his cheeks hid pale spots of fear. He wasn't mad; he was *sad.*

"I—" I started. All my frustration and anger drained away. Dad wasn't a crier. Mom said he hadn't cried at their wedding or at my birth. I'd seen for myself that Dad hadn't cried when Mom had walked out on me. *On us,* I corrected in my head.

He sagged against the glass and rubbed his hand over his face. "What, Sara?" he asked again, this time in a tone of surrender. "What can I do? Tell me what you want me to do. Because I don't know anymore. You say you want to spend time with me. You're mad at me when I have to work all day—even when it's important. But then when I do have time and even suggest celebrating together, you act like you can't stand to be around me."

"That's not true—" My words lacked force. We both knew he was closer to being right than I was.

"I heard you say you wanted to meet that boy later. You'd rather spend time with a stranger than with your own father."

I gritted my teeth, grinding the guilt into a thick paste that coated my tongue. I could barely get the words out. "His name is Sam. And he's not a stranger." *Not anymore,* I added to myself.

"What's his last name?"

I blinked. "What?"

"His last name. If he's not a stranger, then what's his last name?"

I opened my mouth, then closed it. Casting my mind back over the day, I searched for the answer to Dad's question, but I came up empty. Had Sam ever told me his full name? Had I told him mine?

Dad waved his hand, his face weary and strained. "It doesn't matter. Let's go inside—"

I took a step back. "It *does* matter, Dad. Yes, I spent the day wandering all over the city, but you told me to have fun, and that's what I was doing. And you know what? Being with Sam *was* fun. Maybe I don't know his full name, or where he was born, or what shoe size he wears, but I know other things about him. Important things. Yes, we spent time together. And now he's my friend—that's how it works. Maybe if *we* weren't such strangers, we could have spent the day together. Maybe we could have had fun together. Maybe then *we'd* be friends too."

As soon as the words were out, I covered my mouth with my hand. Dad recoiled as though I'd slapped him.

A coldness crept through me, turning my toes, my feet, my legs to ice.

The red spots vanished from Dad's face, leaving behind only the chalk-white fear.

"I didn't mean that," I whispered. "Honest. I didn't."

Dad held my gaze, his green eyes dull and distant. "Yes," he said, "you did."

The coldness rose past my hips all the way to my heart.

Dad looked away, studying the flickering lights around us as though they might spell out the answer to his questions in code. "You're a lot like your mom, did you know that?"

"I'm nothing like her," I said, frowning, but my mouth felt numb.

He didn't seem to hear me. "You are both strong-willed and stubborn. You both speak your mind no matter what. You both have this same dimple that shows up only when you're mad. Frowning makes it more visible, too, you know."

I forced my mouth to flatten into a line.

His own mouth flattened to match. "And neither one of you likes to admit when you've made a mistake."

My inhaled breath felt sharp in my throat. My nose and cheeks tingled. The edges of my vision blurred. A dull roar sounded in the back of my head, a wave that crashed through me, washing away thought and leaving behind only instinct. "That's not true. Mom knew being with you was a mistake. That's why she left." I took another step away from him.

"No, Sara," Dad said, his voice trembling and his face ashen. "That's not why she left."

"Then why?" Those two words ripped through me like thunder following lightning. A stab of energy, then nothing but noise. "Why did she leave?" For eight years I had wondered. I'd waited for Dad to tell me something—anything—about the *why* behind everything that had happened. But he had kept his silence. I think he was afraid to say; I know I was afraid to ask. What if the answer was *me?* That she left because of me? "And why didn't she ever come back?"

Sam

Chapter 30

Sam paced outside the door of the toy store. Boxes were stacked on the other side of the window in neat pyramids and piles. Just beyond was a giant white indoor Ferris wheel. He watched as a mother crouched down next to a small boy and pointed to the slowly rotating wheel. The boy's eyes were bright with amazement and anticipation, locked on the one empty chair as though he could imagine himself already there, hands up, head back. As the chair reached the top of the wheel, the boy rose up on his toes.

When the wheel settled to a stop in front of the boy, the mother smiled encouragingly, gesturing that it was his turn, but suddenly the boy wasn't having any of it. He curled his shoulders inward and shook his head, shy and scared.

Sam shifted his weight and settled his bag on his hip. It seemed impossible that joy could turn to fear so quickly, that the two emotions could occupy the same space, but he knew it was true. It was on display right there in front of him; it was buried deep in his heart.

Sam

When Sara had asked him to stay and had promised to trade her story for his time, his joy had immediately turned to fear. The moment she had disappeared from view, he had been in motion. His first thought had been to get back on the subway and ride the train all the way back home. To put as much distance between him and Sara as he could.

It was one thing for him to tell her *his* story. He was counting on sending that story away with her at the end of the day, never to return. Like tying a wish to a balloon and then setting it free. Or writing a message, sliding it into a bottle, and throwing it into the ocean. You stand and watch it drift away—a dot in the sky or a flash of glass on the horizon—and then it's gone.

But if Sara told him *her* story, then the balance shifted. They would be connected—and stay connected—even if she floated away and disappeared, never to return. The place inside of him that had held onto the memory of Alice and the horror of that night, the place that had been scoured clean by that sacred, inside quiet ever since he'd given that story to Sara, would be filled with a new story. A potentially sad story. One starring Sara and her dad and the mom she never mentioned. He didn't know if he could shoulder that burden again.

But was it fair to expect Sara to shoulder *his* burden all alone? He'd been concentrating so much on the freedom he felt that he hadn't really considered the question.

A small part of him said she was strong and stubborn—she would be fine. But the rest of him knew that it wasn't right.

A story for a story was definitely a fair trade; he'd said so to Sara earlier that very same day.

And Sam never said no to a trade.

So instead of heading toward the subway station, he headed toward the toy store, where he leaned his shoulder against the glass, watching. Waiting. Hoping he was doing the right thing. Hoping his wish would come true. Hoping for rescue.

The mom inside the store took her son's hand and gave it a squeeze. He saw her mouth the words, *Maybe next time.* Together, they headed up the stairs.

He checked the time. Had it been twenty minutes yet? Longer? It felt like he'd been waiting forever. He wondered what he would do if Sara didn't show. Her dad had been pretty upset; Sam figured there was a better than even chance that her dad would forbid her from going back out tonight.

How long should he wait?

He scanned the crowd, not really seeing faces, just shapes and colors. He let the noise wash over him like music. The mixture of hum and roar was comforting, familiar. The sound of movement.

A line of people passed by, and in between the small gap of space between the last two people in line, he saw Sara coming toward him.

He straightened up, pulling his hands from his pockets.

She wore his borrowed jeans and the same red T-shirt. She had the same bag slung over her shoulder, but even from a distance he could see the dark red rims around her eyes, as though she had hidden all her sadness in the one place she wouldn't be able to see it.

He met her halfway, though he didn't remember moving so far so fast.

She stopped in front of him, her arms wrapped around her chest as though she was afraid that if she let go, everything would fall apart.

"If you need to cry, this is the best place to do it," he said kindly.

She breathed out a sound that could have been a laugh but wasn't. "Do a lot of people come to Times Square to cry?"

He shook his head. "Beats me. But when you cry in public, everyone ignores you. Even in a crowd—no, *especially* in a crowd. It can be surprisingly private."

"You know this from experience?"

"I've had my days," he hedged. He personally had not shed a tear since moving to New York, but he knew that people avoided anger as much as they avoided tears. He'd once screamed his throat raw on a street corner and no one had looked twice at him. That was when he'd first learned that isolation could be liberating.

She shivered as though a cold breeze had touched her. "I'm done crying." Her voice was flat, but the tear that dribbled down her face defied her words.

Without a word, Sam reached into his bag and withdrew a travel pack of tissues.

Sara accepted the offering, and this time, the sound she made was closer to a laugh. "Why am I not surprised?"

"I'm not a very surprising person, I guess." Sam had to fight the urge to brush her hair away from her face. Yes, she needed comfort, but whatever had happened had left her fragile. A touch might leave behind a crack. And a crack might be more than she could handle right now.

She dabbed at her face with a tissue, her eyes never leaving his. "You've surprised me all day," she said quietly.

"Were you surprised to find me here?"

Sara cocked her head in thought. "No," she said finally, a touch of wonder in her voice. "No, I knew you would be here. I knew I could depend on you."

A splash of heat hit Sam's heart, warming him from within.

How long had it been since someone had depended on him for something more than to finish a job or run an errand? How long had it been since he'd had a *friend* depending on him? The dog tags hung heavy around his neck and the memory of Alice's sky-blue eyes left him cold.

"You okay?" Sara asked.

"Yeah," he said, suppressing a flinch. Here she was obviously upset, and yet she was the one worried about him. "It's just . . . I'm a little surprised to see you. I didn't think your dad would let you out of his sight again."

To her credit, she didn't turn and look back toward the hotel, but he could see the effort it cost her. Her shoulders stiffened and her mouth turned down in a frown. The small dimple he'd noticed before made a brief appearance.

"I don't think he ever wants to see me again."

"He's your dad—"

"He said if I wanted to go, then maybe I should just go."

"I'm sure he meant—"

"He told me to leave," she said bluntly. "So I did." She pivoted away and started walking toward the subway station.

Sam waited a single beat before catching up to her. "Where are we going?"

"I want to see the Empire State Building."

He touched her elbow, but though it made a shock travel through his fingers, it hardly slowed her down.

"I see it all the time in the movies. It's iconic. It's New York. I want to see the Empire State Building." Her voice broke the second time she said the name.

Sam noticed another set of tears appear in her eyes. But though they trembled on her lashes, they didn't fall. Sara was right; she was done with crying.

"It's the tallest building in the city, right? How tall is it? Like a hundred feet?"

"A hundred and two stories, actually."

"Cool. I want to go all the way to the top."

"That costs extra," Sam warned. He knew she was short on money, and it didn't sound like her dad had sent her out the door with a pocket full of cash.

She shrugged, her mouth sad. "It always does."

"That's cryptic."

Her shoulders slumped. "Everything costs more than you think it does, that's all. And what you get in return is usually not what you wanted. Not really."

"Sara." He touched her elbow again, and this time, she did stop. "So, what is it you want? Really?"

She huffed out a sigh, rolling her eyes. "I told you—to see the Giants play."

Sam didn't laugh. He kept his hand on her arm. Waiting.

She looked down and jutted out her chin. Her mouth turned hard and stubborn. "I want to see the Empire State Building."

Sam waited until she looked at him. The bright lights lit up her eyes like emeralds. He held his breath and slipped his hand down her arm and folded his fingers around hers. When she didn't pull away, he exhaled and allowed himself a moment to enjoy the warmth that sprang up from where they touched. "Then come with me," he said.

Sara

Chapter 31

Sam held my hand all the way to Rockefeller Center.

The plaza felt a little like Times Square—lots of people, lots of energy, fewer signs. The stores lining the walkways were dark, closed for the evening. I wondered why they didn't stay open all night. With all the people still milling around, they would make a fortune.

Next to the wide sidewalk area was the famous spot where the ice-skating rink would be in the winter, and the place where the Christmas tree would stand, dressed all in lights. Tonight there was no tree, no ice, but I still felt like the ground beneath my feet was fragile, a pane of glass that prevented me from falling—but just barely. The only thing keeping me anchored and steady was Sam's hand closed around mine.

I thought back to when he had held my hand in the elevator on our way to Piper's suite. I had the same stomach-dropping sensation now as I did then. But then I had also enjoyed the possibility of a whole day spread out before me, unmapped, unmarred. Now, the day was over, and I felt like I had ruined everything.

Dad was right: I should have stayed in the hotel.

"Pretty amazing, isn't it?" Sam pulled my attention away from my dark and broken thoughts.

He leaned back on his heels and looked up at the towering column in front of us.

I followed his gaze up and up and up along the clean lines of the building, and for a moment the dizzying sense of vertigo that had followed me from Times Square stabilized around me. I felt surprisingly calm standing at the base of the building.

"This doesn't look like the Empire State Building," I said.

Sam offered me a small grin. "It's not."

"Then why are we here? I told you I wanted to go to the Empire State Building."

"No, you said you wanted to *see* the Empire State Building, and the best place to see it is from here—Top of the Rock." Sam's grin grew in size. "After all, you can't *see* the building if you're standing *on* the building."

I put my free hand on my hip and drawled, "You should be a tour guide."

"And show people the famous sites around town? I might as well have Will's job."

I saw the moment when he realized what he had said because his smile wiped away clean.

I squeezed his hand. "Not your fault, you know."

He squeezed mine back but didn't look at me. "C'mon, let's go to the top."

We stepped into the lobby. A giant crystal chandelier hung from the ceiling like frozen rain. The cool blue walls and the white marble steps that circled in a descending spiral made me feel like I was making a grand entrance in some silent movie. The line for tickets wasn't too bad, but it still took us a few minutes to wind through the aisles marked across the floor and then zigzag our way up to the registers.

When we reached the front of the line, Sam leaned his elbows on the counter and smiled at the clerk. "Hi, Lauren. How have you been?"

A girl with long blonde hair and delicate square glasses smiled long and slow, like a cat stretching in the sun. "Well, look who it is. Trader Sam himself—in the flesh. I haven't seen you since the lecture at the library two months ago."

"I've been busy."

Lauren hummed knowingly. She didn't look directly at me, but I felt her evaluating me all the same.

"Listen—my friend Sara and I would like to see the view from the top, but I'm a little low on cash at the moment." Sam patted his bag. "I don't suppose I could trade you for two tickets, could I?"

Lauren rose up on her toes and looked past us to the short line of waiting customers. Apparently satisfied with what she saw, she leaned closer to Sam. "What are you offering?" she asked quietly.

Sam thought for a moment. "I hear Danielle O'Dell is coming to the library next month. I could probably get you tickets—"

Lauren rolled her eyes. "Please. O'Dell is my favorite author. I already have tickets. What else you got?"

Her interruption threw Sam off his stride. "Oh, well, I, uh—" He reached into his bag; I could hear the sound of his hand scrabbling against the fabric.

The line of people shuffled restlessly behind us. We didn't have much time left to barter.

"Will you take this?" I asked, reaching into my pocket and withdrawing the small golden angel pin Rebecca had traded me back in Sam's apartment. She'd said it wasn't really her style, but I thought it was pretty. It was about an inch from halo to hem, and the angel's wings were spread open on either side. There was a small clear crystal set in the spot over the angel's heart. The clasp on the back was a little loose, but not broken.

Lauren's eyebrows rose. "For two tickets?"

I shrugged and moved to close my fingers around the angel.

Lauren's hand flashed out, snatching it from my palm. "I didn't say I wouldn't take it."

Out of the corner of my eye, I saw Sam look from me to the angel and back again. He looked surprised. And maybe even a little unsettled.

Lauren lifted the ID card that hung around her neck and swiped it through the computer scanner. A small click sounded, and she opened a side drawer. Her hand disappeared beneath the level of the counter.

I had a sudden vision of Lauren summoning her supervisor with the push of a button and reporting us for trying to bribe her for tickets. I wondered if she would demand that security escort us out of the building. I stepped closer to Sam.

"You're not going to get us in trouble now, are you?" He said it as a joke, but a set of worry lines appeared next to his mouth.

"Of course not," she said, as though offended we would even consider it. Her voice turned brisk and professional. "My manager always sets aside a few tickets for unexpected VIPs." She brandished two tickets in triumph before handing them to Sam and smiling brightly at us both. "And since you *are* special guests, please accept these complimentary tickets to the observation deck." She lowered her voice and patted Sam on the cheek.

"Always a pleasure trading with you, Sam. We close at midnight. Have fun."

She lifted her hand and waved at the next person in line to step forward, effectively edging me and Sam out of line and toward the elevator bank.

It took less than a minute for the all-glass elevator to whisk us up to the top, and when we stepped out onto the observation deck, I felt like the sky had opened up and all the stars had fallen down to light up the city spread out at my feet.

My mouth opened at the beauty before me, and I stumbled after Sam without saying anything.

He led me around the small knots of people crowded close to the edges, the tourists taking pictures of the view and of each other. The small camera flashes glittered like fireflies.

The Empire State Building rose out of the jagged city skyline in all its glory. Proud and majestic, the building was topped with a glow of red, white, and blue lights. Beyond, a swath of black flowed like a shadow—a river, perhaps. Or maybe just more buildings that were closed and quiet for the evening.

Sam leaned against the tall stone wall, his gaze sweeping across the scene before us.

For as dark as the night was, I was surprised at how much light I could see. Light from the cars traveling the avenues and streets—liquid gold in one direction, red lava in the other. Light from the apartments stacked one on top of the other. Light from the office windows and storefronts. I imagined I could even see the glow that rose up from the distant Times Square like a white mist.

I shivered, but not from the warm breeze that blew endlessly across the observation deck.

My dad was down there, just one small person in an entire city filled with people.

I wondered if he felt as alone as I did. I wondered if he cared.

I pulled out my camera and took a picture. It turned out a little blurry—it was pretty dark and I didn't have a tripod—but I didn't mind. I liked the way it looked like an Impressionist painting with the lights and colors smeared across a black background.

"Like what you see?" Sam asked, breaking into my thoughts. "They don't always light up the building with different colors. I wonder what they're celebrating tonight."

"It's beautiful," I managed, my throat unexpectedly tight.

Sam turned toward me, lounging against the wall and resting his weight on his elbow. He looked down at his hands, his fingers fidgeting restlessly. His brown hair fell over his eyes. "Can I ask you a question, Sara?"

The rest of me tightened up in anticipation and dread. I had promised to tell Sam my story, but I didn't think he'd want to hear it so soon. And things had happened between when I made that promise and when I found him again that would make the telling even harder. I swallowed. "Yes," I answered.

"Why did you trade away Rebecca's angel?"

I blinked. That wasn't the question I was expecting. "We needed to give Lauren something for the tickets."

Sam kept his eyes on his hands. "True, but I had given that angel to her as a gift."

I felt an embarrassed heat rise up in my face. "I'm sorry. I didn't know."

"I hadn't been in the city very long before I met Rebecca. She was new too, and I think we both felt a little out of place. She mentioned once that she wished she had a guardian angel to watch over her, so I found that pin for her."

"She didn't say anything about that when we traded."

Sam waved away my words. "Remember what you said on the subway? That sometimes it's okay to hold on to the good things?" He swept his gaze back over the city. "I guess part of me thought Rebecca would hold on to that pin as a good thing. That's why I was surprised to see it in your hand. And then in Lauren's. But I guess it meant more to me than it did to her."

I folded my arms across my chest, holding onto my elbows with both hands. "Do you want me to try to get it back?"

The breeze ruffled Sam's hair. "No. You traded it fair and square." He lifted his face toward the dark sky, a small, slightly unsettled smile appearing on his lips. "You've sent it out into the world. Maybe it'll come back to you at some point, but maybe not . . ." He looked at me directly, his brown eyes filled with shadows but reflecting pinpricks of light. "Yes, sometimes it's okay to hold on to things. But sometimes it's okay to let them go, too."

SAM

Chapter 32

LETTING GO. It sounded so easy. He had even tried to make it easy, trading away whatever came across his path, but he knew that letting go of emotions and memories was something altogether different. Harder. He wasn't sure he had mastered that yet.

But after today, after Sara, he felt like he was getting closer.

"You think I'm holding on to something I should be letting go of?" Sara asked, her crossed arms tightening like a shield. The angles of her body—shoulder, elbow, hip—sharpened, kept him at bay.

Sam shrugged. "You tell me."

She was quiet for a long time. He stood next to her and they both stared across the city at the tallest building in New York.

"You know," he ventured into the quiet, "I've learned that sometimes you can only see what you want to see by changing where you stand. And standing somewhere unexpected can lead to unexpected discoveries."

She kept her gaze fixed on the buildings rising into the sky. After some time passed, she said, "He promised he was going to take me there today. After he signed the papers, we were going to celebrate by going to dinner and then to the top of the Empire State Building. 'Just you and me—just like in the movies,' he said. But that didn't happen. Do you know what *did* happen?" She didn't wait for Sam to respond. "We spent the whole day apart, and every time we talked today, we fought. The minute we were together again, we fought. We stood in Times Square and yelled at each other and screamed and said—" She shook her head once, sharply, as though physically forcing her thoughts in a new direction.

Sam bit down on the inside of his cheek to keep himself quiet. He didn't want to interrupt the flow of her words and risk her closing down instead of opening up.

"So maybe it's good that we're here instead of there," she said, nodding to the building across the way. "If he comes looking for me, he'll go there. And I won't be there." Her voice held a dark note of pride and anger.

"Do you think he'll come looking for you?" Sam was keenly aware of the weight of his phone in his pocket. Should he suggest she call her dad, if only to let him know she was okay? Was she okay?

"Not in a million years. Not after what he said. Not after what *I* said—"

There was that sharp shake of her head again.

"I didn't think it was that much to ask, you know?" she said softly. "I know his business meeting was important, but I guess I thought he'd still be able to get away for lunch—or dinner. Or something. I thought we'd still be able to do a couple of sightseeing things. Explore the city."

"You did explore the city," he said just as quietly.

"With you." She turned her back to the skyline. "But somehow I'm the bad guy for having fun today."

"Is that what he said?"

"No, but it's how I feel."

Sam took a chance. "What *did* he say?"

"That he was worried about me. That he wanted to make sure I was safe. You know—basic dad stuff."

Sam took a bigger chance. "What did *you* say?"

"During the fight or after?"

"After." Sam knew from experience the importance of what happened *after.* What you said—or didn't say. What you did—or didn't do.

Sara looked down at her feet. Her long hair swept across her face like a curtain. Her body trembled, and her voice, when she finally spoke, was thin and high. "I said that if I had known what kind of man he really was, I would have left with Mom and I would never have come back either."

Sam sucked in his breath as though he'd been punched.

"I know, right? Daughter of the Year award, right here. It's no wonder he told me he'd need some time alone after I said that."

The wind gusted past them. A group of tourists wandered up, talking and pointing out landmarks. Their laughter was light and carefree, but the noise felt abrasive to Sam. He gently touched Sara's arm and led her down the walkway toward an empty spot. She walked automatically, directionless, willing to be guided by his hand.

"When did your mom leave?" he asked once they were alone again. Or as alone as they could be in the heart of a popular tourist spot.

Sara's mouth twisted. "When I was eight."

"Why did she leave?"

A bitter laugh escaped. "You know, it took me half my life to summon up the courage to ask that question, and it took you, like, half a second."

"Do you know the answer?"

"I do now." She shuddered and looked away. "Dad told me. He told me everything."

"You don't have to tell me," Sam offered gently, remembering when Sara had said the same thing to him in Central Park.

"Yes, I do. We traded—fair and square. You told me your story; I promised to tell you mine if you waited for me. You did. Now it's my turn."

She drew in a deep breath. Sam waited, trying to ignore the itch in the soles of his feet that made him want to move, to walk—maybe even to run—away. But no. As much as it scared him, he knew he needed to hear Sara's story. He needed to help her shoulder the burden of her past the same way she had helped him with his.

"I was a love baby. That's what Mom and Dad always said. They said that they loved each other so much that it couldn't be contained in just the two of them, so it spilled over into me. For a long time I thought that was how babies were made. I imagined a hospital full of little empty baby shells and when they were filled up with enough love, they came alive and then the mom and dad took them home to be a family."

Sam smiled, but tried to keep it small.

She caught him anyway and echoed his smile, though a bit self-consciously. "I know—I wasn't the brightest kid growing up."

"At least you had an idea. When my parents gave me 'the talk,' it came out of nowhere. It was like they were speaking another language. I was horrified."

"How old were you?"

Sam shook his head. "Not old enough, that's all I can say."

Her shoulders relaxed, and she loosened the death grip she had on her arms, which was what he'd been hoping for.

"We were a good family—at least, I thought we were. We did stuff together: vacations and parties and holidays. Dad was a businessman—suit and ties to work every day—and Mom worked in an accounting firm. She was great with numbers. One of my earliest memories is of being curled up on the couch next to Mom and watching her do her math problems for work."

"I thought you said you weren't very bright as a kid," Sam said with just the hint of a tease in his voice.

She let the comment slide, her eyes focused into the distance. "When Mom did her accounting, something special happened. She made math look like magic. I mean, where else can you take two different numbers and turn them into something else? Something bigger. And together they always seemed stronger than they were separately."

"Do you still think math is magic?" he asked. It was strange—he had spent all day with her, had opened up his heart a crack to her, but he still hardly knew her at all.

"No. When Mom left, it was like she took the magic with her. No more addition—just subtraction and division."

Sam rolled his shoulders, feeling the weight of her words settle over him. He wanted to say something, change the subject, change the story, but this wasn't something he could take and trade. This was something he needed to learn how to take—and keep.

"I thought for sure she would come back." Sara leaned as far over the wall as she could go, which wasn't very far.

Sam saw a nearby security guard take note of Sara and shift his weight as though preparing to come over if she needed help. Sam knew that when you invited people this close to the sky, you had to keep them safe and secure, and somehow keeping her safe had become his job for the day. He stepped closer to her, feeling oddly protective of Sara, and the guard relaxed.

"Even though she had said good-bye, I honestly thought she would come back. I made up all these stories about where she was and why she left. Like, maybe she was just on a business trip. Dad took lots of those—all the time, to California, to computer conferences—and sometimes he took Mom with him. Sometimes we all went. But I remember wondering, if it was a business trip, why we all hadn't gone with her."

It was easy for Sam to imagine an eight-year-old Sara, her face crinkling up with confusion and worry, her small fists hitting her hips in frustration. He'd seen her do the same thing more than once today.

"Lots of nights, I waited up for her, thinking of all the places she might have gone. The store. The movies. I even dreamed that maybe she'd gone out to a ranch to pick out a pony for me. When she hadn't come back by morning, I would ask Dad where she'd gone, but all he ever said was that she had gone somewhere she couldn't hurt us anymore. I didn't understand that at all. I mean, Mom had never hurt me. She was my *mom.* She loved me, right?"

Sam knew it was a rhetorical question, but the raw pain in her voice compelled him to answer it anyway. "Of course she did."

Sara looked at him, those green eyes of hers cutting him like a laser. "'Of course'? You make it sound so easy. So obvious. But I was eight. I wasn't so sure. When you're eight, all you have are questions. What if she left because of something I did? What if she left because I didn't love her enough? What if she left because she didn't love *me* enough?"

"I'm sure that's not why she left," Sam started, but his words faltered under the heat of her stare.

"I know that," she said. "Now." She took a deep breath. "She left because Dad told her to. And what's more, he told her never to come back."

Sara

Chapter 33

I couldn't believe I had been able to say the words. Tonight, when Dad had finally, *finally,* explained to me the truth behind why Mom had left, it felt like all the words in the world had turned to dust and ash and bone. The lights from Times Square burned my eyes like fire. The noise roared in my ears like a train. My throat closed up and I feared I might never be able to speak or breathe again.

"What?" Sam said, the lines of his face moving and shifting through horror to fear to disbelief.

"I know," I said. "I spent my whole life thinking that it was my mom's choice to leave, and it wasn't. She left because Dad told her to." The idea still rattled through me, as if a rock had been tossed into a well but hadn't hit bottom yet. I looked down the long slide of the building at the small flickers of lights below as cars and busses buzzed along the dark streets. It made me dizzy, but the spinning felt good, almost as though if I turned around long enough, or fast enough, I'd be able to change what was around me. Or, better yet, return to where I started, back before all of this happened.

"Did he say why? I mean, he must have had a reason."

I looked at Sam, whose forehead was buckled with worry, and pulled back from the edge. I sat down and leaned against the stone wall. Pulling my knees to my chest, I locked my hands around my wrists. I hadn't realized how much my fingers had been trembling until they stopped.

Sam sank down next to me, folding his long legs under him, tailor-style. He swung his bag across his hips, tucking it low behind the small of his back so he could lean against the wall with me, side by side. But that left his hands unoccupied, and Sam, never one to stay still for long, tapped his fingers on his knee. I found his familiar fidgeting calming.

I leaned my head down. Sam's profile slanted in my vision, his image distorted where my eye pressed against my knee.

"Dad's reason for sending her away was so obvious, I probably should have guessed it a long time ago. She was cheating on him."

Sam's eyebrows rose, but he didn't say anything.

"The summer before my seventh birthday, Mom stopped going to work. I thought it was because she wanted to spend more time at home with me—she even told me that was the reason—but tonight I found out that she was home because she'd been laid off from her job."

I closed my eyes, trying to remember what she had looked like the day she came home from work for the last time. Had she been crying? Was she mad? The only memory I had was how she'd sat down at the kitchen table and taken off her shoe, only to find the heel had split clean in half. I remembered how she had sat at the table for hours, the broken heel in her hand, crying.

"Mom loved her job. She loved working and being a part of

something important. Dad said he tried to tell her that being part of a family was important too, but I guess there was something in her that wasn't happy at the thought of settling down, of being a stay-at-home mom."

Sam scratched at the side of his neck, but he didn't interrupt.

"Dad said he encouraged Mom to look for another job. He said he wanted her to be happy, and if working—even part-time—could give her that happiness, then that was a good thing." I shook my head, remembering the look in Dad's eyes when he told me this part of the story. The sorrow. The guilt. "So Mom started looking, checking the job listings online, signing up for networking sites. But I guess she had a hard time finding anything that was a good fit. The pay was too low, the commute was too far. There was always something. And then . . ." I trailed off. I didn't want to say it. I couldn't.

"She found what she was looking for?" Sam offered, his voice hesitant, laced with fear.

The knot in my stomach moved into my throat. "More like *who* she was looking for."

"The guy? The one she cheated on your dad with?"

I unraveled the knot enough to speak. "I guess she met him on one of those online networking sites. They were both looking for the same kind of job and they would share tips and review each other's resumes. I guess it got pretty serious pretty fast." I swallowed. "The more time Mom spent looking for a job, the worse things got between her and Dad. And the worse things got between them, the more time Mom spent on the computer, looking for a job. And I guess, at some point, Mom stopped looking for a job and started looking for something else."

"A way out?" Sam suggested quietly. His hand reached for the dog tags around his neck, but he bypassed the chain and rubbed the back of his neck instead.

"Something like that. I guess the relationship was mostly online, but Dad thinks she met the guy at least twice in person."

"He's not sure?"

"Mom *said* she was going out with friends, but by then Dad had his suspicions. And then he found the proof, and that's when they started fighting about it. A lot."

"What kind of proof?"

"Internet history logs. Messages. E-mails. Dad knows everything there is to know about computers, but I guess, there at the end, Mom wasn't trying very hard to keep it a secret anymore."

Sam looked down at his hands which were suddenly still on his legs. "Maybe she wanted to be found out. Secrets can be hard to hold on to."

"It's hard to hold on to a family too." I felt a small rock of rage harden in my chest, and I sat up straight. "But Dad didn't even try. When he found out the truth, he didn't fight for his wife, or his marriage, or for *me*—he just told her to go, and she left." The rock turned jagged around the edges. The laugh that escaped my lips was bitter. "Of course, she didn't fight either. Most divorces end with some kind of custody case, but she didn't fight to keep me with her. I haven't had any contact with her for more than *eight years.* The last thing she said to me was *good-bye,* and then she left, and she never came back. We've never talked about her until tonight. Not really. Dad doesn't even know where she is anymore. It's like she just vanished. It's almost like she never existed."

Tears burned the rims of my eyes, the hot salt stinging like needles. My fingers dug into my wrists. The pain felt good, clean and honest.

"I don't know if I'm madder at my mom for being stupid and

selfish and for cheating on my dad or at my dad for not trying to save our family. I always knew he was weak, but I didn't know he was *that* weak. He just gave up and watched her walk away."

If I'd known what kind of man you really were, I'd have left with Mom. And I wouldn't have come back either.

The memory of my last words to my dad filled my mind like tar—hot and sticky and suffocating. But I wasn't sorry I'd said them.

My dad's last words to me were "Then go." I had a hard time imagining that he was sorry for those words either.

"This guy," Sam said after the initial heat of my anger had dissipated into the atmosphere, leaving me cold and trembling, "did he have a name?"

I nodded, my breath choking me now just as it had hours ago when I'd heard this story for the first time. "Thomas Templeton." I shuddered. I'd thought it was a horrible name when I'd heard it; saying it out loud was worse. "One day, she was Kathryn Nolan, and the next, she . . . wasn't. She was back to being who she was before she married my dad. Before she was my mom."

"Did she marry the Templeton guy?" Sam asked, his eyes narrowing as though I had presented him with an unexpected puzzle.

I shrugged, a headache beginning to throb at the back of my skull. "If she did, I never got an invitation."

Silence fell between us. I was tired. I had hoped that by saying the words, by sharing my story, I would feel better. But all I felt was tired. Tired of hearing the words that had torn me apart; tired of saying them out loud. But they were branded into my bones now, and I would carry them with me like scars for the rest of my life. The thought pushed me past tired and all the way into exhaustion.

"I think I get it now," I said quietly.

"Get what?" Sam looked at me, confused.

"Why you said the accident was all your fault."

He tensed up next to me, his fingers falling flat against his knee.

"Maybe if you hadn't done what you did, the outcome would have been different, but maybe not. You said the driver was drunk. Maybe he would have hit you anyway. Or maybe he would have hit the car in a different spot and Alice would have lived but one of your other friends wouldn't have. There's no way to know." I closed my eyes. "And maybe if Mom hadn't done what she did, the outcome would have been different, but maybe not. No matter how many *maybes* you dream up, you still always feel like it was your fault. Like somehow, you could have changed things before . . . before they couldn't be changed anymore."

Sam was quiet, and after the moment had stretched into minutes, I leaned my head against his shoulder.

"You want to know the strangest thing?" I asked.

Sam's head barely tilted down. It could have been yes; it could have been no.

"As I was walking away from my dad that last time, all I could think about was those pink sugar packets in your bag and how much I wished I had one."

"Why?" Surprise filled Sam's voice.

"Because I knew you could turn one of those sugar packets into the desire of someone's heart. You did it for Jess. And I wanted you to do that for me. I wanted you to take a packet and trade it and change it and somehow turn it into my mother."

I closed my eyes, feeling a weariness all the way down to my soul.

"I hate it," I whispered, "but as mad as I am at her, at my dad, at *everything,* there's still a part of me that wants to see her again."

Sam

Chapter 34

Sam didn't know how long Sara slept on his shoulder. She leaned into him. Her skin was chilled where the back of her hand touched the back of his. He could almost feel the warmth of his body flowing into her as she slept. Her breath was soft against the side of his neck. It was enough to keep him warm too. He considered it a good trade.

As his legs tingled into sleep and his back stiffened, he listened to the murmur of hushed voices and the shuffling of quiet feet. The crowds had thinned on Top of the Rock; it must be close to closing time. The wind curled over the stone barriers, dipping down to ruffle his hair.

For a moment, he thought he wouldn't mind sitting like that forever.

When he'd moved to New York, he'd been running away. He had known it then and he knew it now. But it felt like he'd been running ever since. Always moving. Never stopping. He'd always believed that stagnation killed, and maybe that was still true, but stagnation wasn't the same as stillness.

And, tonight, it was nice to sit and be still.

A guard strolled past, flashlight in hand. He stopped in front of Sam and Sara. "Last elevator leaves in ten minutes. Make sure you're on it," he ordered, but quietly.

Sam nodded in understanding, then turned his head slightly to look at Sara. She might be sleeping in peace, but Sam suspected her dad was still awake, still beyond worried about her. This might be his best chance to help ease his fears.

He carefully reached over and picked up her bag from where it sat on the far side of her hip.

Sara stirred, but didn't wake.

With fingers well trained from months of delving into his own bag of secret treasures, he withdrew her phone. He pressed the text message icon on the phone and found the entry marked DAD. With one eye still on Sara, he typed in a short but—he hoped—reassuring message:

This is Sam—Sara's friend. She's with me. I'll bring her home as soon as she'll let me.

Almost immediately after he pressed SEND, the phone buzzed quietly and a reply appeared.

Where's my daughter?!

Sam hesitated.

Safe. Don't worry, and maybe don't call. She's still pretty mad about things.

Let me talk to her.

She's sleeping.

But she's okay?

Yes.

You'll bring her home?

Promise.

This time the reply took a minute to appear.

Will you tell her I love her?

Before Sam could reply, a second message arrived.

And that I'm sorry for what I said?

Yes.

When he returned the phone to the bag, his fingers landed on her camera. The small rectangle fit nicely in his palm. He could see why Sara liked it. It felt comfortable, familiar. Setting her bag down again, he powered on the camera and trained the lens on Sara's face.

A faint pink had brightened her cheeks. Her eyes moved under closed lids; her eyelashes curled down and away. Her lips parted slightly with a sigh.

A touch of a button and a quick flash of light, and he'd snatched the picture, saving it automatically on the memory card.

He smiled, imagining her face when she scrolled back through her photos from today and saw this one.

On impulse, he held out the camera at arm's length and pointed it back at both of them. He couldn't see to frame up the shot, but he pressed the shutter anyway, trusting to luck that he was at least kind of close.

The flash fired once again, but this time Sara's eyes blinked open.

"Hmm?" she mumbled. "What's going on?"

Sam hurried and shoved the camera back into her bag, feeling guilty that he'd startled her and grateful that she hadn't caught him.

"Sorry to wake you up," he said. "It's time to go."

Sara sat up, rubbing at her eyes with a loosely curled fist like a child might after a nap. A faint pink line creased her cheek from where she had leaned against his shoulder. The pattern matched exactly the black stripe that ran down the sleeve of his hoodie.

He felt a strange and sudden flash of pride at seeing it. Even though he knew it would fade—it was already fading—for a moment, they were connected, like halves of a whole, and that made him happy.

"The elevator's leaving, and we need to be on it," he said.

"Oh, okay." Sara reached for her bag and rubbed her eyes again. "Sorry, I didn't mean to fall asleep. How long was I out?"

Sam shrugged. "I don't know. An hour, maybe? It's almost midnight."

Sara's face paled a shade whiter. She set her mouth in a grim line. "That's it, then."

"That's what?" Sam asked. He carefully unfolded his legs, wincing as the blood rushed all the way down to his toes.

"I failed Piper's challenge. I had until the end of the day, and now it's gone. I missed it."

"Somehow I don't think Piper is waiting by her door with a stopwatch, counting down the seconds to midnight. In fact, now that she's dealt with Paul, she's probably forgotten all about her"—he cleared his throat delicately—"request."

"Still." Sara pushed herself to her feet and swung her bag over her shoulder. She reached down her hand for Sam and leaned back, levering him to his feet. "It would have been nice to have done *something* right today."

The bottoms of his feet burned; it was definitely past time to be moving again. He took a tentative step forward, testing his weight on legs that still tingled and itched as the numbness wore off.

"Can you walk okay?" Sara asked.

Sam tried not to notice the small dimple that appeared next to Sara's mouth as she frowned, but failed. Taking her picture seemed to have brought all his senses to life. He couldn't stop himself from noticing everything about her. The way the spotlights above the doors cast a halo of white around her face. The way the hem of her left pant leg was folded up in a crooked line. The way she held her breath while waiting for his answer.

"Yeah," he managed. "I'll be okay."

She narrowed her eyes to green slits as though suspicious of a lie, and then looped her arm around his elbow. "I can help. It's not far."

Together they made their way toward the glass doors and then to the waiting elevator.

As they descended back to street level, Sam leaned against the wall, stretching and flexing his toes inside his boots as best he could. It hurt, but in a good way. He felt like not only were his legs waking up, but his whole body was too.

"Thank you for visiting Top of the Rock," the elevator operator said with a cheerful grin as the doors opened and the passengers filed out. "Enjoy the rest of your stay here in wonderful New York City."

"How can he have so much energy this late at night?" Sara asked as Sam pointed her toward the exit doors. "He's probably said that a thousand times tonight."

"Maybe he just really loves his job," Sam said as they pushed through the doors and out into the warm spring night. "It's been known to happen."

Sam's cell phone rang. He checked the number; it was one he recognized. What's more, it was the one he'd been hoping to see.

He stepped to the edge of the sidewalk, tugging Sara after him.

"Vanessa? I'm so glad you called," he answered.

Sara's eyes brightened.

"Hello, Sam." Vanessa's warm voice poured through the

connection like honey. "You said not to worry about the time, but I'm surprised you're still up. I was expecting your voice mail."

"I'm surprised *you're* still up."

Vanessa laughed, low and throaty. "Oh, honey, art *never* sleeps. And when the muses call . . ."

"What is it?" Sara whispered, stepping closer, as though trying to hear the conversation. "Can she help?"

Sam breathed in the scent of her hair, her skin, and swallowed hard. His stomach flipped as though he were still falling in the elevator from seventy stories up.

" . . . the artist must answer," Vanessa finished. "Tell me your tale, sugar. Your message said it was important."

"It was," Sam said. "I mean, it is. A friend and I could use your help with an art project. I know it's kind of a strange request, and I know it's way late, but I don't suppose we could come by your studio? Tonight?"

Sara, listening to his side of the conversation, rose up on her toes in hope.

Vanessa hummed into the phone. "Tonight?"

"It would only take a few minutes—I promise."

Vanessa's hum turned into a laugh. "Of course you can come over. Art doesn't care what time it is. When it's right, it's right."

Sam locked eyes with Sara and nodded. She blew out her breath in relief.

"Thanks, Vanessa. You have no idea how much this means to me."

"When do you think you'll be here?"

"We're at Rockefeller Center now—"

"Oh, child, it'll take you forever if you take the subway, even at this time of night. Take a taxi; put it on my bill."

"No, I couldn't ask you to pay—"

"I'm not asking; I'm telling. Take a taxi. Put it on my bill." A hint of steel gave weight to her words.

Sam smiled. "I'll be in your debt," he warned.

"That's what I'm counting on," Vanessa replied, and Sam could hear a matching smile in her voice. "I'll put the kettle on. Hurry along, now. The muses are fickle mistresses; they don't like to be kept waiting."

Sam hung up the phone and looked at Sara, feeling more energetic than he had all day. "Still interested in going on an adventure with me?"

Her smile was all the answer he needed.

He took her hand and headed for Fifth Avenue, where he was pretty sure he could find an empty cab.

Even though the night was dark, the city was still bright and vibrant and alive around him. Walking with Sara, he felt like he'd been traveling in the dark for too long. It was time to turn on the lights and see what he'd been missing.

Sara

Chapter 35

Vanessa's studio in SoHo took my breath away.

Unlike Paul and Sam's apartment, which was an actual apartment with bedrooms and closets and a kitchen, Vanessa's studio was just that—a studio. The only walls I could see were the four walls enclosing the wide open space, and one wall was floor-to-ceiling windows that overlooked the neighborhood. The room felt welcoming and cozy at the same time.

A four-poster bed held court in the far corner of the room, the blankets rumpled as though Vanessa had been summoned from sleep and couldn't be bothered with something as mundane as making the bed. In another corner was a small kitchenette space. Nothing fancy—a mini-fridge, a narrow counter with a sink in the center, an old-looking stove. Next to the counter was a baker's rack with a microwave on it and a few pots and pans. A table made out of an old door stood nearby, surrounded by four mismatched but still oddly complementary chairs.

Most of the rest of the room was filled with easels, boxes of paints, jars of paintbrushes bristle-side up, empty picture frames and mats of all sizes, shadow boxes, and stacks and stacks of paper. Every flat surface was covered with some kind of art supply or image. A tall cabinet stood to one side, lined with a number of small, square drawers, but it was a toss-up if it held jewelry or shoes or more art supplies. My attention snagged on something familiar in the happy chaos around us. Between the cabinet and a workbench was a desktop computer with a huge monitor. A mammoth printer sat on the floor.

"Wow," I breathed out next to Sam as I turned in a slow circle, taking in the room. The photographer in me fairly drooled with delight. I wanted to take pictures of everything. If we couldn't find something for Piper here, then we weren't going to find it anywhere. "This feels . . ."

"Overwhelming?" Sam suggested.

"Amazing?" Vanessa said. She gestured for us to take a seat at the table, the sleeves of her paisley dressing gown fluttering like colorful wings over her white silk pajamas.

"Like home," I finished. I tucked my bag under my chair and ran my fingers over the table. Sam sat across from me, the polished hinges of the door gleaming like splashes of gold set into the dark wood.

Vanessa smiled as though I'd said something delightfully profound and bustled around the kitchen area, selecting three mugs from small hooks hanging beneath a cabinet and tending to the kettle on the stove. "Hot chocolate?" she asked me.

"Please," I answered.

Humming a low tune, Vanessa poured a stream of dark chocolate into a mug decorated with alternating purple and green stripes and handed it to me. The mug was warm in my hands and I inhaled the scent of melting sugar and chocolate.

She nodded to Sam. "I already know what you like."

I raised my eyebrows in anticipation. For all that I felt connected to Sam, he was still a mystery to me. I may have stolen his soul outside the bookstore, but that didn't mean I understood him yet.

"Classic Southern iced tea," Vanessa said. "I brewed up a batch as soon as I heard you were coming." She filled his mug almost to the rim and set it down on the table.

His brown eyes were warm as he smiled and shrugged his bag off his shoulder. With one hand he drew the mug closer. "Vanessa introduced it to me last year. Can't get enough of it." He pulled out a pink packet from his bag. "But I like it with just a hint of sugar." He tore off the top and poured the white crystals into his mug.

I almost asked him for one; I was sure the small granules would taste like wishes.

"There's something about having a sweet beverage while the world is sleeping that is comforting, no?" Vanessa said, relaxing into her chair like it was a throne.

I took a sip of my drink. Pure heaven.

Vanessa took my breath away too. She was tall—taller even than Sam—and thin, with dark hair and light-brown, caramel-colored skin. Her large eyes seemed to be full of laughter and secrets, and I suspected she could see right to the heart of me. She'd piled her hair up into a tidy mess and pinned it with two carved wooden hairpins. Even in the middle of the night, she looked flawless and beautiful.

"I really appreciate you letting us come over," I said.

"It's been a long time since Sam has asked me for a favor." Vanessa wrapped her long fingers around her mug and curved her lips into a circle, blowing on her hot chocolate. "How could I say no?"

"You have in the past," Sam said mildly, looking down as he took a sip of his drink.

Vanessa laughed. "And I might again in the future. But today the answer was yes. Don't you love 'yes' days?"

"What's a 'yes' day?" I asked.

Sam set down his mug but kept his hands curled loosely around it. "It's a day where you find ways to say yes."

"To what?" I looked from Sam to Vanessa.

"To goodness," she said, spreading her arms wide. "To life."

"To things you might otherwise say 'no' to," Sam added. His eyes flickered up to mine, the brown as warm and dark as my chocolate.

"Like saying yes to a damsel in distress?" I asked with a lift of my lips.

"Exactly." Sam matched my smile, and I felt my heart flutter in my chest.

"Then I'm glad today was a 'yes' day," I said.

Vanessa looked between us and her eyes sparkled. She leaned forward. "Sam's message said you needed a Mardi Gras mask. You're a little late for the party this year."

"It's not for me," I said. "It's for Piper Kinkade."

Vanessa leaned back in her chair and pressed her hand to her chest. "Ms. Kinkade asked for one of my masks?"

"Not specifically. But I think she might like it." I quickly explained about my encounter with Piper and how we had failed to save Paul's job. "So you see, it's my fault, and I promised to try to make things right. I thought this might be the answer we were looking for."

"If this is the answer, what was the question?" Vanessa asked.

I lifted my bag off the floor and withdrew the head shot of

Piper. Handing it to Vanessa, I said, "I wrote it all down on the back of this."

Vanessa held the photo by her fingertips, her eyelids fluttering as though trying to sense something within the paper and ink itself. Then she turned it over and read the list out loud, the cadence of her voice adding a musical quality to the words I had all but memorized. "'Original but familiar. A fresh look at something ethereal. Signed one-of-a-kind. No fakes. Nothing pedestrian. Unexpected and bold. Needs to be emotionally moving. Inspiring but not sappy. Must match décor.'"

"Kind of crazy, right?" I said.

"Not at all," Vanessa said with appreciation. She smoothed her hands over the glossy page. "I believe that art prefers rules. For some artists, the worst thing you can say is 'Do whatever you want.' Such permission can be terrifying. I know it is for me. Often it's better if you impose rules or restrictions on a project. Requirements can force you to be creative in unusual ways."

"Well, Piper's requirements seemed a little extreme to me," I said.

"But they have led you here, haven't they?" Vanessa countered. "An unanticipated destination, perhaps, but you must admit, all the best journeys take unexpected detours." She clapped her hands together a single time. "Come. We will take this journey together."

She swept back from the table and glided across the room to the cabinet.

I watched her as she swayed in front of the drawers, her hands dancing in small circles as though she was conducting music only she could hear.

"She's . . ." I shook my head, at a loss for words. "I mean—wow."

"I know," Sam said, grinning. "I thought you might like her."

Vanessa suddenly darted forward, opening the drawers two at a time, her hands flashing and moving, gathering up supplies. The frame of a mask. Sequins. Feathers. Ribbons and glitter and glass beads.

She turned toward us, her face alive and alight with joy. "The muses are calling, my darlings."

"And the artist must answer," Sam answered, giving me a knowing look. He stood up and gestured for me to join him. "Are you ready?"

I lifted my mug in a one-sided toast. "Mmm, not quite. I can't let something this delicious go to waste. You go on ahead. I'll catch up."

"Okay." Sam jerked his head toward the other side of the room where the cabinet of art supplies stood. "You know where I'll be."

I took a sip of my chocolate and wiggled my fingers in a teasing, farewell wave. I was warm and comfortable and feeling good. A little sleepy, maybe, but the nap I'd taken at the Top of the Rock had helped.

I watched Sam walk away, appreciating the fine lines of his legs and the swing of his arms, and the sight reminded me of the first time I'd seen him that day. I fished my camera out of my bag and slouched back into my chair.

Sam and Vanessa had moved the mask-making supplies to a side table, arranging the items and arguing good-naturedly about if the red ribbon was the best choice or the blue. Maybe white? Their voices blended into a low murmur in the background.

Powering up my camera, I switched into review mode, and the last picture I'd taken flashed on the small back screen.

Except the image that appeared wasn't one I had taken. It

was of me and Sam, the flash painting the length of his forearm white, his hand disappearing into the blackness behind the lens. He appeared relaxed and comfortable—more so than I'd seen him all day—and what was even more interesting was that the picture had captured him doing something I didn't think was possible for him: being still. And looking happy about it. The slope of his shoulder, the lift of his arm, the way he had crossed his legs beneath him, every part of him looked sculpted and polished. Like a work of art.

I stared into Sam's eyes that were looking directly into the camera, directly at the me sitting here on the other side, and I felt an idea begin to stir inside me.

The me in the picture was asleep on his shoulder, eyes closed, body curled close, one hand reaching out and almost touching Sam's knee.

I pushed the button to scroll back to the previous picture and saw a close-up of my own face. Still asleep. Still peaceful. The curve of my cheek looked smooth and soft.

Holding the camera closer, I studied the image. I had always thought I looked average, normal. Brownish-blonde hair. Green eyes. Nothing too remarkable. But the face of the girl in the picture was beautiful. Was this how other people saw me? Was this how Sam saw me?

The idea stretched and reached, taking shape.

I pushed the button one more time to reveal the Empire State Building, lit with red, white, and blue lights and dominating the skyline. I had loved the picture when I had taken it, pleased with the emotion that had been captured along with the lights and shadows.

Toggling forward again, I skipped past the picture of me and returned to the one of me and Sam together.

The idea steadied and solidified. I knew what to do.

My hands trembled, both from excitement and from fear. Could I really pull this off? Should I? I wasn't an artist—not really. Not like Vanessa, who ruled her world with magic and muses. Not like Aces, who lived his life with passion and built his own three-dimensional version of reality. Not even like Daniel, who could play music that sounded like the voice of God.

I was just me. But sitting at a table that had once been a door, I thought being me might be enough.

Sam

Chapter 36

"Vanessa?" Sara asked. "Can I use your computer for a minute?"

"Of course, sugar. What do you need?" She looked up from the table, her hands filled with ribbons of all different lengths and colors.

Sara turned her camera over and over like it was a puzzle box she was trying to solve. "There are a couple of pictures I took that I'd like to look at on a bigger screen. You know—see if they are any good."

"You're a photographer?" Vanessa said, delighted. She allowed the ribbons to flutter through her fingers. "It's a beautiful art form." She swept over to the desk with long, graceful strides. Sam trailed along in her wake.

With a touch of her finger, she woke the computer; bright light poured over the keyboard and mouse.

For all that the desk appeared cluttered, Sam realized it was actually quite organized. The cords were color-coded, and there was enough room to work while still keeping the supplies—scratch paper, pens, clips—close at hand. The lamp was positioned perfectly to offer enough light but not so much that it glared off the screen. Clearly Vanessa spent enough time in front of the computer to leave her mark on it and make it feel like home.

Sara joined them at the desk, one hand resting on the back of the chair, the other gripping her camera.

"I've tried my hand at taking a few pictures myself, but I've found that photography requires a certain kind of sight that I haven't mastered yet. I'm still learning how to see the truth through the lens." Vanessa gestured toward a bookcase that stood next to the window. The top shelf was lined with sleek black camera bodies and several lenses standing tall like pillars. A black camera bag sat at the end of the row like a fat bookend.

Sam knew Sara had been taking pictures all day—they'd met because she'd taken *his* picture—but he hadn't seen any of her work yet. It occurred to him that if she'd turned on her camera, she must have seen the shots he'd taken. He wondered what she thought of them. "Do you need my help?" he asked.

"I don't know. Maybe." Sara pulled back the chair and sat down at the desk without looking at him.

Sam heard a tremor in her voice, and he wondered if she was nervous about having an audience present while she reviewed her pictures.

Vanessa selected a small black cord and plugged it into the side of Sara's camera. While the computer hummed, she launched Photoshop Lightroom and quickly closed her open files. In a moment, the screen was fresh and ready for new material. Once the camera and the computer had finished their conversation, a quiet chime sounded, and a window filled with a series of yellow folders opened up on the screen.

Sara moved the mouse, the arrow hovering over the folder

dated today, but she didn't click it open. She twisted in the chair and looked over her shoulder at Vanessa and Sam. She bit her bottom lip. "Um, I'm sorry . . . but, well . . . I mean, I was kind of hoping . . ."

Vanessa smiled. "I understand. Sometimes art demands privacy." She touched Sam on the arm. "Come, Sam. Let's leave her with her muses. There is other work for us to do."

He looked from her to Sara. Part of him wanted to stay with Sara—he wanted her to want him to stay—but it was clear that she needed some space and time alone with her pictures.

"Let me know if you need anything," he said as Vanessa drew him away from the desk. He stepped back reluctantly. "I'll be right here."

"I know." Sara gave him a smile. "I will. Thanks." Then she turned toward the computer and clicked open the folder.

Sam saw a flicker of colors around the edges of her body as the images loaded up on the screen—green, blue, silver, black. He craned his neck, hoping to see at least one of the mystery pictures, but Vanessa tugged on his arm and pulled his attention to her.

"She'll let us know when she's ready to share," she said.

Sam leaned his hip against the small table, frowning. He'd thought they were a team, working together to solve the problem of Piper, but now, just when he thought they'd hit upon the right answer, Sara was suddenly off on her own, pursuing a different course and working on something where he didn't feel welcomed.

He watched as Sara pulled up one leg beneath her on the chair and leaned forward, studying the screen intently. Her hands moved swiftly but confidently over the keyboard. She knew exactly what she was doing—whatever it was.

He sighed and looked down at the table. The blank mask stared back at him with empty, black eyes. He picked up a green ribbon and draped it across the oval sockets. Better, but he still shivered, thinking that no amount of decoration could bring life to those eyes.

"Maybe this mask is a bad idea."

"How so?" Vanessa selected a heavy brocade trim in green and gold and laid it next to the silk ribbon.

"Piper said she didn't want anything fake. What's more fake than hiding behind a mask?"

Vanessa shrugged. "Sometimes wearing a mask is the best way to show our true selves."

Sam flinched inwardly and looked away.

"Art can conceal as well as reveal," she continued. "It takes courage to remove our masks. But it takes greater courage to allow those we care about to remove their own masks when they are with us." Vanessa fanned a row of feathers—all green except for one solitary white one—above the arched eyes. "When we grant others the opportunity to be open and vulnerable, that is when we can see the truth. In them. And in ourselves."

Sam rolled a bottle of silver glitter between his fingers. He thought about the truths he had learned today. "What if you don't like what you see?" he asked quietly.

"You see something in Sara you don't like?" Vanessa frowned.

Sam shook his head, feeling the dog tags shift beneath his shirt. "In me."

Her frown broke into a crooked smile. "That's good. That's how we know we need to change. And *what* we need to change." A strand of hair escaped from the pins, curling by her ear. "But you should know, once you go down the road of change, you'll never be able to wear that old mask again. Are you brave enough to leave it behind?" She met his eyes with a kind but piercing stare. "Are you ready to trade away your fear?"

Sam set down the bottle and pressed his hands flat against the table to keep them from trembling. Bravery had never been his strength, but for the first time in a long time, he had tried today to be brave. For Sara. With Sara. And he was still standing. Maybe he was stronger than he thought.

Vanessa touched his hand. "You are," she said, and for one moment, Sam thought she had read his mind; then he realized that she had simply answered her own question.

But either way it was true. He felt it deep in his soul. He had offered up his story of Alice; he had accepted Sara's story of her fractured family. Maybe he was ready to move on. To move forward. To leave stagnation behind and say yes to life.

He looked at Sara. She leaned back in her chair and reached her hands high in a stretch that pulled her spine straight. She ran her fingers through her hair, scraping it away from her face, and then bent again to her mystery task.

In no small way, he had Sara to thank for this day that had changed everything. She may have stolen his soul, but she'd given it back to him, better than before. He wanted to do the same for her.

"I think," he started, cautious and careful. If he went down this path, there was no going back. "I think I might need to find someone, but I'm not sure where to start."

"The great Sam the finder needs help finding someone?" Vanessa's smile was warm as she inclined her head toward Sara's back. "I don't know—I'd say he's already found someone."

Sam flushed. "Not for me."

Vanessa's eyebrows rose. "For her? Who does she need that she doesn't already have?"

"Her mom."

Sara

Chapter 37

The answer had been right in front of me all day? Who knew?

I knew the minute I opened the folder containing the pictures I'd taken today that I was on the right track. I pulled up my leg, tucking it under me on the seat.

Twelve pictures opened in twelve windows, one after the other, in reverse chronological order:

Sam's portrait of us together on Top of the Rock.

The close-up of me asleep on his shoulder.

The skyline of New York with the Empire State Building in the center.

The picture of Sam on the subway, his head leaning against the dark window, his reflection a smudge of light on the glass.

Two pictures of the birds I saw outside St. John's. One brown, one blue. Both small and nestled in a summer-green tree, their wings as close as a whisper.

The black-and-white photo of Daniel's hand wrapped around mine.

My snapshot of me and Daniel, the walls of St. John's Cathedral rising up behind us, the blurry image of Sam's face as he was caught turning away.

A red, double-decker bus driving past, filled with tourists on their way to their next destination.

The back wall of 24 Frames, where if you looked at the pictures fast enough, a man seemed to be in motion. Sam was in motion too, trying to duck out of the frame, but failing.

A picture of a crowded sidewalk, a bookstore off to the side.

The last picture—or the first, depending on your perspective—was of the same crowded sidewalk, the same bookstore off to the side. But the difference was Sam. He wore his gray Zebra Stripes hoodie and had a book wrapped in brown paper tucked under his arm. The picture didn't show his face, just a portion of his back, his leg extended midstride.

I studied the twelve photographs, amazed at how my day had been captured and chronicled. It wasn't a perfect record: I didn't have any pictures of Piper or Paul or Will or Rebecca. I didn't have any shots of Times Square. I was asleep in two of the three pictures of me.

But even still, as my eyes moved from image to image, I remembered the emotions I'd felt at each stop. I remembered the experience.

Original but familiar—that was what Piper had asked for. There were enough hints in the pictures to place them squarely in New York, but somehow I suspected Piper had never seen *this* side of the city. I had pictures that I felt were fresh and bold and ethereal. There was certainly nothing pedestrian about the picture of Daniel's hand with mine. There was something inspiring about the two birds perched on the tree branch. There was something emotional about the picture of Sam on the subway, his expression unguarded, his eyes lost and thoughtful.

A shiver ran down my back. Was I really going to do this? Could I?

I found myself lingering on the pictures of Sam. There were more of them than I expected. Outside the bookstore. On the subway. On Top of the Rock. But he was also in the one at St. John's. And the one at 24 Frames. He was blurry in both of those, but he was there. And when I looked closely at the picture of the double-decker bus, I could see the gray sleeve of his hoodie with the black stripe down the edge of the frame. He was even in the close-up shot of me—or at least, his shoulder was.

Parts of him were scattered through almost every picture I'd taken.

I clicked through them one more time, front to back, then back to front.

I stopped on the picture of Sam outside the bookstore. It was a decent action shot. The other people in the frame were in various stages of motion—a few in the background were blurry, a few in the front were sharply defined—but Sam was clearly the subject of the photograph. After spending the day with him, I recognized the shape of his body, the set of his shoulders. I could imagine the expression on his face even though it was turned away from the lens: determined, focused. His eyes would have been wide open, seeing everything, noticing everything.

I thought back to that moment when I had taken his picture. I smiled, thinking of all that had happened because I had chosen to follow him. Such a simple decision, almost impulsive, but it had changed everything. It had changed me.

I reached up my arms, stretching my back, and ran my fingers through my hair. I could hear Vanessa and Sam talking about the mask they were working on. It sounded like they were making good progress, and I didn't want to interrupt them. If we gave Piper the mask, then maybe these pictures could be for me.

I bent to the task at hand, feeling the fire of creativity start to burn in my fingers, begging to be unleashed. I gave in and focused on the files in front of me. I tended to each one individually, running them through a gauntlet of Photoshop treatments. Check exposure. Balance color. Crop and straighten and tighten. Highlight. Polish.

For the picture of my hand with Daniel, I pushed the black and white into even starker contrast.

For the picture of the double-decker bus, I bumped up the red.

The cathedral birds were softened until the leaves around them looked like a watercolor.

I debated whether or not to crop out the slivers of Sam that kept appearing on the edges of my pictures. In the end, though, I decided to keep them all. He was too important to the story to pretend he hadn't been there.

The individual pictures prepped and ready, I turned my attention to assembling them into a collage.

First I centered the picture of Sam at the bookstore. I wanted the eye to be drawn to him right away. Then I replicated the picture of the same shot—sans Sam—and surrounded the center photo with a ring of identical images. I rotated and layered the images so they looked as though Sam was walking into a tunnel where three distinct branches broke off and led him in three different directions.

One path led him to St. John's Cathedral and the black-and-white picture of my hand in Daniel's.

One path led him toward Central Park, past two birds that

sat close enough to share secrets, their wings feather-light against the green.

One path led him to Top of the Rock and a view of the city I had fallen in love with. That path also led to the two pictures Sam had taken: the one of me sleeping, and the only one that showed us together.

Along the way, I scattered in the pictures I had taken of movement, of transportation: the bus, the subway, the man walking through twenty-four identically framed pictures.

For the background, I zoomed in on some of the details of my photographs, washing them out into gray and silver and turning the recognizable images into repeating shapes and patterns.

I worked without stopping. My back ached from sitting hunched over the keyboard; my eyes stung from staring at the screen.

The low murmur of Sam and Vanessa's voices reached me, but they weren't loud enough for me to make out individual words or phrases. I thought I heard my name, but I couldn't be sure. I didn't care; I needed to finish the collage. I needed it to be perfect.

I weighed all the options Photoshop offered. I tried new techniques I'd never used before. I placed pictures together, only to move them when I realized they would look better *here,* look stronger *like this.* I moved on instinct. I made decisions with confidence. I knew what I wanted it to look like when I was done, and somehow I knew exactly what to do to make it happen.

Eventually, the voices behind me grew quiet and I risked a glance over my shoulder. Sam was stretched out on Vanessa's couch, his arm over his eyes, his breathing deep and even. I wondered how long he'd been asleep. I realized I didn't have any idea what time it was.

Vanessa remained at her worktable, a pair of tweezers in her hand and a box of sequins at her elbow. She looked up and met my eyes.

"Finished?"

"Almost." I yawned, feeling the fingers of fatigue coaxing me toward exhaustion.

"Happy?"

I glanced at the file on the screen. A sense of peace settled over me. "Yeah," I said. "I am."

"That's good." Vanessa set down her tools and dusted her hands together. "What can I do to help?"

"Can you help me print this off? There are a few other things I'd like to add, but I'll need to do it on a flat surface."

Vanessa stood and stretched. She glided over to the computer and studied what I had done.

She was quiet for so long, my heart started hammering in my chest. I felt like it was good, but Vanessa was a *real* artist. What if she didn't like it? What if she didn't understand it?

She set her hand on my shoulder and squeezed.

I looked up at her, surprised to see tears in her eyes.

"I see the muses have been singing to you tonight," she said.

"Do you really think it's good?"

"I think it's amazing." She selected a few commands, and the printer on the floor clicked and hummed into life.

The paper was slightly warm when it finally emerged from the printer. The collage looked even better enlarged and on paper than it had on the monitor screen. I helped Vanessa clear away the dishes, and she helped me spread out the print on the kitchen table. I stood back, trying to see it from a different perspective. It looked like a real work of art.

But it wasn't quite done.

Reaching for my bag that was still on the floor under the

chair, I asked Vanessa if she had some glue I could borrow. And a black marker. And maybe one of the feathers she'd selected for the Mardi Gras mask.

When she returned with the supplies, I withdrew from my bag the red beads I had received from Aces and the small branch I had taken from the tree in Central Park.

Pressing a drop of glue next to the picture of the birds, I added the leaves to the paper, smoothing them down and overlapping them against the birds' wings so that it looked like they were really tucked into a tree.

"Very nice," Vanessa murmured from behind me.

I moved the glue to the picture of the New York skyline. At every point where there was a glow of red light against the black, I dabbed a spot of glue and added a red bead in its place. When I was done and the glue had dried, the effect was exactly what I wanted. The lamplight reflected off the beads; not only did it make the picture glitter like it was infused with real lights, but it also gave the image a three-dimensional texture.

Aces was right, I thought. *The answer is passion.*

I picked up the black marker and carefully traced the faded handwriting on my palm—the directions from Daniel that had taken Sam and me to Central Park. And to Sam's story about Alice.

With the ink still damp, I pressed my hand against the paper in a blank spot next to the picture of Sam on the subway. *Aces. Cathedral Parkway 110th Street station.* The letters were imprinted backwards, and not all of them transferred cleanly, but I liked the effect.

I placed a white feather along the bottom edge of the collage.

There was one item left to add.

I stepped to the narrow kitchen counter and picked up Sam's

discarded pink sugar packet. It was crumpled along the edges and the top was ripped off, but I didn't mind. In fact, the texture it added was perfect.

I could feel the thin line of granules of sugar still caught in the bottom of the packet, and that made me happy. It was almost like Sam had left a few wishes inside just for me, a few sweet treats that could be traded for something even sweeter.

I glued the packet to the collage next to the single picture of me and Sam. The placement felt right, and, as I stepped back, I knew in my heart that it was done.

"What are you going to call it?" Vanessa asked.

I clicked the lid of the pen in my hand, thinking. After a moment, I leaned down and wrote in the open space along the bottom edge of the picture near the feather: *After Hello.* Then I signed my name with today's date.

Vanessa and I looked at my creation for a long time in silence.

Finally, I touched the edge of the collage with the tips of my fingers and spoke. "Do you like it?"

"It doesn't matter what I think," Vanessa said. She moved her dark eyes from the picture to me. "You didn't make this for me. You made this for you."

She was right. I had poured my heart into the pictures. It was my whole day spread out before me—it felt like my whole life—and I shook my head.

"I made it for Sam, too," I said quietly. "I couldn't have done any of this without him."

I glanced over at the couch where Sam still slept, one arm propped over his eyes. Spending the day with him had been amazing. He had taught me how to see the world around me with new eyes, and how to trade. And together we had learned how to keep, and how to embrace letting go.

I returned my gaze to the collage, letting my eyes travel over the pictures and remembering every moment of this unforgettable day.

"I have to say good-bye to it, though. I have to give it away." It hurt to say the words, but the longer I looked at the collage, the more certain I was of what I needed to do.

"Are you really going to give it to Piper?" Vanessa's gentle voice just about undid me.

I felt a catch in my throat, but I said the word anyway. "Yes."

"Even though she couldn't possibly appreciate it the way you do—or the way Sam would?"

"Yes," I said again.

"Why?"

"Because I promised Piper I would find something amazing for her. Because saving Paul and Sam requires a sacrifice, and Sam taught me that sacrifice means giving up more so that the other person can get what they need. And Piper needs this more than I do. I have it all in here." I touched my chest right above my heart. "And maybe, if I give this to Piper, she'll feel some of what I have felt today. And that would be a good thing to give her."

Vanessa brushed at her eyes with the edge of her sleeve before wrapping her arms around me in a hug.

I drew in a shivering breath, feeling like both crying and laughing at the same time. "I guess I won't be needing the mask after all. I'm sorry you went to all the trouble to make it."

"Ah, but art and trouble go hand in hand. If you cannot be troubled to create art from your heart, than your art will never trouble the hearts of others." She stepped to the worktable and returned with the finished mask in hand.

The mask was designed to cover the forehead, eyes, and nose and was a marvel of color and texture. The sides curved upward into points that ended in shimmering golden ribbons. Strands of beautiful red beads and clear crystals were woven between the green feathers that lined the entire rim of the mask. One pure white feather rose up behind the right eyehole.

"Oh," I gasped. "It's beautiful."

"It's yours," Vanessa said, setting it on the table in front of me.

"Oh, no, I couldn't take this. You worked so hard on it. You should keep it or sell it or—"

"Give it to you," she finished. "If you are going to trade away an original work of art, then you should have something original to replace it. That seems only fair, wouldn't you agree?"

I wanted the mask, I couldn't deny it, but when I reached for it, I found myself hesitating. "Are you sure?"

In answer, Vanessa selected a black box from off a nearby shelf, placed the mask inside, wrapped it with a bright white ribbon, and handed it to me. "The muses are sure."

Sam

Chapter 38

SAM WOKE IN TIME TO SEE the sunrise through the wall of windows in Vanessa's studio. As he watched, the stars seemed to fade behind a screen of sky that gently turned from gray to blue. He could see a few scattered clouds, just faint white lines above the rooftops. The room was still and quiet.

He blinked and rubbed at his eyes. He checked the time on his phone: 5:43. Sitting up, he yawned. He felt like he could have used a few more hours' sleep, but at least he no longer felt beaten down with exhaustion. The last thing he remembered was Sara still sitting at the computer and Vanessa working on the Mardi Gras mask and the clock ticking closer to 3:00 A.M. At some point Vanessa had ordered him to bed, an order he had reluctantly obeyed. He felt bad that he'd fallen asleep while everyone else had stayed up, but it had been a long day.

And being the first one asleep meant that he was the first one up, which had its perks.

He padded past the four-poster bed, being careful not to wake Vanessa or Sara, who were both still asleep, and headed to the small kitchen corner. He had intended to forage for breakfast—maybe some toast or cereal—when the large frame resting on the table caught his attention.

He slowed his steps, then stopped, then dropped into the chair. This must have been what Sara had been working on all night. He couldn't look away. Not that he wanted to. The collage was interesting and intricate. Beautiful. It was strange to see his face in so many pictures and in so many places, but he had to admit, the overall effect was impressive.

He followed the different paths in the pictures to the different destinations, wondering if his life had always had so many options and if he had simply been blind to them until now. He couldn't help but notice how many of the pathways ended up with a picture of Sara.

The buzz from Sara's phone sounded loud in the quiet room.

She had left her bag next to the framed picture on the table. A black box with a white ribbon had been shoved inside, and her phone was balanced on the lip of the bag, threatening to fall out.

Sam snagged it and checked the incoming text. As he suspected, it was from her dad.

Sara? Where are you?

Sam could sense the worry and fear in those four words. Then he noticed that the same message had been sent every ten minutes since five o'clock.

He had promised Sara's dad that he would bring her home. It was time to make good on his word. Part of him felt guilty using Sara's phone without her permission, but he couldn't let her dad worry in the dark forever.

Hey. This is Sam. We're at my friend's place in SoHo. On our way to TS soon. Need to make one stop first, OK?

The reply appeared so fast Sam knew Sara's dad must have been waiting by the phone.

Sara's okay? She's safe?

Yes.

She's coming home?

Yes.

When?

Soon. Sam didn't want to commit to a time. He wasn't sure how long it would take to arrange a meeting with Piper.

Sam expected another instant question, but when there was a slight delay, he wondered if Sara's dad had said all he was going to say. Then the next text appeared, and Sam understood the hesitation.

Has she forgiven me?

Now it was Sam's turn to hesitate. He didn't know the answer and he didn't dare bluff and say yes, even though he knew that was what Sara's dad wanted to hear.

His thumb hovered over the keypad, then he quickly typed the safest message he could manage.

We'll be there soon.

There was another pause, then two more texts in quick succession.

Okay.

But our flight leaves at noon.

Sam blew out his breath. That changed things. JFK was always busy—figure two hours at the airport, plus at least an hour to get there. Add in the time it would take to get from SoHo to Times Square—twenty minutes; no, better make it thirty—and that left approximately two and a half hours to meet up with Piper at the Plaza and get Sara back to her hotel with enough time to make her flight with her dad.

And that was assuming they left right now.

Sam glanced over his shoulder. Sara stirred in her sleep, her hand rubbing at her nose.

He didn't want to wake her—she'd been up all night—but it looked like he didn't have much choice. The familiar demand for urgency stirred inside him, erasing any lingering weariness he felt.

Got it, he texted, then set the phone back in Sara's bag.

Even though he was acutely aware of the time slipping away, he couldn't help but spend a few minutes studying Sara's picture. He'd never seen anything quite like it. He supposed it was possible that Sara had saved the file on Vanessa's computer, but even if she printed out another copy, it wouldn't be the same. It would be close, but it wouldn't have the green leaves, the red beads, the white feather. It wouldn't have Sara's fingerprints—literally—on the canvas. It wouldn't be infused with her memories or her life the way this one was.

He brushed his fingers over the last picture he'd taken—the one of the two of them together—then traced the path back to the center picture, the one of him outside the bookstore.

As he leaned over the table, his silver chain slipped free and swung from his neck. The rising sunlight caught the flat surface of the engraved dog tags and made them shine. He caught them in his hand and ran his thumb over the names. He had worn them for so long as his own private burden of guilt and secret shame. But Sara had taught him that letting go was sometimes as important as holding on.

With a swift pull, he yanked on the chain, feeling it snap. The ends slithered free. He separated the tags from the St. Christopher medallion and weighed them in his palm, considering his options, choosing the path he wanted to take.

Reaching for his messenger bag, he placed the tags into a

small zippered pocket so he wouldn't lose them. Letting go didn't mean throwing away, after all.

Glancing back at Sara, still sleeping, he rolled the circular medallion between his fingers, thinking deeper, longer. Then, reaching for the half-empty bottle of glue that stood by the picture, he added the token of St. Christopher to a small white spot next to the center picture, pressing down hard to make sure it wouldn't slip or fall off.

He liked how it looked. What's more, he liked how it made him feel.

Sara

Chapter 39

"*I can't believe you did that,*" I said, tracing the medallion with my finger.

The taxi slowed for a red light, and Sam reached out to brace himself against the front seat.

"I can't believe you did everything else," he said. "I'm amazed you finished it all in one night."

I yawned. "Don't remind me. I'm still tired."

"You can sleep on the plane."

My yawn turned into a grimace. "Again—don't remind me."

I had woken to the sound of Sam's voice saying my name. Even though I had been groggy with sleep, *that* was a memory I would never forget. He had barely given me time to open my eyes before he'd dumped a ton of information on me, the bottom line of which was that if I wanted to see Piper before my plane left for home, I had to get up and get moving. Now.

I wasn't ready to leave New York; there was still so much I wanted to see and do. And part of me wanted to see and do it all with Sam, even though I knew that was impossible.

I told him about the picture and how I wanted to give it to Piper—and why. To his credit, he took the information in stride and didn't protest my decision.

Sam told me he'd texted my dad, which, once I got over my initial wave of anger, I realized was actually a really nice thing to do. But it didn't make the thought of seeing him again any easier to stomach. We'd said terrible things to each other. I had run from him; he had let me go. I hadn't called him, or texted him, or even really thought about him since Sam and I had left Top of the Rock. I knew I needed to apologize for leaving him, but I didn't know if Dad would forgive me. I didn't know if I could forgive myself.

While I hurried through breakfast—half a glass of juice and a few bites of a granola bar—I saw Vanessa press some bills into Sam's hand. She had insisted on paying for the taxi—again. I hoped Sam could convince her to accept something in trade for all the help she had given us. She deserved something wonderful, like diamonds, or a building named after her.

Before we ran out the door, picture in hand, Vanessa stopped us long enough to give us each a hug. In my ear, she whispered, "Always listen to the muses, sugar. They will never lead you astray."

"I will. Thank you," I said, squeezing her back.

Then we were off. Down the stairs, to the street, and into a taxi that would whisk us uptown to the Plaza Hotel and the completion of our quest.

The driver maneuvered past a bus with barely an inch to spare. I shuddered at the close call; one day was not enough time to get used to driving in New York.

I touched the medallion again and shook my head. "This was your grandfather's," I said, awed. "I know you said you'd trade it if the right thing came along, but I'm giving this to Piper. I can't just take your medallion and give it away."

"Yes, you can," Sam said. "This isn't a trade. It's a gift. And that's what you do with gifts—you give them away."

I thought of the mask Vanessa had given me as a gift, tucked away in my bag, the eyes opened wide like it was my own personal muse that could watch over me.

For all that we were in a rush, he seemed perfectly relaxed. He leaned back against the seat, and, for once, his fingers were motionless on his knee. No endless tapping. No restless energy pouring off him in waves. The calmness suited him, I decided.

"Besides," he said, touching the silver circle with one finger, "St. Christopher watched over both of us yesterday. It's only fair he have a place of honor recognizing his contribution."

I smiled. "He did bring us some good luck."

"Only the best."

The taxi pulled up in front of the Plaza Hotel. The building looked the same as it had yesterday—a beautiful gray exterior with flags hung at an angle above the front doors. Today, though, I knew what—and who—was inside. I could only hope that this time we would have a different ending to our meeting with Piper.

Sam paid the fare, and we headed into the lobby. I carried the framed print with both hands.

"How are we going to get in to see Piper?" I asked. "Without Will to buzz us through, I mean."

Sam smiled. "I have a plan."

Whereas yesterday we'd sidestepped to Will's station, today Sam strode directly up to the front desk.

"Sara Nolan to see Piper Kinkade, please," he announced to the uniformed employee. "That's Sara without the *h*," he added in a mock-whisper, as though that detail would make a difference.

I tried to keep my surprise in check and still look official at the same time. This was Sam's big plan? Did he really think this was going to work?

The employee checked a clipboard, flipping pages and swallowing hard. "Um, there's no one on the list by that name. So—"

Sam leaned his elbows on the desk and gestured for the clerk to come closer. "You're new here, aren't you"—Sam squinted at the gold name tag—"Harold?"

Harold's nervous glance darted right then left as though he were afraid of being identified as the new guy. "May I . . . uh, may I ask what your business is with Ms. Kinkade?"

"Let me give you a bit of advice, Harold." Sam's smile was charming and effortless. "You should *never* pry in Ms. Kinkade's personal business, and you should *never, ever* keep her waiting. We have a special delivery, so why don't you call her up and let her know we're here."

Harold swallowed and, after a moment, reached for the phone. He turned his back to us, and I took the opportunity to bump Sam's arm with my elbow.

"What are you doing?" I hissed. "This is never going to work."

"If I know one thing about Piper, it's that she loves special deliveries. She'll be intrigued enough by the promise of a surprise that we should be able at least to secure a pass into the elevator."

Harold turned back to us, his face ashen. "Follow me," he said with a quaver in his voice.

Sam grinned. "Thank you, my good man."

I felt a laugh tickle the back of my throat and I quickly turned it into a cough as I followed Sam to the elevator.

Harold swiped his ID card through the reader, and when the chime sounded, he said, "You have five minutes."

The elevator doors opened and we darted inside.

I held my breath as we ascended to the top floor. My heart thudded in worried anticipation. We'd come so far and done so much. Would it be enough? Would Piper like our gift enough to give Paul his job back—and, by extension, Sam?

Or had we spent the day on a fool's errand?

No, I couldn't believe that.

I looked up at Sam, who was watching the numbers tick higher and higher as the elevator closed the gap between us and our destination.

"Don't worry, Sara," he said without looking at me.

Someday I was going to figure out how he managed to see everything around him.

The doors opened, revealing the pristine white hallway I remembered. There were the same tables. The same mirrors on the walls. The same plush carpet rolling all the way back to a pair of wooden double doors.

The difference now was that Piper stood in the center of the hallway, waiting for us. She held a squirming Bootsie in her arms, the small dog sporting an even smaller hot-pink cast around one leg.

Neither one looked happy at all.

"I told the new boy downstairs I didn't want to be disturbed and what does he do? He calls me—before noon! on a Sunday!—about some random delivery that I don't even remember ordering. My old assistant never would have let this happen." Her eyes snapped with anger. "This better be good, or else I'll have to fire the new guy too. It's been a bad week for that." She frowned. "Maybe I'll fire him anyway. Wait—" She stopped mid-rant and narrowed her eyes at me. "I know you. You told me you worked for that bookstore, but when I called over there to have them fire you, they said no one named Samantha worked there. And then they hung up on me. On *me!*"

Bootsie growled, and Piper shifted her pet into the crook of her other arm.

"I . . . uh, I'm sorry about that. My name is Sara, and it's true I don't work for the bookstore." I handed the collage to Sam so that I could reach into my bag and pull out the head shot I'd carried with me for the past twenty-four hours. "But you asked me for this. Yesterday."

I held out the glossy photograph, and she took it carefully with her free hand, pinching the paper between two fingers. "I asked you for a picture of me?" She raised her perfectly arched eyebrows in disbelief.

Blushing in embarrassment, I shook my head. "No, not exactly." I gestured for her to turn the picture over. "You asked me for that."

I watched as she skimmed my notes, her lips moving ever so slightly as she read.

When she finished, I gestured to Sam, who flipped the frame around to display the collage on his outstretched arms like a living easel.

"And so I brought you this," I said, and held my breath.

Piper dropped the head shot to the floor and stepped forward. Tapping her finger against her lips, she examined the artwork from the top all the way to the bottom where I had signed my name. After an excruciatingly long minute, she jerked her head over her shoulder.

"Put it in there," she ordered Sam. "I'll have someone hang it up later." She turned to me. "I like it. Who's the artist?"

I gulped. "Me?" I said, hating that it sounded like a question.

I saw Sam slip into Piper's apartment, and I felt a small pang of loss in my heart. I knew giving the collage to Piper was the right thing to do, but it had all happened so fast.

I cleared my throat and tried again. "I mean, I am. It's my work."

She examined me as closely as she had my artwork, from the top of my head all the way to the bottom of my feet. "You have good taste," she finally said. "For someone who works at a bookstore." Then she turned her back to me in what was a clear dismissal.

I didn't bother to correct her. Once she returned to her apartment, I would lose my chance to set things right. It was now or never.

"Piper?" I called out, feeling the rush of adrenaline that only comes from fear—or from doing something dangerous. "What about Paul?"

She turned slowly to face me again. "What *about* Paul?"

"You fired him because I didn't bring a piece of artwork back to you in time. But I did bring you something—something you liked. And so I think you should give Paul his job back," I said, my voice gaining strength the longer I spoke.

"And you know him—how, exactly?"

"He's my brother," Sam answered from behind her. He closed the apartment door and walked back down the hallway toward us.

Piper watched his every move, eyes narrowed, lips pursed.

"And, trust me," he said, stopping at my side, "you have no idea what you've lost by firing him. You'd be smart to bring him back."

She pinned me with her eyes. She looked so young and innocent, but I could see the shrewd and careful mind behind her gaze. It was no wonder she'd made such a successful career for herself. She lifted Bootsie and pressed a kiss to the top of the dog's head.

I took a step closer to Sam.

The moment seemed to lengthen to the breaking point, then reached beyond. My heart pounded so hard it hurt. Sweat tickled along the nape of my neck. Sam brushed the back of his hand against mine, and I knew he was feeling anxious too.

Then Piper shrugged. "Fine," she said. "Tell him to be here at eight tomorrow morning." She turned on her heel and sauntered back to her apartment.

The sound of the door closing cut the tension, and all the air rushed out of my lungs in one enormous, grateful sigh.

We'd done it.

My hand reached for Sam's, our fingers automatically locking together. I looked up at him, and he looked at me.

And then we both started to laugh.

Sam

Chapter 40

They were still laughing when they left the hotel and stumbled back onto the sidewalk, falling over each other with comfortable ease.

"Success!" Sara crowed, throwing her hands up in the air like she'd scored the winning touchdown. "Though I was a little worried there at the end. She was so mad at us and at poor Harold." She shuddered. "I still don't know why Paul wants to work for her. She's scary when she's mad."

"I guess she hasn't read the book yet," Sam said with a grin.

"What book?"

"The one we brought to Piper. The one that started all this."

She looked at him in surprise. "*That* book? What was it? You never told me. And Piper wasn't exactly chatty about it either."

Sam tried to force his mouth into a serious line, but failed. "*Anger Management for the Celebrity Soul.*"

Sara's mouth rounded in honest surprise. "You're kidding."

"Nope. Piper—if you hadn't noticed—has a bit of a temper."

"I'd noticed," she drawled.

"It's why I didn't want to say what it was. Stuff like that is personal. She wouldn't want something like that to get back to her fans."

"Clearly not."

"I mean, can you imagine if her fans knew what kind of a person she really was?"

"The mind boggles."

They looked at each other for a moment, then dissolved into laughter again, turning the corner and leaving the hotel behind.

They walked along the sidewalk for a few blocks, Sam tried to aim their route toward Times Square, but he wished he could take a few detours. There was a shop down the street that had the best bagels. And the International Center of Photography was on 43rd Street and Sixth Avenue—they would practically walk right past it. Sara would go nuts there.

There just wasn't enough time.

The morning was still cool and fresh, though Sam knew that by noon, it would turn muggy and oppressive. By noon, the clouds that were skimming high in the air would plod sluggishly across the sky.

By noon, Sara would be gone. Back on a plane that would carry her through miles and miles of that same cool air all the way to Arizona.

He'd heard about the dry heat of the Arizona sun, but he'd never actually experienced it himself. He wondered if the heat would sap the color from Sara's face, drain her energy, and burn away her vitality. He hoped not. He wanted to remember how she looked in this exact moment of time: her green eyes sparkling, her lips parted in a smile, her face lit with joy.

Once noon came and went, it would be all he'd have left of her.

He pushed away the thought.

"Thanks for an amazing adventure, Sam," she said, looking up at him.

He laughed. "Who would have believed we would be victorious in our quest?"

"I'll be honest, at times, I had my doubts."

Sam's laugh softened into a sigh. "So did I." He kept his hand twined with hers and hoped she wouldn't pull away. "But I knew if anyone could do it, it would be you."

Sara tilted her head to the side. "Wow. You're braver than I am."

"I don't know—I think you're pretty brave."

"And stubborn," she added. "I'm equal parts stubborn and brave. Remember? That's what you said to me when we met."

Of course he remembered. He doubted he would forget anything about that meeting.

"Which reminds me." She let go of his hand and opened the mouth of her bag. Digging in the depths, she finally emerged with a small 3x5 framed picture. "Here. This belongs to you."

Sam took it from her and held it carefully with both hands. She had framed the picture of him walking away from the bookstore. Written in small letters along the edge of the white mat was the caption: SAM. She'd signed her name in the corner.

He looked at her, feeling overwhelmed.

"Vanessa helped me with it once we were done with the collage. Do you like it?" she asked, rocking up onto her toes, her fingers twisting into a knot of nerves.

He nodded, not trusting himself to speak.

"I'm still not sorry I stole your soul," she said. "But I'm glad I was able to give it back."

He tightened his hands around the frame, holding on as if

he were afraid to let go. He opened his mouth to speak, but the words he wanted to say felt rusty and raw. He cleared his throat and tried again. "In more ways than one."

Her face filled with color, soft and warm. "I just wanted to say thanks. For everything."

He swallowed. His heart picked up speed in his chest. He thought about that night eighteen months ago when he had driven along a country road on a dark night with a blue-eyed girl. Then he thought about last night when he had stood on a building that seemed to reach to the stars with a girl who had green eyes. Both nights had changed his life, but in such different ways.

"Do you believe in fate?" he asked.

"I don't know. Maybe a little. Why?"

"I believe sometimes people come into your life at exactly the right moment to give you exactly what you need at that moment."

She bit her lip and looked at the framed picture in his hands. "You think it was fate that we met?"

"It kind of feels like it, don't you think?" he said with a shrug.

"Yeah," she said after a long moment. "It kind of does." She gave herself a little shake, like waking up from a dream. "Though it's hard to believe that all I needed was a little pink packet of sugar." She smiled ruefully. "You know, I traded that sugar packet all the way to Top of the Rock, but I never did get to see the Giants play."

He matched her smile. "You didn't really want to see the Giants play, though, did you?"

"No," she admitted, looking down. "I only said that because I knew what I really wanted wasn't possible." She sighed. "All these years, I kept wishing that my mom would come home, that I could see her again—just once. But now that I know the truth, I guess I just have to accept the fact that she's gone and, if she hasn't come back by now, she's not coming back."

Sam took a deep breath and lifted her chin with his finger. "I've been trading for a long time now. I've found a lot of interesting things. I've met a lot of interesting people."

Her eyes were the green of spring, of new life.

She looked up at him with so much trust that he had a sudden moment of doubt. Was this the right thing to do? Or would this just lead her down a path that would end in heartache? He thought about the collage she'd made and how all those different paths had been marked out for him. If there was even a chance that one of the paths in Sara's life would lead to joy, then he had to do this.

He would have wanted her to do the same for him.

"One thing I've learned, though, is that you work and you try and you trade, but sometimes you don't always find what you want."

Sam carefully placed his framed picture into his messenger bag and withdrew a small square piece of white paper, which he held out to Sara. "And sometimes you do."

Sara

Chapter 41

I took the card Sam offered to me. "What's this?"

He scrubbed his hand through his hair and shifted uneasily on his feet. Nervous Sam had returned. I wondered why.

All that was written on the card was a phone number with a New York area code. I flipped the card over to see if there was anything written on the back, but it was blank.

"What's this for?" I asked again.

Sam swallowed. His fingers drummed on his leg; he couldn't seem to decide if he should keep his hands in his pockets or not. "If you're serious about getting what you want, then you'll want to call that number."

I felt a hard, cold panic settle in the pit of my stomach. Sam was a magician when it came to finding things. He had said it himself—he could find anything. Was it possible he had found in one day what I had spent half my life looking for?

"Is this . . ." I had to stop, my breath catching in my throat. "Is this my mom's phone number?" My voice cracked. Yes, I had said that was what I wanted, but I suddenly felt unprepared to have it so close. I wasn't ready to hold the answer in my hand. I wasn't ready to face her.

"No," Sam said quickly. "It's not her number. But you said your dad didn't know where your mom was anymore. That number will put you in touch with a friend of Vanessa's who knows a guy who knows a guy who might be able to help you find your mom." His smile was the slightest bit crooked on his face. "I guess you still have a little more trading to do before you get to the end."

I pressed the card between my palms and brought my hands up to my mouth as though I could breathe in the possibilities. "Oh, Sam . . ." I said, feeling tears rise in my eyes.

"I know it's a lot to handle. And kind of a surprise—but, I hope, a nice surprise." He looked down at the tops of his boots. "I can't promise that James will be able to find her for you, but if anyone can, it'll be him."

All the words I wanted to say seemed small and inadequate compared to how I was feeling.

"I wanted to leave it up to you," he continued. "You know, for when you wanted to call. That way you can talk about it with your dad. See what he thinks."

A frown threatened to interrupt my good mood. "I doubt my dad would think this is a good idea."

"You weren't the only one she left behind," Sam said quietly. "Your dad sacrificed a lot—he *lost* a lot—as well. But he loves you. And maybe he's just been looking for his own happiness—same as you. Maybe you should give him a chance to find it again."

I thought about Sam's words. I was still mad at my dad for keeping secrets from me, for not fighting for our family like I thought he should have, but underneath the simmering anger I felt was a truth I wasn't ready to acknowledge: There was more to the story. There were things about my parents' divorce that I still didn't understand, questions I hadn't known to ask. Maybe Sam was right. Maybe, before I made a decision I couldn't change, I should give my dad another chance to explain.

Maybe, before it was too late, I could try to trade my anger for understanding and build a better relationship with my dad. Starting with my apology for making him worry about me all day and night.

I looked down at the business card in my hands, amazed that something so small could be such a large burden and such an amazing opportunity at the same time. "How can I ever repay you for this?"

He lifted a shoulder in that familiar half-shrug of his. A dark shadow of embarrassed pride stained his cheek. "It's what I do. I'm a finder."

"Still. This seems like it goes way beyond the kind of thing you normally find for people. Don't you usually charge some kind of finder's fee or something?"

Sam brushed his hair out of his eyes. He hesitated, then said, "I can think of one thing that might cover it."

"Name it and it's yours."

"A kiss," he said, his voice unexpectedly soft and shy. "If you don't mind."

My heart flipped in my chest.

Slowly, he stepped closer to me. Close enough to place his hand on my wrist. Then he slid his hand upward, his fingertips just skimming the surface of the skin. The fine hairs on my arm stood up as if electrified. I could feel the slightest tremor pass through him, as though he had to concentrate on keeping his movements slow and even.

My breathing was suddenly anything but slow or even. I

focused on the details of him that I had come to know so well over the last twenty-four hours: the way his brown eyes turned a shade darker when he was deep in thought, the slant of the leather strap of his bag as it cut across his broad chest, the curl of his hair as it fell across his forehead, the smell of smoke and sky and endless motion that was uniquely New York, uniquely Sam.

His hand reached the bend of my elbow, then continued traveling all the way up to the curve of my neck. He rested his thumb along the length of my collarbone.

I was sure he could feel my pulse increase as my heart tripped into overdrive in my chest. I couldn't seem to breathe as deeply as I wanted to. All the nerve endings in my body felt like they'd been lined with glitter. I wondered if, when I closed my eyes, I would see myself glow on the inside.

I couldn't look away from Sam, though. I didn't want to. All the times I had imagined my first kiss, it had never been anything like this.

He kept his dark eyes locked with mine as he reached out and brushed a strand of my hair away from my face. His fingers left behind a trail of warmth.

Closing the distance between us, he drew me into his arms until we were almost touching along the leg, the hip, the shoulder.

Cupping my face in his hands, he leaned down until his forehead touched mine. The slope of his nose brushed against my cheekbone.

I could feel the nearness of his lips next to mine, the heat from his mouth as he breathed out the words, "Just . . . one . . . kiss."

I felt a corresponding heat answer inside of me. I slipped my arms around him, thrilled at how natural it felt to hold him and to be held by him.

When his lips pressed against mine, I closed my eyes, feeling like a sun was rising in my chest, pouring light into my fingers and toes. In that moment, it was as if all the noise around me—the crowds of people talking and moving and shouting, the taxis crawling through the narrow lanes of traffic, the music thumping out of open windows and passing cars, all the thousands of sounds that made up the heartbeat of New York City—suddenly fell into silence.

The only thing I could hear was my own blood pulsing in my ears. The only thing I could feel was the touch of Sam's mouth on mine. I kissed him back, lifting up on my toes as though I might fly away.

Much too soon, Sam pulled back from me ever so gently, though he kept his arms locked loosely around my waist. A delicate shiver traveled all the way through his body, and he smiled.

"*That* was exactly what I have been looking for."

I couldn't reply; I was too busy trying to remember how to breathe.

After a few moments, he turned his head and rubbed his cheek along the curve of my head. I could feel his prickly stubble against my scalp. "Sara?"

"Mm-hmm?"

"I hate to have to ask, but what time is it?"

"I don't want to know," I said.

"I promised your dad you wouldn't miss your flight."

"Sa-am," I said, my whine making his name into two syllables.

"Sa-ra," he mimicked.

I frowned and he laughed, swiftly bending down to kiss the dimple that appeared by my mouth.

"Don't be mad at me," he said. "I don't want you to go. But—"

I sighed, knowing what was coming next and hating it.

"But you can't stay here, either," he finished.

I leaned my forehead against his shoulder and spoke into his chest. "I know."

We stood together for another moment before Sam stirred, separating us back into two people. "Sara—"

I recognized that tone, and it sent chills like arrows through the warmth that still filled me. "Don't," I said, looking up at him fiercely. "Don't say it. I don't want this to be good-bye."

"I don't want this to be good-bye either," he said. He pulled two tattered sugar packets from his bag and held them out to me. His eyes danced with light and life. "So, tell me, Sara without an *h*—what do you want?"

The last time Sam had asked me that question, I hadn't known what to say. This time I did. Aces had given me the answer.

"I want my life to be filled with passion."

Sam chuckled under his breath. "That's a tall order."

"But not impossible. Someone once told me that if you don't know what you want, you'll never get it."

"I see. And something tells me that a smart girl like you will find a way to get whatever she wants."

"Hey, I learned from the best."

"True." Sam granted me that point. "But I think there is one lesson left." He bounced the sugar packets on his palm. "Instead of saying good-bye, let's say hello instead."

I lifted a packet from the palm of his hand. "How is this going to become a hello?"

"The same way it became two tickets for Jess, or a coupon for a free manicure. You trade your packet; I'll trade mine. And if we keep them moving, eventually we'll find what we're looking for."

"This little packet will bring me all the way back to New York?"

Sam smiled. "You never know. Maybe my packet will take me all the way to Arizona."

I grinned, catching the spirit of the adventure. "Are you proposing another quest?"

"You game?"

I turned the small packet over in my fingers. "Yeah," I said. "I am."

"Good." He tucked the square of sugar into his pocket. "Then the next time I see you, we'll have a proper hello."

I raised an eyebrow, feeling a matching lift of hope in my chest. "And what comes after hello?"

"Anything. Everything. Whatever you want," he said. "Just as long as it's not good-bye."

He held my eyes for another minute, then took a deep breath and stepped out of my arms. "So, I'll see you around?" he said, his voice holding the slightest hint of a question.

I curled my hand into a fist around my sugar packet and nodded.

He settled his bag more firmly over his shoulder, tugging at the sleeves of his hoodie, rocking his weight on his feet as though trying to decide how much effort it was going to take him to leave.

"Then I'll see you around, Sara," he said.

When he turned and stepped into the flow of pedestrians, I had an overwhelming sense of déjà vu. The moment was just like the picture I'd taken of him yesterday—the one where he was already walking away from me—but this time I knew I wasn't supposed to follow. This time, I knew it was okay to let him go.

I thought back to the inside quiet I had felt visiting St. John's Cathedral and in Central Park and again on Top of the Rock. I wanted that feeling all the time. And if that meant letting go of my anger and my fear, then that was what I was going to do.

I checked the clock on my phone. I still had time. I turned my face toward Times Square, toward where my dad was waiting for me. I had so much to tell him, so much to ask him about. So much to apologize for and to forgive.

I started walking, my steps quick and sure. In one hand I held the card that could lead me to my mother; in the other, I held the packet that could lead me back to Sam.

Both were equally thrilling to me.

I didn't know if either one would work out the way I wanted them to, but I knew for sure that I was going to try.

Gotta keep moving, I thought. Then I picked up my pace, eager to see what my future would turn out to be.

Acknowledgments

This book started with a dream. I remember dreaming the first scene—I saw Sam outside the bookstore as clearly as Sara did, right down to the Zebra Stripes hoodie and the military-green messenger bag—and I woke up knowing I wanted to write a story about him. And as I got to know Sam and Sara, their story was even better than I originally dreamed.

Thank you to the excellent team at Shadow Mountain—Chris Schoebinger, Heidi Taylor, Emily Watts, Heather Ward, and Tonya Facemyer—all of whom support me in more ways than I can count and who make the whole process feel effortless.

Thank you to my alpha and omega readers: Cindi Cox, Jen Shaw, Valerie Hill, Becca Wilhite, Ally Condie, Pam Anderton, Dennis Gaunt, and, of course, my mom. Their feedback and insight encouraged me and kept me on the right track.

A special thanks to two Facebook friends: Lisa Nickolson Green for suggesting the name Chasing Pages for the bookstore, and Addison Kanoelani for suggesting the angel pin that Rebecca trades with Sara.

And thanks to my sister-in-law Tammy, who introduced me

to the music of Matt Nathanson. And thanks to Matt Nathanson for coming in concert last fall and bringing Scars on 45 to open for him. And thanks to Scars on 45 for the song "Heart on Fire." That song and their music—and Matt's album *Modern Love*—provided much of the soundtrack for this story to take shape.

And, as always, a special heartfelt thanks to my family—specifically my too-amazing-for-words husband, Tracy. He believes in me even when I don't; he is my heart's desire. And I wouldn't trade him for all the sugar packets in the world.